Forged in Blood

Rise of the Giants Series: Book 4

Theo Mann

The Invisible Publishing Company

Rise of the Giants Series

Book 1: Rise of the Giants
Book 2: Clan of Heroes
Book 3: The Fate of All Traitors
Book 4: Forged In Blood
Book 5: Hidden Kingdom
Book 6: Igniting the Flame
Book 7: The Angler War
Book 8: Rise of the New Race

Contents

Chapter 1   1

Chapter 2   7

Chapter 3   11

Chapter 4   19

Chapter 5   27

Chapter 6   35

Chapter 7   41

Chapter 8   49

Chapter 9   57

Chapter 10   61

Chapter 11   67

Chapter 12   73

Chapter 13   79

Chapter 14   83

Chapter 15   87

Chapter 16   93

Chapter 17   103

Chapter 18   109

Chapter 19   113

Chapter 20   119

Chapter 21   125

Chapter 22   131

Chapter 23   139

Chapter 24   147

Chapter 25   153

Chapter 26   159

Chapter 27   165

Chapter 28   169

Chapter 29   173

Chapter 30   177

Chapter 31   183

Chapter 32   191

Chapter 33   197

Chapter 34   203

Chapter 35   207

Chapter 36   213

Chapter 37   219

Chapter 38   225

Chapter 39   231

Chapter 40   237

Chapter 41   241

Chapter 42   247

Keep Reading   253

Sign Up Once--Get all Theo Mann's free books including brand new   255
releases

About Theo Mann   257

Also by Theo Mann (so far)   259

Chapter 1

Hammer and his men stood on top of a high hill and stared down at a line of people making their way across the countryside. Shadow and his Godless band wound through the jungle on their way back to their long camp in the gorges.

"Now what are we going to do?" Lonion asked.

Hammer turned away and didn't look at Shadow's band again. "We're going to go out on our own," Hammer replied.

"How can we do that?" Vuco asked. "Going out on our own is a death sentence in this jungle."

"No, it isn't. We've been out on our own since we were uninitiated boys. We already run our own band. That's what we'll do now." Hammer turned to Lonion and the other uninitiated boys. "You boys aren't old enough for initiation. You're the oldest Vuco. You'll initiate first when you get to the right age, so start preparing yourself for that. The rest of you should get ready before then. Start deciding what creatures you plan to fight and prepare yourselves for how you're going to do it."

The uninitiated boys exchanged glances. "You can do that?" Ziti asked.

"Do what?" Hammer asked.

"You can initiate us? I didn't know you could do that."

"We're all initiated Godless men. We can initiate anyone into manhood." Hammer turned to survey the girls in the group.

Fifteen men had left Shadow's band to support Hammer. Five girls came with them, including Vina, Hammer's sweetheart, and Sema, Cross's sweetheart.

Cross and Sema stood there holding hands in front of everyone. She huddled close to his side and didn't show any sign of letting go of him.

"I'm grateful for your support," Hammer told Cross. "I never intended for you to leave your family."

Cross's eyes darted around the group of men. "I suppose I've been a member of your band all this time. I don't see that I could suddenly change that—and what he did was wrong. He shouldn't have stepped out of line the way he did. I couldn't sit by and let him get away with it."

"I'm still grateful."

Sema's constant presence brought Hammer back to the problem at hand. The other three girls were also already attached to Hammer's men. Masha belonged to Lucky. Eleph belonged to Ant and Daora belonged to Earthquake.

That made twenty people in Hammer's band not counting the uninitiated boys.

"You all heard what Hangman said," Hammer went on. "None of you can marry until the girls come to the age of gathering. Follow the law or we'll be shunned by everyone. Our children will never be able to go to the gatherings. We didn't leave Shadow's band so we could break the law. We'll follow every Godless law and make ourselves a real band. You only have to wait a little while—and I'm waiting, too. We'll all marry and then no one will be able to stop us from going to the gatherings with everyone else."

Some of the other couples exchanged glances. Hammer made a mental note to keep an eye on his men to make sure they followed the law. He was a full Kral now with full responsibilities, including this one—especially this one.

Hangman's warning imprinted itself on Hammer's mind. Hangman would always be Hammer's Kral even now after they separated probably forever.

Hangman knew what was important. He had impressed on Hammer and his comrades the need to follow the law. None of them could go alone.

Hammer saw the truth written all over this situation. His band would fade away and die off without the gatherings. They would have to interbreed because they wouldn't be able to bring in new women from outside.

The opposite would happen if he and his men only held out a few more weeks until these girls came of age. His band would grow and get stronger. Their families would establish territory and become a Godless band he could be proud of.

These couples just had to wait a little while longer.

"We need to find territory," he decided. "We need to withdraw from Shadow's land and find our own place."

"We could search for a hundred miles and never find that," Stray pointed out.

"There *is* nowhere else that isn't already someone's territory," Pitch added. "We're in Godless territory. Everywhere belongs to someone."

"You're wrong," Hammer countered. "Not everywhere is controlled by a Kral—and even if it was, we could travel back to the northern valley. It's unclaimed and it would be safer, now that the Renegade Clan isn't tracking Aster anymore."

"We can't travel all that way!" Vuco exclaimed. "We just traveled all the way here. We can't go back."

Hammer shot him a hard look and then cast the same glare around the group. "You followed me to make me your Kral, so I'll make the decision if we go or if we stay. You'll follow my decision or go out on your own away from the rest of us. We won't travel north—not yet. I have a better idea. We'll go back to the Ashtaw Valley and domesticate the creatures the way Mora said."

"The Renegade Clan is there—and the Bounty Hunters," Ant pointed out.

"We can defeat them with the Ashtaws," Hammer replied. "We've done it once already. We would be able to do it more easily if we domesticated them and trained them for combat. The valley is Godless territory. It's ours by right, but no other band is claiming it. It's perfect for us."

No one made a sound. No one mentioned if they agreed with him or not.

He crossed another line within himself right at that moment. He couldn't think anymore about whether anyone agreed with him or not. That no longer mattered.

He made his own decisions. He was Kral now. His people either followed him and obeyed him or they didn't. That was the Godless way. It was everyone's way.

He turned away. He couldn't let himself dwell on Hangman anymore, either. Hammer led the way down the hill into the jungle. He didn't run this time. The men had to walk so the girls could keep up.

They traveled faster than pregnant women and mothers with tiny children. The long, long journey, both from Renegade country to the northern mountains and from the northern mountains to here—Hammer would never forget that journey as long as he lived.

Pregnant women and mothers with young children needed territory. They needed protected, defended camps where they didn't have to travel around and where their enemies and dangerous creatures couldn't get to them.

Hammer had some time before any of these girls got pregnant, but he needed to establish territory before that happened.

He kept his eyes and ears tuned to everything moving in the jungle. He had never put himself in charge of these girls' protection before—not as directly in charge as this.

Hangman had always been the one responsible for everyone's protection. The journey back to the valley made Hammer all too aware of the real implications of his decision to leave Shadow's band.

Hammer had never really considered himself Kral of his own separate band—not really. Hangman had said that Hammer was Kral of his own separate band, but Hammer always made himself subordinate to Hangman's leadership. All his men did.

It never once crossed Hammer's mind to leave Hangman's band—not really. He toyed with the idea when he thought he might have to take Vina away, but he never really let himself think about what it would be like.

That was the reason he didn't leave before. He didn't realize that until now. He didn't leave because he still considered himself Hangman's subordinate.

Hammer himself stayed under Hangman's protection. Hammer grew up under Hangman's leadership. Part of Hammer's innermost being always considered himself a boy compared to Hangman.

All that had to change now. Hammer himself was responsible for the girls' protection—all of them—not just Vina's. He was responsible for everyone's protection, including his men.

The party camped in the trees that night. The girls sat close to their men—much closer than they would have if they had still been part of Hangman's band.

Sema put her arm around Cross's shoulders and rested her head against him. She never would have done that in front of Hangman and her family.

Vina squatted next to Hammer. He let himself hold her hand and finally look up into her eyes. "Everything will work out," he murmured under his breath. "We'll get married and find territory where you and the other girls can be safe."

"I know," she murmured back. "I know you'll make a good Kral."

He found it difficult to hear that coming from her, but looking away only brought him around to seeing all the other couples.

He had to establish himself soon so the uninitiated boys could go to the gathering. Four years. He had four years to build this band into a respected Godless force in whatever territory they claimed as their own.

"We're getting low on food," Scarecrow pointed out. "We should hunt."

"We have enough to get to the valley," Hammer decided. "We'll hunt when we get there."

"Do you remember that waterfall on the southwest side of the Ashtaw Valley?" Cross interjected. "It ran down into some rocky chasms and valleys. We might find a protected spot there to make a long camp."

"Good idea," Hammer replied. "I think we should establish a temporary camp on the east side of the valley—the side farthest away from the Renegade and Bounty Hunter invasion. We'll set up there where we can process our kills. That will give us a base where we can explore the area and find a more permanent location."

"How will we deal with the invaders when we have so few men?" Ant asked.

"We'll deal with them the same way we've been dealing with them all along. We'll set up ambushes and surprise attacks. We'll use the creatures as much as possible." Hammer scanned the surrounding jungle. "You girls should start working on the harnesses as soon as we get to a fixed camp."

"We should have Mora with us." Masha's voice quavered. "She would know what to do."

"Mora isn't here," Hammer snapped more harshly than he meant to. "We'll just have to figure it out for ourselves—and we already know what to do because she already told us. We have to do exactly what we did before. We have to use Fogpo branches to tame the creatures, get them used to us, and find a way to ride them."

"We would be miles off the ground if we tried to ride them," Scarecrow pointed out.

"But imagine if we could," Cross added. "Our enemies wouldn't stand a chance—and we would be too far away for our enemies to hit us. They wouldn't be able to scratch the Ashtaws. The Ashtaws could just step on them and it would be over."

"That wouldn't protect our camps," Scarecrow countered. "The Renegade Clan and the Bounty Hunters don't have our law of confronting their enemies. They would sneak around the Ashtaws and attack from another direction."

"That's enough speculation," Hammer interrupted. "We'll never find a perfect situation because none exists. We'll go and do it either way. Things will go wrong and we'll figure out how to correct it. That's all."

His tone silenced everyone. They went back to eating, but no one ate much. The weight of their decision hung heavy over all of them.

At least, the weight of their decision hung heavy over some of them. A few acted light and carefree about it. Cross actually acted much happier and more relaxed than Hammer remembered seeing him act in a long, long time.

In fact, Hammer couldn't remember seeing Cross this happy ever. He lived under his older brother's shadow—and Shadow's shadow.

Cross leaned back against a tree trunk and grinned at Sema in outright smirking glee. He rubbed her back and used his fingertips to comb her hair out of her face.

Hammer couldn't remember Cross ever acting so openly affectionate toward her. The weight of worlds lifted off his shoulders, now that he no longer had to tiptoe around his father and brother.

His behavior unnerved Sema. She kept casting glances at Hammer and the others, blushing, and squirming in her seat. Her reaction only delighted Cross more.

He gazed up into her eyes beaming and smirking in delight. He expressed the excitement and relieved delight all the rest of the men should have been feeling. They were all going to marry the girls they loved.

Hammer should have felt that excitement and relief. He was going to marry Vina. No one could stop him now. No other Kral would come along and take her away to the gathering to marry another man.

None of the other men even seemed to realize how big this was and how truly happy they should all be about it.

The absence of the older men cast a pall over the group. Hangman wasn't here, but the other men's presence meant almost as much if not more. Viking wasn't here. Red wasn't here. Wildling wasn't here. None of Red's men from the northern band were here.

No one was here to tell the younger men what to do. No one was here to tell Hammer what to do. They were completely on their own with no safety net to catch them if they fell.

They would stand or fall on their own. No one would ever find out if they all died out here. They would disappear into the landscape and the rest of the world would go on as though Hammer's band never existed.

Chapter 2

"Go up into the trees and stay there until we come back," Hammer told the girls. "We'll see what's happening up at the Ashtaw Valley before we make any decisions."

"What about hunting for some more food?" Eleph asked. "We're all out."

"Not yet," Hammer replied. "Just wait a little longer. No one will starve before we see what's happening with the valley."

"Hunting means lighting fires," Vina pointed out. "We won't be able to hunt even after you come back."

"Just go up into the trees. We don't have time to argue about it now." Hammer turned to his men. "Let's go."

The men took off at a run through the jungle. It ended fifty yards away where the mountains rose around the Ashtaw Valley.

Hammer didn't look back to see if the girls obeyed him. He was going to have to start flexing his authority a lot in the coming months—maybe even for years.

He had to establish his authority as Kral. He saw that now. None of these people really thought of him as their Kral before, either. They all made themselves subordinate to Hangman.

Maybe none of these people really thought they would ever leave Hangman's band. Maybe Hammer's men thought they would all just stay there as Hangman's subordinates forever.

Hammer's men also considered Hammer as subordinate to Hangman. Hammer's own men never thought of him as their Kral. He had to change that now. He might even face challenges to his leadership. He would have to deal with those.

The men gathered on the hilltop. They had stashed their Fogpo branches on this hilltop during their first campaign to the valley.

A hush fell over the men at the sight of thousands of Ashtaws grazing in that valley. Most were so tall that Hammer wouldn't even have come up to the creatures' knees.

"We could never ride one of those," Omen murmured. "Look at them! They're huge!"

"We have to find a way," Hammer replied. "It won't work to domesticate only the smallest Ashtaws the way we did last time. That was only a temporary solution."

"I don't understand what you mean," Ant chimed in. "Why couldn't we do it that way? It worked, didn't it?"

"The young ones will grow up," Hammer replied. "They'll get bigger. Then all the time and effort we put into domesticating and training them will go to waste. We have to take on the adults or at least be preparing to ride the adults once we train them as juveniles."

"How on earth would we ride one of *those*?" Lucky asked. "How would we even mount them?"

"You heard what Mora said," Hammer replied. "We have to train them to stoop down toward the ground—but they probably wouldn't even need to do that much."

Ant frowned. "I don't understand."

"Think about it. Those ropes—the line she called the reins that lead from the creature's head harness to our hands—they would be too long if we rode on the Ashtaws' backs."

"What's the solution?" Scarecrow asked. "It's the only place to sit."

"No, it isn't. She said some of these people used harnesses and platforms tied around the creatures' backs and the people rode in those. All we have to do is train the creatures to lower their heads to the ground, put on the head harness, and then attach another harness around the creature's neck. That's where the rider will sit—high up on the Ashtaw's neck close to the head."

"It would be dangerous to sit that high up," Scarecrow remarked. "We might fall out and get killed when we hit the ground."

"Please," Hammer sneered. "We aren't here to protect ourselves. If you want to be safe, go back to the trees and hide with the women. We're doing this. It's the only way to defeat our enemies and establish our own territory." He surveyed the surrounding terrain. "It's a good country—the best. I'm not surprised the other Clans want to take it."

"I think it's a good idea," Cross interjected. "This was our band's traditional territory for generations before the Renegade Clan invaded. We should get it back."

"Do you know if the band lived down the canyons to the southwest?" Hammer asked. "Do you know where the band kept their camps?"

"I can't tell you that. I'm sorry," Cross replied. "The Renegades drove our people out of this country before I was ever born. I wish I could help you, but I can't—not in that way."

Hammer found himself smiling at Cross. He had the most cause to regret separating from Shadow and Hangman—yet Cross was being the most helpful, the most supportive, and the most enthusiastic about this whole project.

Hammer never understood why Cross always ran with Hammer's band—except that they were the same age. Maybe Cross always needed to distance himself from Hangman without openly challenging or abandoning Hangman's leadership.

Cross always followed Hangman's leadership. Hangman never had a more loyal supporter than Cross—except for Viking and Alien, of course.

Running with Hammer's band was the only way Cross could get out from under his brother's shadow without outright challenging or insulting Hangman.

Hammer's feelings instantly softened toward Cross. He was one man at least that Hammer didn't have to worry about.

He turned his attention back to the Ashtaws. "Mora said the riders used to give their mounts voice commands. Riding closer to the head will make that easier. They wouldn't be able to hear us if we rode on their backs."

Omen rubbed his head. "I don't know about this....."

"I don't see any sign of the Renegades or Bounty Hunters. Let's return to the girls, find a place to set up camp, and do some hunting. That will give us the time and materials to make these harnesses before we try again."

Hammer started to turn away. Cross grabbed Hammer's arm to stop him. "Not so fast. Look. There they are."

Everyone turned around to see a party of Renegades snake across one of the far hills across the valley.

"They're still here," Omen murmured. "They must be trying to take this valley, too."

"If they can see us, we can see them," Scarecrow remarked. "They already know Godless are in the area. Now they know we didn't actually leave."

"We wouldn't be able to get near them without them seeing us." Hammer turned his back on the Renegades. "Let's get out of here. We'll deal with them later. We'll be better able to deal with them in the jungle anyway."

The men retreated down the hill to the trees. Hammer looked up into the trees to make sure the girls were still where he left them. He made eye contact with Vina, but a twig snapping in the jungle startled him into spinning around.

All the men whirled that way and drew their weapons when they saw a mob of Bounty Hunters coming straight for them. The Bounty Hunters outnumbered the Godless by two to one.

Hammer made a split-second decision. "Into the trees! Get into the canopy now!!"

He launched off the ground and scrambled into the treetops. His men followed him—all but Stray. He hesitated and faced the enemy holding both his drawn blades. Hammer called out to him to come on, but Stray didn't respond. Hammer couldn't wait any longer.

He took a running jump off the branch underneath him, launched himself into open space, and grabbed hold of a flexible sapling not far away.

The sapling bowed under his weight and sagged close to the ground. The trunk bent all the way over and lowered him down right next to Stray.

The Bounty Hunters didn't see him in time. They concentrated on the one Godless man still standing in front of them. They would cut him down instantly.

Hammer grabbed Stray by the arm and the sapling snapped back taking both men with them. Hammer's fingers slipped on Stray's sweaty skin.

Hammer's hand slid all the way down to Stray's wrist and locked. Both men whizzed upward out of the Bounty Hunter's reach. Hammer let go of the sapling at the top of its arc and let go of Stray's wrist while the two men hovered there for a minute.

They both dropped onto the branches beneath them while the Bounty Hunters ran around on the ground trying to decide how to get to the Godless after all.

Hammer didn't wait around. He signaled to his men and the girls. The whole band took off streaking through the canopy to put as much distance behind them as possible.

Chapter 3

Hammer came to rest on a branch far away from the Ashtaw Valley. He squatted there and searched the surrounding canopy for any sign that the Bounty Hunters might be following the band.

The rest of his party caught up and gathered around him. Stray squatted on a nearby branch. "What were you thinking?!" Hammer demanded. "I told you to get into the branches. Didn't you hear me?"

Stray looked away. "I don't know what happened. I just didn't react in time. I could only think I had to confront them and fight them. I'm sorry. I don't know what happened."

Hammer let the matter drop, but it still bothered him. Was this the first glimmer of insubordination? Stray never bucked Hamer's leadership before.

Hammer took that moment to evaluate all the other men in his party. The only man here he felt absolutely certain he could rely on was Cross.

Ant was the shortest of the group, but he had a compact, powerful build that made him a lot more intimidating than his bigger comrades.

In a way, his size made him more intimidating than much bigger men like Viking and Alien. Any man would have been taking his life in his hands if he underestimated Ant.

He also had much darker skin than any other Godless man Hammer had ever met. Hammer didn't understand why Ant's skin was so much darker. Hammer had known Ant's mother back in Ceon before she died. Hammer also knew the Renegade who fathered Ant.

Both of Ant's parents had the same light brown complexion, straight, black hair, and black eyes as everyone else in this country. They couldn't have passed down anything to make Ant so much darker.

He wore his hair long, loose, down, and flowing except for two locks right at the corners of his forehead. He braided those off to the side to keep his hair out of his face.

The bends of both braids around his face gave him a strange look. That was how he got his name. He really did look kind of like an ant with his powerful, iron frame, dark skin, and those corners of hair sticking out from his head like an ant's antennae.

Earthquake was the tallest and most powerful of the group. He reminded Hammer of Viking's gentle, easy-going nature. Earthquake even fought with an enormous battle axe the way Viking did. Earthquake would probably grow up to be a lot like Viking.

Earthquake even had a scar on his face in almost an identical position as Viking's. That was the most bizarre part about all of this. Earthquake was almost an exact copy of Viking only much younger.

Pitch and Lucky had both grown up tall, lean, agile, and extremely fast. They both had to slow down to accommodate their friends when the party moved around.

The twins didn't wear their hair the same way. It was one of the few ways someone who didn't know them could tell the twins apart.

Pitch braided his hair and wrapped the braids with hide strips. He wrapped the strips so tightly together that the braids formed solid rods hanging from the back of his head.

Lucky also braided his hair, but he wore it in one single braid starting from his forehead, hugging his scalp, and running backward along the top centerline to his neck where it ran down his back to his waist.

The braid looked like a Gorlock's spine ridge, but no one ever mentioned the resemblance. The twins' younger brother Omen also braided his hair. He did it in dozens of much smaller braids that he twisted into a knot on the back of his head.

He grew up slightly shorter than his brothers and he didn't develop their speed and agility. He turned out to be too grounded for that.

He had a way of planting himself in one spot, digging in, and making a stand there. Nothing could move him once he did that.

He shrank in on himself, rooted himself to the earth, and woe to anyone or anything that came against him because he simply would not back down.

Bugs had a jittery way of squirming and fidgeting at the worst possible times. He always glanced around at everything and his eyes darted everywhere even when they had no reason to.

He had a small, slight build and made a lot of people nervous, including his own comrades. He wasn't the most pleasant man to travel with, much less wage any kind of combat campaign with, but Hammer couldn't find any other fault with him.

He ran, fought, and worked as hard as the others. He just never developed their power. Hammer couldn't understand why, but then again, he didn't think about it too much.

Scarecrow got his name from the constant scowl he wore on his face all the time. He had a gruff, abrasive, hostile attitude toward everything—except that he didn't. He just acted like he did and he had the size to reinforce it, although he didn't get as big as Earthquake.

Scarecrow had a heart of gold underneath all that smoldering fury. He would do absolutely anything for his comrades and to protect his band even though he glared at them all in murderous rage all the time.

He never let it out—not at his comrades. He did let it out when he faced the enemy. He went berserk and raged through them in unbridled bloodlust.

Hammer sometimes wondered if Scarecrow had to try really hard to quell that fury when he finished killing and came back to his friends, but that never happened.

Scarecrow could switch it off instantly and go straight from slaughtering his enemies to sitting with his mother and helping take care of his younger siblings.

Scarecrow was Thuron's older brother by five years. Hammer had never seen Scarecrow be anything but kind to all women and anyone smaller, younger, and weaker than himself.

And then there were the uninitiated boys. Thuron absolutely worshiped Scarecrow. Hammer recognized only too well the look of blissful awe with which Thuron looked up to his brother. Hammer used to feel that way about Hangman, Viking, and Alien—especially Alien.

Lonion didn't look at Hammer that way because, one way or the other, Lonion somehow admired Hammer too much even for that.

Lonion kept quiet around Hammer—exactly the way Cross used to keep quiet around Hangman. Cross went to extraordinary lengths to support and maintain his brother's position.

Now Lonion did the same thing for Hammer. Lonion turned himself into a perfect warrior for Hammer's mission. Lonion never indicated by word, deed, or facial expression that he ever questioned Hammer, not even in the privacy of his own mind.

Lonion's support overwhelmed Hammer with unspeakable gratitude. He needed all the supporters he could get.

He had no problem accepting questions from Vuco and Ziti. Hammer remembered how much he questioned Hangman and his men in those early days.

Hammer didn't question them to challenge or cast doubt on their seniority and leadership—quite the opposite. He just wanted to understand their way so he could follow it.

He would never forget how kind, understanding, and patient they acted toward him back then. They never once told him not to ask questions.

He and his boys just wanted to be Godless. Hammer wanted to be one hundred thousand and ten percent Godless.

The older men understood that and encouraged it. Hammer encouraged it in the younger boys. Every man in their party encouraged it.

Lonion didn't take the early role of acting as any kind of leader to the other three. Ziti did that. He was by far the biggest, smartest, and shrewdest of the four boys.

Ziti also wore his hair loose and down. He didn't braid it at all.

He took extra pains to comb his hair every day. It glistened and shimmered in long, black waves when sunlight shone on it. The others teased him about his long, flowing, almost feminine locks, but he only laughed along with them and left his hair the way it was.

Thuron wasn't even fourteen yet, but he was rapidly catching up to his brother in size, height, weight, and sheer brutal power when it came to combat. Thuron copied Scarecrow in his ferocity and battle fury nor did Thuron continue it once the battle ended.

Thuron had a calm, earthy, almost childlike personality. Nothing disturbed him. He never hated his enemies the way Scarecrow did, not even when Thuron was killing them.

Hammer couldn't tell how Vuco reacted to Aster's execution. They had been as close as any couple here. Then Vuco had to stand aside and watch Hammer and Hangman feed Vuco's sweetheart to the ants.

Vuco didn't talk about that. He didn't show any emotion over losing Aster. He never offered a word of protest at the time or afterward.

Vuco went on after Aster's death as if she'd never existed. Hammer never even saw Vuco looking off wistfully into the distance.

Vuco showed the most hesitation at leaving Shadow's band and accepting Hammer's leadership, but Hammer expected that from such a young boy.

Hammer expected a lot more of it than he got from the other three. Their cooperative attitude unnerved him. He expected more resistance.

Lonion somehow faded into the background of Ziti's leadership, too. Anyone more assertive and powerful than Lonion seemed to have the same effect over him.

No one could doubt Lonion's bravery and energy when it came to accomplishing the band's mission. He just didn't have a single leadership bone in his body. He wasn't made that way.

Ant looked around at the surrounding jungle. "I guess we're far enough away from them now. We could hunt and light a fire."

"You do that," Hammer ordered. "Take Scarecrow, Bugs, and the boys and go hunting. You can build your fire at the base of these trees. The rest of us will spread out and keep an eye on the countryside to make sure no one comes to attack you while you work."

The party split up. Hammer once again told the girls to stay where they were until the hunting party came back. He caught Vina making eye contact with him before he left. Her eyes communicated so much.

Their relationship would change after this, too. He was starting to understand that as his relationship with all his comrades changed. He and Vina had been sweethearts all this time. They had been teenagers for most of it.

He had never been a Kral before. She would become a Kral's wife. She would become a leader among the women and tell them what to do.

She would be the one to organize them to defend themselves if the men got caught outside their camp and couldn't make it back in time to defend the women.

He couldn't talk to her about that now. He didn't know when or where he would be able to talk to her—about anything.

He and his men would have to establish a permanent camp somewhere with proper shelters before he and Vina could have a private conversation. How long would that take?

He wouldn't be able to do it tonight. He separated all his men and posted them in a wide circle around the spot where they left the girls.

Ant and the others didn't take long before they killed a full-sized Gurlg. Hammer heard the creature squawking long before it fell silent.

Everyone returned to the same location and descended to the ground. The girls built a fire and started cooking the Gurlg meat the hunters brought back.

Hammer divided the rest of his men into watches to keep track of the area overnight. Those working at the fires kept their weapons close at hand to defend the women in case any of the band's enemies got past the watch.

The rest of the band settled down by the fire to spend the night on the ground. Hammer found himself studying the group again.

Of course he considered Vina the most beautiful of the five girls, but an outside observer would have picked out Daora as the most beautiful.

Vina had a round face and a cheery expression and demeanor. She had a way of putting everyone at ease with her easy, accommodating ways.

Daora's sculpted, finely drawn features matched her much more serious personality. She carried herself with regal poise and elaborate dignity in everything she did even if she was just washing the blood off her hands after cutting up a piece of meat.

Masha usually kept her eyes downcast. She had a cringing, timid, frightened way of always huddling closer to anyone bigger and stronger than herself. She did it a lot whenever Lucky sat near her, but she even did it around any other man.

She didn't do it as a way of starting anything with them. She just made herself smaller in reaction to them being bigger, stronger, and more of a threat.

She did this even when nothing around was threatening her. She always did it even around her mother and the other women.

Eleph couldn't have been more different. She had a fierce, driving, unrelenting personality that complemented Ant exactly. Hammer never questioned what Ant found appealing about her. They were two of a kind.

She walked and talked fast, worked her hardest, and did everything with maximum effort and determination even when it wasn't anything particularly important.

Cross and Sema were two of a kind, too. She usually kept quiet, but in a much more thoughtful, observant way than Masha. Sema had a kind of simple beauty that never imposed itself or drew attention to itself—just like everything else about her.

She watched and listened to everything going on around her, but she did it much more directly than Masha did.

Hammer always got the sense that Sema was evaluating his decisions and making up her mind if she agreed with them or not.

Talking about anything in front of her always felt like taking the matter to some kind of tribunal that would rule whether the idea or decision was any good or not.

He found himself as much concerned by her evaluation of his decisions as any of his men. She would have been an asset to any band—and she always backed up Cross. She gave him her undivided loyalty, help, and support in everything he did.

Hammer settled back and enjoyed the hot, juicy food he was putting in his mouth. He hadn't enjoyed fresh meat in a long time—too long. He might not enjoy it again for another long time.

Twenty-three people. He had twenty-three people to build a band, establish a territory, and defeat his enemies.

He needed to do that soon before the Renegades and the Bounty Hunters overwhelmed Hammer's band with numbers. He wouldn't get a second chance to come back from it if they did.

Chapter 4

Hammer paused at the top of the hill again and looked down at the Ashtaws. They never stopped grazing unless something spooked them into a stampede.

He and his party watched a flock of Boultars attack the herd on the opposite side of the valley. The Boultars tried to snatch young Ashtaws away from their mothers.

The Boultars triggered another stampede of Ashtaws charging toward the Godless, but the stampede didn't last long.

The Ashtaws ran into all the other Ashtaws in the herd. The young Ashtaws ran between the legs of all the much larger adults. The Boultars couldn't go after these giant creatures. The Boultars had to break off and fly away.

The surge of Ashtaws blended in with the rest of the herd and they all went back to grazing.

"The Renegades aren't there anymore," Ziti pointed out.

"They're still there," Scarecrow muttered. "They're always there. We just can't see them."

"Let's circle the valley and check out the canyons to the southwest," Hammer suggested. "We need a camp."

The party headed off to the right to circle the valley. The men brought the girls with them this time. Hammer didn't want to leave them in the trees where the Bounty Hunters knew where to find the girls.

At least he could see the landscape from up here. He would be able to see if any of his enemies came after the party.

Big rocks dotted the ridgeline in a few spots. He sent his men and the uninitiated boys out there to scout the route before the girls got anywhere near it. The last Renegade ambush haunted Hammer now. The Renegades had hidden behind rocks outcroppings just like that.

Shadow's men had saved the party that time, but the Renegades could have wiped out Hangman's band if Shadow hadn't turned up when he did.

The men and boys stayed up on the rocks and waved Hammer's party forward. The men continued to travel across the top of the rocks to make sure the way stayed clear all the way south.

Hammer didn't see anything to concern him—except that everything concerned him. He kept seeing all the potential hazards and threats that could put his people in danger.

He even had to keep an eye on the skies. Boultars patrolled the Ashtaw herd all the time in search of any unprotected juveniles. The Boultars would just as soon come after people if any happened to wander into view.

Hammer would have to take Boultars into account when he selected the band's long camp. Protecting people from the air would become even more important once these girls came of age and started having children.

None of the party saw anything on their way around the valley. Sema and Eleph kept just as sharp a lookout on the surroundings as the men did.

Vina got preoccupied with helping Masha. Masha's agitation got progressively worse as long as Lucky stayed out of the group scouting to rock tops.

Hammer didn't ask why Masha found everything so terrifying. She had been like this for as long as he had known her—since her earliest childhood.

He assumed something must have happened to her in Ceon. One of the Renegades might have attacked her even then—or maybe just frightened her into thinking he would.

The party stopped again when they got to the farthest southern tip of the valley. "Where did you find this waterfall?" Hammer asked Cross. "I didn't see it. You lead us to it and show us where you think would be a good spot to camp."

Cross led the way after that. Hammer took a position in the far rear where he could guard the party. He climbed into the rocks a few times so he could see the whole valley.

He still didn't see any Renegades or Bounty Hunters, but he agreed with Scarecrow. They were there.

The Renegades worked hard to drive the Godless out of this territory and take it as their own. The Renegades wouldn't let it go without fighting to keep it.

The Bounty Hunters didn't want the territory. They knew the Godless were here. The Bounty Hunters didn't need any better reason than that to come after the party.

The Bounty Hunters also knew that the Godless had women with them. The girls would offer an irresistible temptation for the Bounty Hunters to track down the party at all costs.

Hammer should have gotten his people as far away from this country as possible. That would have been the smart thing to do. He should have taken his band straight north to the one place in the world he knew the Renegades and the Bounty Hunters were not.

The northern valley was so much more defensible than this place, too. He knew for certain his people would be safe there—because they would be alone.

A cluster of ideas stopped him from leaving. For a start, he and his band were already here. Staying here saved them a journey of months or maybe even years.

These girls would come of age soon enough. Then they would get pregnant. Hammer didn't want to travel anywhere with pregnant women ever again, especially not now that he was the one responsible for their survival.

The Ashtaws also presented a unique opportunity he just couldn't pass up. He would become all-powerful if he could just find a way to harness their size and strength. No one would be able to stand against him.

Shadow's warning proved the most powerful motivator of all. Hammer's band would be alone in the northern valley. Their children wouldn't be able to go to the gatherings.

The band would die out eventually if they went that far north. Their only hope was to establish themselves here in the south—close enough to attend the gatherings and bring in new blood.

Resentment ate away at Hammer's guts when he remembered Shadow's words. Hammer had to prove Shadow wrong. Hammer had to raise this band from a bunch of unruly teenagers and turn them into real Godless warriors.

He had to bring his people to the gatherings and force the other Clans to accept him as Kral. He couldn't back down until he proved Shadow wrong.

Cross came to the waterfall. Hammer hadn't seen it before during his patrols around the valley. Then again, he and his men usually split up to patrol different locations. Hammer had never come to this part of the valley before. He never would have seen the waterfall before.

Cross hunted around until he found a pathway down into the bottom canyons. The path wound through a crooked maze of rock walls. It reminded Hammer of the bare, lifeless northern country Red and his men came from.

Dense jungle choked the canyons. The canopy grew high above the party's heads. Sheer cliffs jutted even higher above the tallest trees.

Vines and creepers snaked all over the cliff walls. The thick canopy protected the party from any attack from the air—any Boultar attack from the air.

The canopy wouldn't protect the party from Krakelows or other jungle creatures, but the party would have faced those anywhere.

Cross led a long way down into the canyons. He couldn't possibly have known where he was going. He kept going until he entered a flat labyrinth of tight defiles between towering cliffs. No one could descend those cliffs to threaten the party.

He turned off into a different canyon and came to a wall at the far end. It met up with the two side walls to form a box canyon with only one narrow entrance in and out.

He turned in all directions examining the surrounding cliffs. "This is as good as it's going to get, I say. I saw we make this the place."

"Outstanding work, brother," Earthquake exclaimed. "This is perfect."

"You girls get started building yourselves some shelters," Hammer ordered. "Make yourselves comfortable. We'll be staying here for a while."

The girls grabbed each other, hugged each other, and jumped up and down in delight before they all got to work.

"Now what do we do?" Ant asked.

"We're going back to the valley," Hammer replied. "I'm starting to think Mora was right about just about everything. We need to lead the Ashtaws down here away from the valley. There are plenty of Fogpo trees around. We'll keep the Ashtaws here while we tame them and build the harnesses where our enemies can't interfere."

"We need to keep patrolling the valley," Scarecrow growled. "We need to make sure none of the other Clans establish themselves there. They might get too strong for us to remove them."

Hammer agreed and said so. He didn't mention that he and his men would be able to demolish any invading Clan as soon as the Godless trained the Ashtaws to fight.

He wanted to hurry up and get started on that. He wanted to hurry up and get to the part where he could flatten any enemy at will with no trouble. That would take time. His band had to defend themselves and guard against any intrusion in the meantime.

The men returned to the valley and then spent a few hours cutting, gathering, and stacking Fogpo branches.

Hammer decided to follow the band's original plan. He and his men would carry the branches into the valley, lure the Ashtaws to follow, bring them up here to give them a feast of Fogpo leaves, and then carry the branches down into the canyons.

He already knew which canyon he would keep the Ashtaws in. It was protected from the air and big enough for adult Ashtaws to live in. The curved cliff walls would make it harder for the Ashtaws to escape. They would find it easier to stay and browse in the canopy.

He chose a spot on the ridgeline much farther south from where Hangman's band had made its original campaign to mount the Ashtaws.

Hammer couldn't take the creatures down the cliffs near the waterfall. He had to lead them farther southeast and circle back through easier terrain, but he still knew it was possible.

He and his men were just returning to the ridgetop with another armload of branches when Thuron got Hammer's attention. Thuron did it silently. That was never a good sign.

Thuron pointed out a different group of Bounty Hunters—or maybe it was the same group the Godless saw last time.

The Bounty Hunters weren't coming after the Godless this time. The Bounty Hunters didn't see the Godless. Hammer's men were too far away and they had been behind the ridgeline until right this minute.

The Bounty Hunters dropped over the side and entered the valley itself. They climbed down the hillsides getting closer to the herd. The Bounty Hunters tried to get near the Ashtaws, but the Bounty Hunters didn't bring Fogpo branches with them.

"What are they doing?" Bugs muttered. "Are they trying to tame the Ashtaws, too?"

"It doesn't look like they know what they're doing," Cross remarked. "Maybe they just realize that *we* want the Ashtaws for something. Maybe the Bounty Hunters want to figure out *why* we want the Ashtaws."

"It doesn't matter because we're going to eliminate these bastards." Hammer dropped his armload of branches. "Come on. We're going to reduce their numbers as much as we can."

He took off running around the ridgeline. His men followed him behind the ridgeline where the rocks would conceal their approach.

He slowed to a walk and crouched behind the rocks searching for the first glimpse of the Bounty Hunters. He and his men had to eventually work all the way back up to the ridgeline before they saw the Bounty Hunters again.

The Bounty Hunters got within thirty yards of the nearest Ashtaws. The huge adults snorted in deafening booms when they saw people approaching.

The creatures tossed their heads, stamped their feet hard enough to shake the ground, and a few even charged the Bounty Hunters. The Bounty Hunters turned and ran for it all the way back to the ridgeline.

Hammer and his men retreated deeper into the rocks. Ant, Scarecrow, Thuron, and Lonion climbed up to elevated positions above the unsuspecting Bounty Hunters. Hammer stayed on the ground, drew his blades, and braced himself to take these enemies down.

Something clicked in his mind at that moment. This valley—this was his territory. No one would ever take this place from him. An enemy Clan's mere presence here insulted him as Kral.

He would destroy anyone who set foot here, starting right here, right now—today.

The Bounty Hunters kept glancing behind them to make sure the Ashtaws didn't follow. The Bounty Hunters must not have observed ahead of time that the Ashtaws never climbed the side ridges of their valley. They went straight back to grazing.

The Bounty Hunters gasped for breath, turned away to leave the valley, and came face to face with Hammer's men coming out of the rocks.

Hammer attacked without mercy. Ant, Scarecrow, and the others leapt down from above and cut all the Bounty Hunters down in a few seconds.

"We ought to be able to do something useful with these bodies," Pitch remarked. "We shouldn't just leave them here to rot."

"They won't rot," Scarecrow pointed out. "The Boultars will take them."

"We should use them as a warning to the Renegades and other Bounty Hunters," Omen suggested. "We should send them a message that we're here and we're staying."

"You're right," Hammer agreed. "Skin and bone the Bounty Hunters. We'll feed the flesh to the Boultars and stake up the skins and skeletons on these rocks for the others to find."

The men worked on that for the rest of the day. The men got covered in blood and threw hunks of flesh far down the valley for the Boultars to feast on.

In the end, the Bounty Hunter skins made an extremely gruesome effect on the rocks. Hammer ordered his men to leave the heads attached. The Godless gouged out the Bounty Hunter's eyes and removed their tongues.

The band tied the remaining grisly flaps of skin to the rocks with ropes twisted from the jungle. The band arranged each body with the arms and legs spread out.

The skins looked like flattened versions of people tied down and held captive there. Everyone could see that the dead people were Bounty Hunters.

The party stood back and admired the effect. The dead Bounty Hunters covered twelve rocks all along this side of the ridge.

"That's perfect!" Omen breathed. "We should have thought of this a long time ago."

"We'll do this with all our enemy dead," Hammer decided. "We'll leave these around the whole valley to announce to the world that this is our territory."

"What about the canyon camp?" Lucky asked. "Do you want to leave warnings there, too?"

"No, not there. That will only attract our enemies' attention and alert them that we're keeping something of value there. Let's get started leading the Ashtaws down the canyons. I want to get them to safety before we do anything else."

Chapter 5

The men returned to their Fogpo branches, but Lonion spotted another group of Bounty Hunters before the Godless men could even pick up the branches.

"We'll just keep attacking them as long as it takes," Hammer decided. "I don't want any of them to see what we're doing."

The men circled the ridge to the other side of the valley. These Bounty Hunters were not trying to approach the Ashtaws.

The Bounty Hunters traveled fast following the northern ridgeline. They looked like they were trying to catch up with the patrol that Hammer's men just killed.

Hammer and his men moved in to strike down this patrol, too, but the instant they broke cover to attack, a party of Renegades burst out of the nearby rocks and pulled the same sudden surprise attack on the Bounty Hunters.

The two groups locked in combat right in front of Hammer. He checked himself and then backed his men away so they wouldn't get involved. Both the Renegades and the Bounty Hunters tried to split out of the conflict to come after Hammer's band instead.

Renegades and Bounty Hunters pulled each other back into the fight by attacking the other side from behind. No one could break out of the skirmish.

Hammer retreated. The animosity between the Renegades and the Bounty Hunters was his greatest asset. He would be stupid not to exploit it and let them kill each other instead.

He and his men returned to their pile of Fogpo branches. Hammer looked down at the Ashtaws and sighed.

"The sun is going down. We should wait on this until tomorrow. Then we'll send out patrols to make sure we get rid of the other two Clans. I don't want to take the Ashtaws out of the valley when one of the other Clans might see us."

"The other Clans will always be around," Cross pointed out. "We'll probably never get rid of them completely."

"We can at least stop them from seeing us take the Ashtaws. We won't do it right in front of them. That would show our hand. We can domesticate the Ashtaws somewhere else—somewhere the enemy Clans won't see us. Let's get back to the canyon camp and see how the girls are getting along."

The men returned to the canyons. Hammer already felt himself coming home as soon as he entered the steep cliffs. They offered such a sense of peace and protection.

The men stopped at the end of the box canyon and stared at the girls working around the area. They had stripped out a large section of the creepers and undergrowth to create a clearing at the farthest end of the canyon.

The girls had left the vines and trailing fronds on the walls themselves. The vines hung over and shielded the clearing from the air. That left the ground bare underneath the roof of foliage.

The girls had constructed five identical four-walled shelters around the clearing—one for each girl. The girls had also constructed seven three-walled shelters for the men.

Two fires burned in the middle of the camp. The jungle diffused the smoke so it traveled through the canopy instead of straight up into the sky.

The girls had gone hunting—or some of them had. They had killed a small Dushag and were in the process of cooking it on a spit.

All the girls burst into proud grins over their handiwork. The girls gathered around to greet the men as if they were all really married couples.

The single men and uninitiated boys assembled at the open shelters. Hammer sat down next to one of the fires while Vina kept working.

"How is everything up at the valley?" she asked.

"Everything is good at the valley. The enemy Clans are still there, but we'll keep fighting them there. Hopefully they won't find out that you and the girls are down here."

She sat down next to him and handed him a bowl of the cooked meat. He saw her acting as his wife. She might as well be. She would come of age in a matter of weeks.

"They know you have women here," she remarked. "They'll keep looking for us."

"I know, but they'll look in the eastern jungle. That's where the Bounty Hunters saw you before—and the Renegades know the other Godless live east of here. Both Clans know we retreated there after our last confrontation. They'll think the same thing now. You girls should stay down here. Don't tip them off that we set it up any differently."

She looked down at the food in her lap. "There ought to be a way to wipe them all out. Hangman's band did it. We should be able to do it, too."

"Hangman's band didn't wipe them out completely," Earthquake remarked from his place across the fire. "That's why these Bounty Hunters are here. They followed us to find out who slaughtered the Bounty Hunter's village."

"We don't know that," Vina corrected. "They could have come from anywhere."

"There is no way to wipe out an entire Clan," Hammer added. "No one has ever done that before."

"I bet there is a way," Vina went on. "I bet you could do it if you sent someone inside their Clan."

"What do you mean by, 'send someone inside their Clan'?" Hammer asked. He wasn't sure he wanted to hear this.

"We did it in Ceon," she told him. "We killed all those Renegades and we got away. We only did that because we were already there. We were inside their Clan. They didn't think they had to guard us because we were there for so long. We could do something like that again."

"They wouldn't leave *us* unguarded. We're Godless," Earthquake countered. "Both Clans know we're Godless. They would never take us into their Clan."

"They do it all the time," she corrected. "That's how we wound up in the Renegade Clan. The Renegades captured our mothers."

"But none of our mothers was Godless before," Hammer pointed out. "I can't even think of any Godless captives the Renegades took before."

"Of course you can!" Vina exclaimed. "They took Mora as a captive! That's how Hangman found us! You've all heard the stories. The Renegades assaulted Shadow's whole band. The Renegades would have taken all the Godless women if the men hadn't stopped them. The Renegades would have done the same thing to us in the northern valley. That's the whole reason Aster led them to us—so they could retake us."

Hammer frowned. "What exactly are you suggesting—that you and the other girls get yourselves captured by the Renegades? You can forget about that."

"I wasn't going to suggest the other girls do it. I could do it. I could infiltrate the Renegades—or one of the Bounty Hunter patrols."

"No!" Hammer snapped. "No. Just no. You aren't going anywhere near them and neither are the other girls. Forget it. You can put that thought right out of your mind."

"It's the only way....."

"It isn't the only way!" Hammer countered. "It isn't the only way by a million miles. How can you even suggest that after what we've already seen—and don't even get me started on what the Bounty Hunters would do to you if they captured you. Kuvik already told us what they do to their captives. No female of mine is going to go through that."

"I could get inside their camp and pull an attack like he did," she insisted. "They wouldn't expect that. They would think another captive would be helpless. Kuvik proves it can be done. We don't even know how many of them he killed all by himself. I could go inside and you could stalk them from the outside. I could do something big—like he did—and you could attack from the outside at the same time. That would wipe them out."

Hammer stared at her as a million ideas collided in his brain. He would never in a million years send any female to get herself captured by either the Renegades or the Bounty Hunters. He would never let that happen as long as he had the breath in his body to stop it.

Hammer and his men grew up in the Renegade Clan and so did all five of these girls. Cross was the only person here who didn't know what the Renegades were truly capable of, but something told Hammer that Cross already knew, too.

Hammer grew up watching the Renegades brutalize his mother and the other women. The Renegades brought in other captive women and put them through the same nightmarish ordeal.

Girls who grew up in the Clan could face the same treatment from their fathers, brothers, uncles, cousins, and any of their male relatives' friends. No female was safe in the Renegade Clan.

The boys grew up under the same brutal regime. They grew up learning to toughen up and start acting the same way if they hoped to survive.

Hammer grew up hating his father, Darso. Hammer grew up watching Darso brutalize Cheina right in front of Hammer, Aster, and Lonion.

Darso didn't care if his children saw him abuse their mother. He wanted them to see. He felt he needed to teach his sons the Renegade way so they would grow up to do the same thing.

Hammer made a decision early in his young boyhood to kill Darso one day. Hammer decided to free his mother and younger siblings. Then the Godless came and did the job for him. Alien killed Darso and the Godless freed all the captives.

The Renegades couldn't hold a candle to the Bounty Hunters when it came to brutality. They made a science of it.

Kuvik's story about how he freed Yoa from the Bounty Hunters—it all came back to Hammer now. Kuvik *did* strike a blow from inside the Bounty Hunters. He did it from right inside their village while he was still an injured captive himself.

What if....? What if Hammer could do something like that—without putting Vina and the other girls in danger? Wouldn't that be worth it?

Hammer stood up and walked out into the dark jungle. His ears told him so much about what was and wasn't going on out there.

He didn't hear any sign of humans coming closer. He heard all the usual jungle creatures moving around. He could let them because his people were safe—for now.

His decision to keep fighting the enemy Clans at the valley—he knew in his gut that it was the right decision. It was the best way to divert the enemy Clans away from the canyon camp.

He climbed into the canopy and squatted on a sturdy limb to listen to the night noises. They calmed him. He didn't hear anything to alarm him.

He was still sitting there when Earthquake climbed up and squatted down next to him. "How is it looking?" Earthquake asked.

"It's all quiet. This place really is the perfect spot. Cross saved us."

"I want to talk to you," Earthquake began.

Hammer turned around. "What about?"

"Daora is the oldest of the five girls. She'll come of age in two months. I want to know what if anything you want me to do before I can marry her."

"You don't have to do anything. Just marry her and move into her shelter. That's all you have to do. We all know you two are together."

"Are you sure?" Earthquake asked. "Are you sure I don't have to do anything?"

"What do you think you have to do? This isn't an initiation where you have to fight anyone for her."

"I know. I just thought....you know....we don't know everything about the Godless way—and we've broken so many rules before. How do we know we aren't breaking one now?"

"Alien didn't have to do anything when he married my mother. Hangman gave his permission and Alien and Cheina started living together. That was the end of it."

Earthquake shrugged. "You're right. I didn't think of that."

"The only thing you could do to make it official would be to go to the gathering and we already know we aren't going to do that. Anyway, imagine we did go to the gathering and the five of us met these five girls with another Godless band on the way. We could pair off and not go to the gathering at all."

"No, we couldn't. We would have to go to the gathering anyway even if we paired off right away."

"Fine. Think about it another way. The five of us are one year older than these girls. We would have gone to the gathering last year if we hadn't gotten isolated in the northern valley. We might not have found wives at the gathering, so we would be entitled to go again this year—at which time we could pair off with these girls and the result would be the same in the end."

Earthquake made a face. "That's stretching it, isn't it?"

"It doesn't matter if it is because we aren't going to the gathering. You're accepting the decision of your Kral to marry Daora when she comes of age. You already have the decision of your Kral, so you don't have to do anything."

Earthquake grinned at him. "Great! Thank you."

"It would be pretty ironic if I made you jump and dance to marry her when I plan to marry Vina in the same way. Who would give me permission—Shadow? I don't think so."

"What will you do if he comes back to this valley the way he did last time?"

"I'll inform him that this is my territory now and I'll take it as an act of war if he enters it without my permission. I'll inform him that he and his band will always be welcome as guests as long as he treats me with the respect due another Kral. If he can't give me that much, then we're going to have a problem—but I don't think we will. He would only come here to keep track of the enemy Clans. He'll retreat once he finds out we're here."

"What do you plan to do about the enemy Clans? What did you think of Vina's idea?"

"I think it's a good idea—or it would be except that there is no way I would ever send any female into that, especially not her."

"Then how can it be a good idea if you don't implement it?"

"I didn't say I wouldn't implement it."

"How could you implement it if you didn't send her?" Earthquake's head shot up. "Oh, no. No, no, no. No way! Hell no! Are you insane?"

Hammer cocked his head to study his friend. "What's wrong?"

"You are NOT going yourself. Are you out of your mind?! You can't go!"

"I have no idea what you're talking about."

Earthquake shot to his feet. "We need you! You're our Kral! The safety of the whole band rests on you! Don't you get that?! You have to stay! Send one of us! Send me! I don't care who you send. You can't go!"

"When did I say I was going to go?"

Earthquake threw up his hands and spun away. "I don't believe this! We've been on our own for less than a week and you're already doing something like that this!"

"What's your problem?"

Earthquake spun around fast and pointed in Hammer's face. "You know what you're doing? You're doing exactly what Hangman would do. This is exactly the kind of stunt he would pull. He would go and get himself captured by his enemies so he could strike them from the inside."

Hammer bit back a smile. "Thank you. I take that as a compliment."

"Will you listen to yourself?!" Earthquake hissed. "You aren't Hangman and you can't get yourself captured! It's too dangerous! You heard what Kuvik said about the Bounty Hunters."

Hammer nodded. "I heard every word."

Earthquake stared at him with huge eyes for a second. Then Earthquake let out a loud gasp of exasperation and took off into the canopy on his way back to the camp.

Hammer settled back down on his branch and stared off into the darkness. It breathed with night noises, but they all sounded good, now that he knew his people were finally safe.

Chapter 6

P itch, Lucky, and Omen came to squat down next to Hammer the next morning. He poked up the coals in the fire in front of him and turned another piece of Dushag meat on the spit.

"Are we going for the Ashtaws today?" Omen asked.

"He already said we can't do that until we check that the enemy Clans aren't watching," Lucky pointed out. "We have to scout the whole valley perimeter before we do anything with the Ashtaws."

"That could take all day," Omen pointed out. "We wouldn't get back here until sundown. Then we would have to do the same thing tomorrow."

"That's for him to decide," Lucky insisted. "You don't tell your Kral how to make decisions."

"I wasn't trying to tell him how to make decisions," Omen replied. "I just asked."

The other men interrupted by coming over to them right then. Everyone else debated the same question.

Earthquake didn't mention the conversation he had with Hammer last night. Hammer never actually admitted to Earthquake that he planned to get himself captured by the Renegades.

Hammer would be able to handle that. He would never get himself captured by the Bounty Hunters. That would have been moronic.

He didn't know how Kuvik survived it—except that Kuvik didn't know beforehand what he would be facing when he got captured. He just dealt with the situation in front of him.

He didn't talk about how difficult it had been for him to resist the Bounty Hunters' brutality. He glossed over that, but some hint still snuck through in the way his voice shook when he talked about it.

Hammer already knew what to expect when it came to the Renegade Clan. He would much rather face that.

Earthquake couldn't actually come right out and tell anyone that Hammer planned to get himself captured. Earthquake only speculated that Hammer decided to take a page out of Hangman's book.

Hangman never shied away from risk. He thrived on it. He didn't seem to function as well without it.

Hammer might not be able to accomplish as much as Hangman would have been able to accomplish in the same situation.

This was definitely the best way to get close to his enemies and strike a decisive blow. He couldn't do that by picking off patrols of five and six men at a time. That would never bring safety to his territory.

He went through the morning meeting with his men and confirmed Lucky's assessment. The men had to check the enemy Clans' status and location before the party made any move with the Ashtaws.

Hammer and his men took their leave from the girls and climbed back out to the valley ridgeline. Nothing moved out there. The Godless had the valley to themselves.

Hammer ordered the men to circle the valley from the eastern side. Earthquake gave Hammer a hard look, but Earthquake still didn't intervene. He wouldn't and he couldn't—not without challenging Hammer's decision in front of the whole group.

The men set off at a run. They had to pass the pile of Fogpo branches on the way. Omen was right about the trip around the valley taking too long. The party wouldn't get back here until evening.

Hammer decided to feed them to the Ashtaws before he and his men went home that night. He made up his mind to cut Fogpo branches every morning and feed them to the Ashtaws every evening no matter what else the Godless were doing.

The Ashtaws would get used to the party. The Ashtaws would become accustomed to these regular food deliveries. Then the Godless could start touching the Ashtaws, getting them familiar with the feel of ropes on their skin, and start teaching them word commands.

Hammer didn't stop now. Scarecrow, Thuron, Lonion, and Bugs scrambled into the rocks and ran on either side of the party. None of the men raised the alarm about any enemy in the area.

The trail turned a corner at the end of the rocks. Hammer could see everything in front of him and on both sides. The whole country was empty.

He picked up speed. Maybe he and his men would make it back to their pile of branches earlier than they expected. Maybe they could make a start with the Ashtaws after all.

He drew abreast of the last rocks. Bugs, Stray, Earthquake leapt off the rocks at the same moment—and then a bunch of Bounty Hunters sprang out from between the rocks.

The Bounty Hunters had hidden themselves there where the scouts couldn't see them. None of the Godless would have been able to see these Bounty Hunters until the exact moment when the Godless stood directly over the Bounty Hunters' hiding places.

Bounty Hunters swarmed out of the rocks by the dozen. Five attacked Hammer. The other Bounty Hunters scattered to surround the rest of Hammer's men.

Hammer's hands flew to his blades. He didn't even get a chance to draw them before four Bounty Hunters tackled him down on the ground.

He struggled and fought to free his arms, but they all piled on top of him and then one of them kicked him in the head hard enough to knock him out.

He floundered back to consciousness in total darkness. He couldn't see a thing, but he felt someone carrying him somewhere.

They carried him off the ground. He didn't feel anything solid underneath him like the ground or a floor or anything. He only felt rough, strong hands holding onto his arms and legs to lift him up.

They had tied his ankles together and his wrists behind his back. A rough black sack covered his head so he couldn't see anything.

He tried to twist his body to see how tight the ropes were. His captors responded instantly by dropping him on the ground and attacking him a second time.

They beat and kicked him all over his body and then someone kicked him in the head again. Maybe it was even the same person.

Hammer didn't pass out completely this time, but the blow stunned him enough to make him stop struggling. He swam in a daze long enough for them to pick him up and carry him somewhere else.

He didn't struggle this time. He had planned to get himself captured by the Renegades. Now he found himself the Bounty Hunters' prisoner. This was not good.

Kuvik. Kuvik did it. Hammer could do it, too. He just didn't have a clue what he would do.

Did the Bounty Hunters capture the rest of Hammer's band, too? Were all his men here with him somewhere? They could escape together.

He wouldn't be able to do anything as long as the Bounty Hunters kept him tied up like this. They had disarmed him, too. The Bounty Hunters went back to carrying him. He felt them walking for a while. Then they put him on some kind of sled made out of hides.

The sack over his head stopped him from seeing how they pulled it over the ground. Knowing that didn't help him come up with a way to escape. He had to pay attention. He didn't want to escape. He wanted to survive long enough to strike a blow from the inside.

If he couldn't do that much, he could at least find out where the Bounty Hunters had rebuilt their village—or built their new village—whichever it was.

Kuvik had hit them from the inside. He had also led the Godless back to the Bounty Hunter village to kill even more of them and free more captives.

Hammer couldn't do any of that right now. He lay still on the sled and thought about his problem—or he thought about it as well as he could in between fading in and out from all these blows to the head.

The beating after he struggled somehow damped his will to resist. He hesitated to do anything even though no one would be able to tell he was struggling.

He tested it by twisting the ropes again. The Bounty Hunters had tied them so tightly around his wrists and ankles that the ropes cut into his flesh.

That pain made him stop trying, too. He could take a lot of punishment. He'd already suffered mistreatment from the Renegades and plenty of pain and trouble with the Godless. This pain acted differently on his mind.

Darso's mistreatment had only made Hammer angry and more intent on getting revenge. Now the pain and attacks made him cringe and want to hide—like Masha. That's what he was turning into. He was turning into someone just like her.

Thinking that should have fired his resolve to strike back at these people, but thinking it only made him ashamed of himself. What if he couldn't strike back? What if he got stuck with the Bounty Hunters forever?

He must have dozed off. He woke up when the sled stopped moving. More rough hands picked him up, threw him on the ground, and gave him another, much more severe beating. They didn't stop until they knocked him out again.

He woke up lying on his side on the cold, hard ground. The cold air around him bit his skin. It smelled like nighttime out there.

The sounds in his ears confirmed it. He was outside somewhere in the jungle in the middle of the night. He heard all the normal night creatures moving around in every layer of the canopy.

He turned his head from one side to the other, but he still couldn't move. The Bounty Hunters had left him tied up here. Was anyone sitting out there to guard him? Did the Bounty Hunters abandon him here to die?

All those sounds crushed in on him with the unbearable weight of dread. Any creature could come along and devour him. He wouldn't be able to defend himself.

What if the ants came? What if Abnormits came? What if a Krakelow came?

The minutes dragged by. They blurred into eternity. His mind started to play tricks on him. Was he hearing day creatures out there? Was he hearing creatures he'd never heard or seen before? Was he even still in the same part of the country?

He should have felt it if the Bounty Hunters carried him that far away from his original territory. They couldn't have. He didn't feel himself traveling faster than a person could walk.

The sled moved with a steady, jarring, walking rhythm of someone pulling it. He couldn't have traveled more than a few days' journey away from the Ashtaw Valley.

He rested his head on the ground to try to get some sleep, but a slam startled him awake. He heard footsteps coming toward him, braced himself for another blow, and someone yanked the sack off his head.

He had half a second to see that he was in fact lying on the ground in the jungle, but the Bounty Hunters didn't abandon him. He was really starting to wish they had.

Five of them attacked him again and pounded and kicked him all over his body. They avoided his head this time.

He howled and roared in agony, but they showed no mercy until they left him battered and bloody on the ground.

One of them kicked Hammer's shoulder to roll him onto his back. This turned out to be the worst torture yet. His weight rolled onto his bound hands and made him yell out in agony.

The guy slammed his foot down on Hammer's shoulder to pin him in that position. "Where's the rest of your band?!" the guy snapped. "Where are they hiding?!"

"I don't know!" Hammer roared. "I don't know where they are!"

"You're lying!" the guy snapped. "You patrolled the Ashtaw Valley and attacked our men! Were you the one who skinned them and put their skins and skeletons on the rock for us to find?"

"Yes!" Hammer bellowed and then burst out in hysterical laughter.

He probably shouldn't have, but his pain, exhaustion, and pure fear made him reckless. He didn't care anymore what happened to him as long as he got the last laugh at their expense.

Another Bounty Hunter stormed up to him, kicked Hammer hard in the crotch, and then ground his foot hard into Hammer's genitals to wring the torturous pain from his body.

Hammer gave up trying to be brave and collapsed howling and sobbing on the ground. "I don't know where they are!" he roared. "They went east—to rejoin the other Godless!"

The Bounty Hunters didn't stop. Did they know he was lying?

He could only writhe in torment until they moved off and left him lying there moaning and seething in agony. He rolled onto his side, but not before they crushed his hands under his own weight.

The Bounty Hunters held a murmured conference to one side. He couldn't hear them and didn't try too hard. He had bigger problems.

He glanced around and realized he wasn't in the jungle after all. He was outside, but the trees ended a dozen feet away from him. Another Bounty Hunter village sat right behind him. He recognized it from Kuvik's attack.

The same sturdy houses dotted a cleared area with a ring of trees surrounding the village on its other side. The village looked identical in every other detail. He wouldn't have known them apart if he hadn't seen the first village torched to the ground.

He even recognized the large hall on the other side of the village—the hall Kuvik had set on fire to start the assault.

Golden light streamed from the open doors at both ends of the building. The voices of dozens of men bubbled out of the walls and flooded the night.

Hammer's heart sank when he realized where he was. None of his men were here. He was alone with who knew how many Bounty Hunters. He wouldn't be able to strike a blow against anything by himself.

Chapter 7

The Bounty Hunters came back over toward where Hammer lay on the ground. He squealed in pathetic terror when he saw them coming to beat him up again. He could have faced it if he could just fight back.

They didn't give him the chance. They beat him twice as hard this time and kicked him in the face a dozen more times. They bloodied him and maybe even broke some bones in his face. He couldn't be sure, but it sure felt like that.

They didn't kick him hard enough to knock him out. They just let him feel what it was like to lie here totally defenseless and not be able to do a single thing to stop them.

They eventually stopped and carried him the rest of the way into the village. Kuvik's descriptions of the place came back to Hammer. He remembered them in much more detail than he realized.

He thought when he first heard about Bounty Hunter society that the other captives must be cringing, pathetic weaklings if they didn't at least fight back to free themselves.

Now he got a completely different picture of why they didn't. Kuvik said the Bounty Hunters beat the captives into submission and didn't stop once they untied them and let them start moving around to do work in the camp.

Hammer didn't understand any of that until now. He didn't understand how this helplessness could play such a poisonous trick on his mind.

He just wanted it all to stop. He wanted to hide from any more beatings. He didn't want to fight if it meant getting beaten like this again. Darso's mistreatment never affected Hammer like this, but Darso never tied Hammer up.

The Bounty Hunters threw him into a bare shed. They dropped him on the floor from three feet up so he crashed down on his bound arms and got hurt again. The Bounty Hunters only laughed at his pained moans, locked him in, and left him there.

He collapsed on the floor and let misery take over. One of the other Godless men would marry Vina now. Hammer would become one of the living corpses he'd seen in the Bounty Hunter camp—the prisoner-slaves who ran off instead of joining the Godless.

Some other man would take over as Kral of Hammer band. Earthquake would probably become Kral—or maybe Ant or Scarecrow.

Hangman never went through this agony and despair. He would have been able to face this. Even Kuvik did it.

He started out as a Hungry Ghost. He rose to become one of the strongest Godless men out there. He was Godless even if he never initiated.

Hammer just couldn't face it. He couldn't think about anything but lying here and waiting for the Bounty Hunters to come back and beat him up again.

They would keep doing it until they completely crushed his will to resist. They would keep doing it until he couldn't even think straight. They would reduce him to a skeleton—a cringing, hopeless, mindless skeleton they could order to do anything.

He would cooperate and flinch if they even raised their hand to threaten him. They would keep beating him anyway to make sure he never raised his head even to look around him or make eye contact with anyone.

That was where this was going. That was how he would end up if he stayed here, but he still found it impossible to act. How could he act when he had no weapon and no way to free himself?

He must have faded out again. He woke up and went through an identical panic when the shed door burst open and another group of Bounty Hunters stormed in.

They started over with another identical beating. He felt himself starting to detach from reality, but they broke off much sooner this time, picked him up, and carried him out of the shed.

He must have passed out for longer than he realized. It was night again.

They carried him across the dark village, carried him into the big hall where dozens of other Bounty Hunters stood around talking, and dumped him in a corner with ten other bound captive men.

None of them were Godless men. He wilted in relief when he didn't recognize any of them. His men weren't here.

He didn't see the big chair where Kuvik said the Bounty Hunter leader used to sit. The guy must be dead now if the captives killed him in the last assault.

That didn't stop the Bounty Hunters from enjoying themselves. The noise in the hall escalated until three men approached the line of bound captives. All of them had been beaten black and blue. They looked as terrible as Hammer felt.

The Bounty Hunters cut loose the two captives on the far end, dragged them and shook them to their feet, and put weapons in their hands.

The Bounty Hunters shoved the two captives into the middle of the hall and all the Bounty Hunters moved back to give the two captives space.

The two men faced each other, but they didn't engage—not right away. Hammer remembered Kuvik's story about fighting the Crusher. This was the Bounty Hunters' entertainment.

They used their captives as slave labor. The Bounty Hunters used their female captives as sex slaves. This was just another example of how the Bounty Hunters used their captives for their own purposes.

Neither of the two captive men could move very well. Their injuries made them limp every time they took a step. Both men kept flinching and looking around at the Bounty Hunters instead of at each other.

One of the Bounty Hunters lost patience at last and jabbed one of the captives with a spear. The Bounty Hunter did this from behind so the captive didn't see in time.

The spearhead stabbed him in the back of the ribs. The captive guy spun around to confront his attacker. The Bounty Hunter brandished the spear at him again and waved him closer to his would-be opponent.

The captive guy took a long time before he summoned the nerve to turn his back on the Bounty Hunters and face his counterpart. The captive guy kept waiting for the Bounty Hunters to stick him again.

The two captives eventually faced each other and started fighting. The noise spiked off the charts. The Bounty Hunters cheered, yelled, clapped each other on the back, and pointed and gestured to the combatants.

Hammer glanced down the row of other bound captives. His turn would come. The Bounty Hunters would make these men fight each other. The Bounty Hunters would eventually come for him. It was only a matter of time.

He scanned the room and the light started to come back on in his mind and soul. This would at least get some weapons into his hands. He might be able to do something with them.

He wouldn't be able to do anything against this many Bounty Hunters. They would all be looking straight at him. He might be able to take down two or three or maybe even as many as seven or eight.

The rest would take him down. He couldn't let that happen. His band needed him. They needed a strong leader. They followed him this far.

They would only survive if they domesticated the Ashtaws and established territory in and around the valley. No one else in the band had the will to domesticate the Ashtaws. He had to get back there—and that meant surviving to get out of here.

That one moment when he glanced around the hall—he froze to the floor and his heart stopped. A bunch of captive women moved through the crowd of Bounty Hunters. Hammer didn't notice them before now.

None of them were Godless, either, but he definitely recognized one of them. She was a short, petite young woman. He stared at her for a second before he fully believed that she was really here.

She wore a short shirt down to her midsection. A rough skirt cut out of sewn hides covered her legs down past her knees.

Old, discolored bruises marked her face. Part of her hair had been cut off too short, but it was definitely the same girl.

She had beautiful, delicate features like Daora's. This girl would have easily been as beautiful as Daora if the girl didn't look so absolutely awful.

She jumped and flinched every time the Bounty Hunters near her yelled out at the combatants. She did her best to move through the crowd and pass around a hide skin stitched into some kind of water-carrying bag.

The men nearest her kept snatching the bag out of her hands. She jumped and cringed away from them every time they did this, but they didn't notice.

They yanked the skin away, tipped it up, and guzzled down the contents before they shoved the bag back at her. They completely ignored her other than that.

Hammer watched until the third time one of the men took the bag. The liquid inside overran his mouth and trickled down his cheeks. It wasn't water. It was dark red in color.

What did Mora call it? Alcohol. She said it made the Bounty Hunters' minds fuzzy and blurred their judgment. It was definitely doing that now. The guy wiped his arm across his face and went back to cheering the captives in their fight against each other.

Neither of them fought—not really. They just pretended.

They waved their blades at each other and slammed them against each other, but neither of the combatants tried to get around each other's defense. They just kept up the performance so the Bounty Hunters wouldn't attack again.

The girl moved on through the crowd. She only made it ten feet before another nearby Bounty Hunter accosted her, grabbed her from behind, mauled her body through her clothes, buried his head into her neck, and started pulling up her skirt right there in the middle of the commotion.

Her features screwed up in misery and terror, but someone jostled them before the guy could do anything. The impact threw them apart and she raced away into the crowd.

Hammer stared after her and scrambled to clear his thoughts. He knew that girl. She was Rosta, Thomion's daughter.

She had the status in Ceon of something like a princess back. No one would have dared to lay a finger on her there. She lived a charmed life compared to everyone else, especially the children of captive women.

Hammer had grown up with her, but she refused to believe his stories about Darso's mistreatment. She refused to believe anything Hammer told her about what really went on in her father's village.

Rosta didn't approve of Hammer's desire to get revenge on his own father. She also didn't approve of Hammer's plan to get his mother and younger siblings out of the village, out of Renegade territory, and take them to some other Clan.

He had been too young then to know which Clan to take them to or even in which direction he should take his family. He never got that far toward planning his escape.

Something terrible must have happened for Rosta to wind up here as the Bounty Hunter's captive slave. She must have been living this nightmare for a long time.

Something terrible happened, all right. The Renegades' captives fought back and killed almost everyone in Ceon. The captives and the Godless killed Thumion, too. Rosta must have been left alone.

That must be how the Bounty Hunters caught her—or maybe some other Renegades took Rosta under their protection and the Bounty Hunters captured her from them. Hammer wouldn't find out unless he asked her.

She wasn't here anymore and he couldn't ask her now.

Her presence brought him back to his senses instantly. He had to talk to her and he had to get her out of here. He just had to figure out how to do it.

His gaze migrated back to the two captive men pretend-fighting. The Bounty Hunters yelled at them to pick up the pace and make it a real fight. Then the Bounty Hunters lost patience. Two of them grabbed their spears and jumped out into the open floor.

They jumped between the two combatants so the captive men faced the two Bounty Hunters one on one. The Bounty Hunters attacked. The two captives had to fight much harder to defend themselves, but their injuries slowed them down.

Hammer relaxed on the floor. His turn would come. He would have to make a good show, but even if he won, the other spectators would probably kill him anyway.

The two captives' pretend-fight weakened and exhausted them in their injured state. They couldn't keep their weapons up.

One of the Bounty Hunters struck down the captive closest to Hammer. The Bounty Hunter retreated into the crowd to the praise and congratulations of his comrades.

The other captive held up better. Desperation gave him strength and energy. He fought back and even landed a few blows on his opponent.

The Bounty Hunter lost his temper. All that alcohol must have made him irrational. His attacks became disordered and sloppy, which gave the captive more openings.

The captive finally made a lunge, slashed the Bounty Hunter across the chest, and smashed his blade against the Bounty Hunter's spear to hack it out of the Bounty Hunter's grasp.

The captive guy raised his blade to destroy his enemy, but right at that moment, another Bounty Hunter rushed out of the crowd behind the captive and impaled him through the back with a different spear.

The captive froze there with the bloody spear shaft sticking all the way through him. He looked down at the spearhead while he still held his blade raised above his head.

He tried to turn around to see the person who attacked him—and then drooped. His weight pulled the spear to the ground and the dead captive collapsed on the floor.

The place erupted in noise. All the Bounty Hunters rushed in, surrounded the killer, patted him on the back, and congratulated him on his victory. No one paid the slightest attention to the two dead captives.

The celebration went on for a long time. Everyone forgot about the other captives lying bound and helpless on the floor. Hammer cast another glance around for Rosta, but he didn't see her.

One hour followed another. Hammer kept waiting for the Bounty Hunters to come over and get another two captives to fight each other, but the Bounty Hunters got so preoccupied with talking and drinking together that they didn't come back.

The throng of Bounty Hunters stopped Hammer from seeing what happened to the dead captives. Other women brought drink for the Bounty Hunters to share.

Some of the men dragged these women away and didn't return. Is that what happened to Rosta? Was she being held as some Bounty Hunter's slave right now?

The sky outside was already starting to get light by the time some of the Bounty Hunters came back, picked up Hamer and the other captives, and carried them away to different parts of the village.

The Bounty Hunters put Hammer back in the same shed. They must have been so addled by drink that they forgot to beat him up this time. They locked him in and left him there.

Chapter 8

D aylight crept over the shed. The little building had been constructed so sturdily that no light came through any cracks between the thick boards.

The light squeaking under the bottom of the door told him it was daylight outside. The sun heated up the walls and turned the shed into a sweltering furnace.

Hammer couldn't lie on the floor anymore. His body hurt too much and the pressure on his arms and sides became unbearable.

He squirmed around for over an hour before he worked himself into an upright position sitting on his seat. He leaned against the wall with his bound wrists behind him and his bound ankles in front of him.

He wasn't exactly comfortable like this, but it was better than nothing. He would just have to lie down again if it got too bad.

Now the question was how he could get the hell out of here—and take Rosta with him. All the men and girls in his band knew her. He could take her back to them. She would find a place there. No one would harm her again.

He wished now that he could have gotten his hands on one of the weapons in the hall. He wished now that he could get his hands on any weapon at all.

His hunger started to get the better of him, but his thirst got much worse. He was just looking around for some way to cut these ropes when someone unlocked the shed door.

He froze and braced himself for another beating, but the door opened and he stared in shock when Rosta walked in.

She stopped on the threshold and stared down at him in slack-jawed disbelief. She definitely recognized him. His face must not be so bruised after all.

She recovered immediately, cast a hasty glance behind her, and pulled the door shut. Then she stood there for another long moment of silence before she entered the shed.

She squatted down in front of him, but she refused to look at him or even talk to him. She put a basket in front of him and took out a large wooden plate loaded with roasted meat.

"What are you doing here, Rosta?" he whispered. "How did the Bounty Hunters capture you after Ceon?"

"Don't talk to me, Kalo," she murmured over her shoulder without looking up. "We could both get in trouble."

"How could we get in trouble more than we already are? Talk to me. I can get you out of here and take you somewhere safe. You could get a knife and cut these ropes. I know someone who rescued a girl from the Bounty Hunters. I could do the same thing for you."

"You're the reason I'm here," she snapped under her breath without looking up. "You killed my father."

"I didn't kill anyone who didn't deserve it—and I never saw Thumion during the fight! The Godless killed him!"

"You all did it," she barked. "You all wiped out the village and you left me there alone. What did you think was going to happen?"

She glanced around at nothing, but she made sure not to make eye contact with him. She took two containers of water out of her basket.

One was a sealed water bag like the ones he saw her carrying last night. This one definitely had water in it. Beads of clear moisture clung to the outside like she'd just filled it before she brought it in here.

The other was a large bowl full of water. She soaked a piece of furry hide in the water and started cleaning the blood off his face. She did it roughly and made him flinch. She didn't try to be gentle.

"Rosta....listen to me....." He winced again and had to stop himself so he could reason with her. "I would have taken you with me if I even knew where you were when the battle ended. All the captive women and their children went with the Godless. We live in a good country—all of us. We're all Godless now. You would be safe with us. No one would harm you. I swear it."

"You're only making a fool of yourself, Kalo," she muttered and wrung her hide out before she started cleaning the blood and muck off his neck. "You never cared about me."

"Stop it!" he blurted out. "You're like my sister. Come on. We can leave here together."

She finally looked up and stared right into his eyes. "Your family went with the Godless, too, didn't they?"

"Yes. We all did. They welcomed us and treated us like as own. They don't maraud, capture, or brutalize anyone. All the boys are there—Lonion, Hitrio, Ethio, Carro—all of them."

Her expression started to soften. "Are Cheina and Aster there, too?"

Hammer winced, but not because she hurt him. She wasn't even touching him. "They're both dead now."

Her features closed up in front of him. She shut down, threw her hide rag into the bowl, picked up her basket, walked out the door, and locked it again without another word.

Hammer wilted against the wall. So she did blame him for her getting captured. He supposed she was right. He should have gone looking for her if he cared about her so much. He should have at least made sure she was safe.

He assumed at the time that she ran away. She wasn't a captive like the others. She had every reason to think the Godless planned to kill her the same way they killed all the other Renegades.

He didn't know for certain, but not all the other freed captives might have thought of her the way he did. She was Thumion's daughter—and she did participate in Mora's captivity.

Hammer would never know how much she participated in the captivity and mistreatment of anyone else in the group. She could have been one of the enemy in that situation.

She wasn't now. She was just another captive like him.

He had to make it up to her somehow. He had to correct his mistake. He had only been a boy back then. He had been too thrilled to escape with the Godless and finally take his mother, brother, and sister to safety. He didn't think of anything else at the time.

She left the food and water there for him, but she didn't leave him any way to eat or drink it. He might conceivably have been able to pull the seal off the water bag, but he wouldn't be able to drink it without freeing his hands.

She was out there somewhere right now—and she was in danger. Some Bounty Hunter could be brutalizing her right now. Dozens of them could be doing it. Hammer couldn't save her—not like this.

She wouldn't step out of line to bring him a weapon and run away with him. She had no reason to trust him or to put herself in even more danger by helping him escape.

He doubted she would be able to escape on her own. The Bounty Hunters had beaten her down along with all the other captives. She wouldn't think to try to escape. The consequences would be too severe if she failed and got caught.

His hunger and thirst became unbearable. He lowered himself onto his side and spent a long time hitching himself toward the plate of meat. He had to use his lips and teeth to inhale one of the pieces into his mouth.

Then he collapsed on the floor to chew up the food. He relaxed and stared at the rafters before he picked up another piece.

Uncorking the water bag would be a completely different problem. He would have to be careful to use his teeth to pull the stopper. He would have to get his mouth around the top of the bag before all the water rushed out. That would be interesting.

He took his third piece of meat….and realized in that moment that he was staring at the door. He didn't think before that he was working himself into any particular position.

He blinked up at the door while he chewed his third piece of meat. The door had metal hinges, some of which weren't as sturdy as the rest of the building. The door also had a metal latch and a metal lock.

This shed must have been built in ancient times. No one used metal fixtures like that anymore. No one knew how to make them—or maybe the Bounty Hunters scavenged them from somewhere.

That wasn't possible, either. The Bounty Hunters didn't do stuff like that. They didn't build things—so how did they build that big hall?

Maybe they captured Followers to do it for them. The Bounty Hunters wouldn't be the first Clan to exploit the Followers' knowledge for their own gain—or maybe the Bounty Hunters found this village already intact.

None of that mattered because some of the hinges and part of the door plate bent away from the surrounding boards. The boards all looked solid and freshly cut. They wouldn't have lasted since ancient times.

Someone must have cut them recently and attached these plates and hinges to build this shed. Whoever did that left hammer marks and bends in both the hinges, the plate, and the fasteners that held all of them in place.

Hammer stopped chewing while he thought it over. Then he swallowed his mouthful and ate another piece while he made up his mind.

Daylight angled through the crack under the door. He should wait for nightfall before he escaped, but his maddening thirst got the better of him.

He ate his fifth piece of meat before he humped his aching body over to the door. It took a long time for him to sit up on his seat and then pivot onto his knees. He couldn't move well while he had his ankles tied together.

He had to lean against the wall to balance so he could push himself up onto his feet. Then he had to shuffle and hop to the door and turn his back to it.

He fingered the door latch and found some sharp corners he could use to cut the ropes, but the metal corners weren't big enough nor did they stick out far enough for him to get to them.

He examined the hinges and came up with the same problem. None of them was big enough, sharp enough, or in the right position for him to cut the ropes.

He stood there floundering in desperate confusion. He had to think of something and he had to think of something now. How the hell could he get out of here?

His thirst drove him crazy. The heat coming through the walls demanded that he drink something immediately before he passed out from heat exhaustion.

He stretched out on the floor again. He would have to drink a lot and he would have to drink fast. He wouldn't be able to re-stopper the bag once he opened it.

He inched over to the bag, took the stopper between his teeth—and froze. He had it. The solution was so simple. Why didn't he think of this before?

He rolled over and worked himself up onto his seat again. God, he was so stupid for not thinking of this before.

He started to maneuver his hands into the right position when someone started rattling the door lock again.

He threw himself over onto his side and lay there facing the plate of food and the water bag. He stared at them in forlorn defeat like he really couldn't figure out what to do with them.

Rosta entered the shed again, put the basket on the floor, and picked up the water bag. "Too bad," she mused. "You won't get any more until tomorrow."

"Help me, Rosta," he rasped more hopelessly than he actually felt. "At least give me some water. You wouldn't deny me that, would you?"

She compressed her lips and groaned. "I shouldn't. I should leave you to suffer the way you left me to suffer."

She ripped the stopper out of the bag and held it to his lips. He gulped down the water as fast as he could. He drank as much as he could hold before he collapsed panting and gasping for air.

She shoved the stopper back into the bag, put it and the food into her basket, and cast a hard look down at him lying bound and broken on the floor.

"I'll come back for you, Rosta," he husked. "I promise. I'll get you out. You'll be free and safe."

She snorted at him and walked out. She slammed the door and locked it behind her. She didn't even dignify his promise with a response. He couldn't exactly blame her for that.

He acted the instant she shut the door, twisted back onto his seat, and hitched himself forward so he could scoot his bound hands under his backside.

It wasn't as hard as he thought it would be. He really was an idiot for not thinking this before. He bent all the way forward and brought his bound hands under his feet. Now he had his hands in the front.

He ignored the pain in his wrists and used his fingers to untie the knot binding his ankles together. Now he could stand up and walk around, but he had to force himself to stop and think.

He couldn't leave the village until nighttime. Even then he would need a weapon to at least free his wrists. He considered just running for it into the jungle and waiting to free his wrists then.

Then he remembered that the shed door was locked. He would have to overcome that.

He went back to the door, turned his back to it, and studied the latch with his fingers. He found what he needed when he touched the pins holding the latch and plate in place.

The Bounty Hunters or whoever built this shed used straight metal nails. The nails must have been made in ancient times, too—or they looked like it.

Whoever built this shed had driven the nails part of the way into the wood and then hammered the nails over sideways to fix the plate into position.

The process made the nails flake and crack. They weren't sharp enough for him to cut the ropes, but the process weakened the wood, the nails, and the plate. The whole thing shifted slightly when he tried to tug the nails free.

He tugged harder and the door banged against the post. He had to be careful not to attract any attention. He didn't want anyone coming along and discovering him with his ankles untied.

He made up his mind that, if anyone did come, including Rosta, he would lie down on the floor real quick and put his feet behind him so he still looked tied up.

He kept working the nail around in circles until he twisted it all the way out of its hole. The process didn't take as long as he expected it to.

The plate slumped to one side when he removed the nail. The plate itself moved far enough out of line for the bolt to slip out of its socket. The door was unlocked.

He stopped there, turned around, and stared at it for a long time. He could leave whenever he wanted to, but he didn't want to—not yet. He had to wait for nightfall.

He returned to the other side of the room, moved his hands behind him, and stretched out on the floor where he had been lying before. He twisted around to hide his feet behind him.

He maneuvered the loose ropes behind him, too. No one would see them—unless the Bounty Hunters came to get him again.

Chapter 9

H ammer woke up and his eyes immediately snapped to the shed door in front of him. The latch plate still slumped over on its side. No light came from under the door anymore.

The Bounty Hunter village lay in silence beyond that door—or it would have lain in silence if not for the noise coming from the hall. He could hear it from here.

That sound drove him to his feet. The Bounty Hunters might come to get him any second to go fight in the hall. Then all his plans would come to nothing.

He sat up, moved his hands back to the front, and eased the door open. He peeked outside and then inched into the open before he sprinted for the nearest trees.

He didn't care where in the jungle he wound up as long as it wasn't here. He ran a long way before he dared to stop. He still couldn't free his wrists—and he needed a weapon.

At least he was out of the village, but he found his attention drifting back there. Rosta was in there. He made her a promise. He had to keep it.

He snuck back to the tree line and peered at the light coming from the hall. Was she in there? Was she serving the men their drink again?

He circled the village without coming out of the jungle. He used the undergrowth to conceal himself and inched silently around the village to its far side. He huddled in the bushes just a few feet away from the hall entrance.

The noise beat on the walls and echoed out into the night as usual. More captive slaves went into and out of the hall. He didn't see Rosta anywhere.

He couldn't leave without at least trying to help her. He waited until the other captives passed out of sight.

He stepped into the open and inched to the corner of the building. The walls hid him from view. No one could hear a thing with all that noise pounding inside.

He snuck closer to the door and stole a peek inside. Two more of the captives from last night fought in there while all the Bounty Hunters cheered, drank, and shoved each other in drunken ecstasy.

Hammer spotted Rosta right away. She stood in the middle of the crowd getting jostled and shoved by different men when they tried to take the drink bags from her and when the men gave them back.

Hammer's heart sank. He wouldn't be able to get her out—not tonight. He would have to wait and then he might get recaught.

He turned around to go back inside the trees when someone shouted behind him. He glanced behind him and spotted four other captive men rushing toward him. He didn't recognize them in the dark.

He spun away and ran for it, but they caught up with him first and tackled him to the ground. They punched and thrashed him much harder than the Bounty Hunters ever did.

The Bounty Hunters never saw or heard a thing. None of them came out of the hall.

The captive men punched Hammer in the face hard enough to stun him and took advantage of his confusion to drag him into the hall.

They dumped him with the other bound captives and these four men kicked him down on the floor to make him stay there. They stood guard over him so he couldn't get up.

The previous fight was just coming to an end. One of the combatants killed the other. One of Hammer's captors went over to have a private conversation with one of the Bounty Hunters. The captive guy had to yell into the Bounty Hunter's ear to make himself heard.

So now the captives were helping their oppressors capture other people. This shouldn't surprise Hammer. It hardened his heart against the captive prisoners. They didn't help him. Rosta didn't help him—not even for a chance at her own freedom.

The other Bounty Hunters held the victor at spearpoint to make him stay where he was. He still held the weapon he used to kill his previous opponent. Hammer saw exactly what was about to happen. He saw, he knew, and he welcomed it.

The same captive guy came back, cut Hammer's wrists free, and they hauled him to his feet before they shoved him into the middle of the floor.

The Bounty Hunters turned their spears on Hammer next. He grabbed the dead guy's blade. Now Hammer had two things going for him. He had a weapon and he had his hands free—the two things he had against him a few minutes ago.

He caught Rosta watching from the crowd, but she turned away and left the minute he made eye contact with her. There was only one thing left to do—get out of here.

He turned his attention to the other armed captive. The packed crowd of Bounty Hunters blocked Hammer's path to either of the doors at the two ends of the building.

He wouldn't even have minded making himself a coward by turning tail and running for it. Desperation made him reckless.

He and the other armed captive eyed each other. They had to fight each other, but that wouldn't help get Hammer free. Not even killing this man would do that.

Neither of them engaged right away. Hammer's opponent sized him up. Hammer couldn't be sure about the rest of the captives in this camp, but this man must have some combat experience. He knew exactly what he was looking at.

Hammer sized the other man up at the same time. Hammer could beat him, but Hammer didn't want to. He didn't want to kill another captive—not unless whoever it was got involved in imprisoning Hammer.

He didn't have time to deal with those people. He raised his weapon and the same determined look came into his opponent's eyes. He hardened his features and came forward to meet Hammer.

They engaged more than any of the other captives had. Hammer's opponent actually tried to kill him. He would succeed if Hammer didn't defend himself.

He let his opponent get the upper hand. Hammer deflected the guy's swipes and thrusts. Hammer never let the guy's blade come too close.

Hammer backed off. The Bounty Hunters parted and flowed around to the other side of the room to give the two combatants space.

Hammer eventually worked himself and his opponent away from the center of the room. The Bounty Hunters shoved both men back in the other direction.

A few Bounty Hunters aimed spears at Hammer's back to stop him from retreating any further. He couldn't get any closer to the doors. He had to come up with another way to get closer.

He blocked another few thrusts from his opponent's blade and made a desperate bid to change things before his opponent got the better of him.

Hammer waited for the guy to make another thrust. Hammer responded by tackling the guy flat on his back.

They rolled back toward the middle of the room. The Bounty Hunters went nuts. They cheered louder and some even came forward to push the combatants one way or the other.

Hammer couldn't pay attention to the Bounty Hunters. The man in front of him turned out to be a lot stronger than Hammer gave him credit for.

The two men grappled and wrestled on the ground. Neither could use their weapons at this close range.

Hammer's opponent took him down right away, scrambled to get on top, and punched Hammer a few times before going for his blade. Hammer couldn't let that happen.

He took advantage of the maneuver to throw the guy off. Hammer threw him a lot harder than he should have. The guy rolled across the floor and landed fifteen feet away from the doors. Hammer scrambled to his feet, charged the guy, and tackled him a second time.

Their momentum carried them both to within five feet of the doors. The Bounty Hunters were too excited to care or notice.

The combatants split apart again. Hammer rolled onto his feet, faced his opponent, and they both raised their weapons to reengage.

None of the Bounty Hunters noticed the two men standing so close to the exit. The fight must have convinced the Bounty Hunters that the two combatants wouldn't do anything else.

Hammer took one look at his opponent. Hammer didn't look at the doors. His opponent must have thought the same thing. The guy bellowed out loud, charged, and raised his blade to attack.

Hammer really did turn tail and run that time. He pretended he was so scared of the guy's attack that Hammer whirled away and bolted—straight outside, across ten feet of open dirt, and he plunged headlong into the trees.

He didn't stop running until he buried himself in the shadows.

Chapter 10

Hammer staggered a few hundred paces, glanced around, and gulped trying to slow down his racing heart. His throat and lungs hurt from the effort of getting this far away from the Bounty Hunters before they caught up with him.

He couldn't keep running. He was making too much noise. He would attract the Bounty Hunters straight to his location. His breathing alone made too much noise. He had to slow down, calm down, and quiet down before he did anything else.

He scrambled into the branches, climbed all the way to the highest canopy, and hid in the foliage. He could have gone back into the Bounty Hunter village to find Rosta, but his recent experience with the other captives made him think twice.

She might sell him out to the Bounty Hunters. She might alert them that Hammer was here. She might even attack and kill him herself.

Kuvik's story made up Hammer's mind for him. He couldn't fight these Bounty Hunters by himself. He needed his men—and he didn't even know which direction to travel to find them.

The sound of footsteps in the jungle snapped him back to high alert. He huddled deeper in his hiding place and strained his ears to hear where the Bounty Hunters were searching for him.

He didn't have to see them. He tracked them with his ears and controlled his breathing so they would never find him. They kept stopping and listening for any sound of his movements.

The Bounty Hunters didn't survive by being good at moving around in the jungle the way the Godless did. They didn't understand how to move around in the jungle at night. They made a lot of noise—noise that didn't fit in with the rest of the jungle sounds.

The Bounty Hunters blundered everywhere, made a lot of noise, and talked loudly about where Hammer might be and how far he might have gotten away from the village.

They eventually moved off into another part of the jungle, but Hammer stayed where he was. He didn't want to travel anywhere if he might accidentally wind up traveling in the wrong direction.

The Bounty Hunters came back eventually. They had to come back on their way to return to the village. They talked the whole time about where they would look for Hammer once the sun came up.

He waited for their voices and footsteps to retreat all the way to the village. Silence descended over the jungle except for the usual night noises.

He tied his weapon to his waistband, buried his head in his arms, and passed out. He could finally relax here. He was as safe as he was going to get for now.

He woke up when daylight started to creep through the branches. He looked around him. This canopy didn't tell him anything.

He climbed all the way up to the highest, smallest branches where he could look over the top to survey the countryside. He caught a single glimpse of the mountains to the east. The Ashtaw Valley was over there.

He descended immediately, but he stayed in the treetops. He could travel faster, more safely, and he would be able to hear the Bounty Hunters coming sooner if he stayed up here. He would also be able to respond better when they did come.

He took off running as fast as he dared through the branches. His injuries slowed him down more than he liked to admit, but he kept moving. He didn't care about anything other than getting back to his band.

He traveled until sunset and kept going through the following night. He sensed himself nearing the point of exhaustion before he broke out of the trees into the bare, rugged country around the mountains.

He couldn't relax even here. The Bounty Hunters were here, too—and so was the Renegade Clan.

He made it to the top of the ridge just as the sun peeked over the highest mountains. Ashtaws covered the valley floor.

He considered crossing it and heading down the gorges to meet up with the Godless at their camp. He changed his mind when he saw his men circling the ridge on their morning patrol.

They saw him coming a long way off before he got there. He didn't try to hide himself. He didn't want to surprise them into attacking by mistake.

They had no reason to attack when they saw someone coming alone. Then he got close enough for them to recognize him.

They stopped in their tracks and gaped at him in horror. "Hammer!" Lucky gasped. "What happened to you?!"

"You saw what happened to me. I had a run-in with the Bounty Hunters—but that's okay because I found out where their village is. We can pull another raid on them the way we did with Kuvik."

"A run-in!" Bugs practically yelled. "You call this a run-in?! You look awful!"

Hammer tried to shrug that away. "It was just a bunch of beatings like Kuvik said. It could have been worse." He looked around. "What's happening here? Are you finding anything on your patrols?"

His men opened and closed their mouths a dozen times before anyone managed to say anything.

Ant broke the silence first. "The Bounty Hunters seem to have pulled back for now. The Renegades haven't been coming around as much, either. We don't know why. We just wanted to keep an eye on things."

"That's perfect," Hammer replied. "We can take advantage of their hesitation. Let's go."

He took a few steps forward to pass them going in the other direction. None of the men moved. "Take advantage of their hesitation how?" Pitch asked.

"To domesticate the Ashtaws—or at least get them out of the valley so we can start domesticating them." Hamer furrowed his brow at his men. "That is what we were trying to do, isn't it?"

His men exchanged glances. He saw right away what the problem was.

"Did you think I wasn't coming back?" he asked. "You should know better than that."

"We weren't sure...." Ant replied. "No one wanted to step forward to take your place, but we thought we ought to at least talk about it."

"Well, now you don't have to. Come on. Let's go. We should get started before the enemy Clans come back."

They still didn't follow him. "You should go back to the camp, brother," Scarecrow remarked. "You need to recover first."

"No, I'm fine." Hammer frowned at them all again. "What's the matter? I told you we would domesticate the creatures."

"Maybe we shouldn't," Omen remarked.

Hammer froze in his tracks. This was the first outright protest he'd heard so far. "Why do you say that?" Hammer asked.

"We have enough trouble just defending this country. The enemy Clans will keep attacking. We need all our men to fight them. We can't spare anyone to domesticate the creatures."

Hammer glared at him. "Are you finished yet? Are you challenging me as Kral? Are any of you?"

"No, of course not," Omen blurted out. "I'm just saying this whole Ashtaw project might be a bad idea."

"How do you suppose we can fight our enemies without the Ashtaws?" Hammer struggled to keep his voice down. "The Renegade Clan took this territory from the Godless long before even Shadow was born. What hope do you think we have of holding this land on our own with just fifteen of us? What do you say we should do if we don't domesticate the Ashtaws? Do you say we should move on and go back to the northern valley right now?"

Omen squirmed. "Maybe we should."

"And what happens when we have children and they need to find husbands and wives?" Hammer countered. "Then what will we do? Will we travel all the way back down here through enemy territory so we can go to the gathering?"

"At least we would be alive then," Lucky pointed out.

"We're alive now," Hammer countered. "We're already sitting on the one weapon we could actually use to get rid of these enemy Clans. We got lucky before. They only sent a few patrols against us. They'll figure out that we're trying to retake this land. They'll send out more men to attack us. We really won't survive without the Ashtaws."

Pitch, Lucky, and Omen exchanged glances. Hammer felt his patience wearing thin.

"So let me get one thing straight before we go any further," he went on. "Did you or did you not have a conversation about who would be Kral after me?"

"We had a conversation about having a conversation about it," Cross informed him. "We had a conversation where we decided we needed to have a conversation about it and decide who would be Kral after you. We didn't make any decisions."

Hammer cast one more evaluating glance over the men in front of him. Omen, Pitch, and Lucky acted the most hesitant and maybe even resistant to domesticating the Ashtaws.

That didn't make them traitorous or disloyal. Whoever was traitorous and disloyal—if anyone was traitorous and disloyal—they didn't show it.

"Well, I'm still Kral until one of you challenges me," he went on. "As long as I'm Kral, we're going to stay here and start working on domesticating these creatures. I've heard your objections. I understand them and I'm taking them into account. Now let's get busy."

Chapter 11

Hammer walked off down the ridgeline heading south. He didn't want to waste any more time on these petty conflicts. He only cared about one thing—who would step out to challenge him.

He never doubted Cross. Hammer didn't doubt Ant, Scarecrow, or Earthquake, either. A challenge could have come from anyone else if it came at all.

Hammer didn't know anything about challenges except that they involved a battle to the death between the challenger and the ruling Kral.

No one ever had challenged Hangman the whole time Hammer and his men were growing up in that band. No one ever dared to challenge Hangman.

He had an easy way of accepting when people disagreed with him or made suggestions that conflicted with his decisions. He didn't take offense nor did he consider it treachery or disloyalty. He just dealt with it.

Hammer couldn't remember Hangman ever having to even think about someone potentially challenging him. The band had too many other more serious problems.

He had the unwavering dedication and loyalty of all his men. A man would have to be idiotic to question Hangman's judgment. They always went along with Hangman's ideas and followed his orders without question.

Hammer never had to think about that before, either. None of his men had ever questioned his judgment before, but he had never been Kral before—not really.

The men returned to their side of the valley where he ordered them to gather Fogpo branches the way they did before. Hammer helped them do it. Then the whole party got to work weaving long lengths of rope. He took the opportunity to evaluate the rest of his men.

Their names were Bear, Mammoth, Acrobat, Eager, Falcon, Flawless. He knew each of them as a brother. He never thought he would ever live to see the day when he would doubt them—in anything.

They all worked as willingly as ever, but the undercurrent of resistance didn't go away.

None of them revealed anything while they worked. He didn't see any of them acting any more friendly toward Omen and Lucky.

Hammer shook those thoughts out of his head. He couldn't start doubting Omen and Lucky—or Pitch. Hammer's band had been so solid from the very beginning. They had all been through too much together.

Hammer cringed when he saw Vuco working with Pitch and Omen. Would these naysayers end up corrupting the uninitiated boys? Hammer couldn't let that happen.

He wasn't in a position to stop it—not now—not without making himself look weak and paranoid. He just had to keep going.

They didn't finish their work until late in the afternoon. He sent Bugs and Flawless to scout the valley for any intrusion while the rest of the men returned to the canyons.

The women went through an equally horrified series of reactions when they saw Hammer alive and injured—at least, they acted like he was injured.

Vina made a fuss over him and made him sit down while she brewed him some Gooji juice. "I don't need it. I'll be fine," he told her. "You don't need to make a big deal about it."

She wouldn't listen. She would have gone out into the jungle right then and there to gather Gooji sap for Hammer, but Scarecrow told her to stay where she was. He went out himself.

Hammer relaxed in front of Vina's shelter. He wouldn't stay there tonight, but he still considered it his house.

She sat down next to him and shared her food with him. He did let her put leaf paste on his injuries, but most of it was just bruises.

"You should rest for a few days," she told him. "You should take some time to heal before you go back out."

"I can't. We have to get ready to attack the Bounty Hunters' village."

"Did you do anything while you were there?" Earthquake asked.

"What do you mean by 'do anything'?" Hammer asked. "I got beaten up."

"Vina's idea was for one of us to go inside the Bounty Hunters' village and weaken them from within." Earthquake shot him a look across the fire. "I wondered if you went on purpose for that reason."

"I didn't go on purpose. You saw me get captured. Didn't you see me fighting back?"

Earthquake shrugged. "It wasn't as clear as all that after the way you were talking the other night."

Hammer turned back to his food. "We have to go back as soon as possible. Rosta is in the Bounty Hunters' village. I promised I would go back and get her out."

Half a dozen heads shot up. "She is?" Ant asked. "Is she okay?"

Hammer only shrugged again. "No one in the Bounty Hunters' village is okay, especially not anyone who got taken as a captive. I'm going back for her with the Ashtaws or without them."

"How did she get there?" Stray asked.

"I can only imagine that she got there in the usual way," Hammer pointed out. "She blames us for killing Thumion and leaving her on her own."

"But...." Lonion frowned to himself. "I don't even remember seeing her then. She wasn't around when we left with the Godless."

"She wasn't around because she thought we would kill her, too," Hammer agreed. "She must have run off or hidden until we all left."

"She *should* have run off or hidden," Eleph cut in. "I would have killed her myself if I saw her there."

"Why would you kill her?" Omen asked. "She never captured anyone."

"She helped them," Eleph spat. "She helped her father and her father's men. She helped subdue resistant captives. She helped break their resistance. She supported the Renegades." She grimaced and turned away. "You didn't see. None of you was there."

Hammer didn't ask what she meant. "She's a captive herself now," he announced. "She's going through all the worst treatment anyone can expect from getting captured by the Bounty Hunters—and she blames us for that. I said I would go back and get her and I will. I won't leave her there."

"Did she help you get out?" Sema asked. "Why didn't you bring her with you then?"

Hammer looked away at nothing. "She didn't help me. She doesn't trust me. I don't think she even understands what it means anymore to be somewhere safe with people who will treat her well. She might have been trapped with the Bounty Hunters for a long time."

"Are we really launching a campaign against the Bounty Hunters to rescue one woman?" Omen asked.

Hammer turned on him a lot more venomously than he should have. Hammer shouldn't have lost his composure, but it happened automatically.

"What exactly is your problem, brother?" Hammer snapped. "I told you before that we would eliminate the enemy Clans from this territory. I told you that before I ever found out Rosta was a Bounty Hunter captive. I told you we would domesticate the Ashtaws to use against our enemies. Why don't you go back to Shadow's band if you have a problem with that?"

"I would never do that!" Omen blurted out. "I didn't mean that, Hammer! You have to believe me."

"You make it sound pretty clear that you disagree with this course of action. Are you in or out?"

"In, of course!" Omen stammered. "I didn't mean to contradict....."

"And yet here you are contradicting again. You already stated your position on domesticating the Ashtaws. It's my decision and I made it. I didn't ask you if you agreed with it."

Omen averted his eyes. "No, of course not. I won't mention it again."

"You'll have to do better than not mentioning it again. Don't even think it again. I already made the decision. That's all you need to know."

Tense silence fell over the group. Vina took that moment to hand Hammer the basin of Gooji juice. He made the most of it by gulping down the juice so he wouldn't have to talk to or even look at anyone.

He could live with contradictions. He could even live with protests and people disagreeing with his decisions. Where did he draw the line? None of his men had stepped out of line—not yet.

He summoned an almighty effort to turn his attention to Vina. "How have things been here? You and the other girls haven't seen any sign of invaders, have you?"

She didn't look up to make eye contact with him. "No, nothing like that. Everyone was just.....they were worried when you got captured. Some people said you weren't coming back and we needed a new Kral. That's all."

He heard what she didn't say. He slipped his hand into hers. "I'll always come back to you. You don't have to worry about me."

"You'll always come back until the day you don't," she murmured to the ground. "Any day could be that day."

"It won't be now. We'll get married and have a family and grow old enough to see our children grow up. I'm certain of it."

She only shrugged. "I wish I could believe that."

"Do you want to know how I know it will happen? It will happen because I'll live long enough to face Shadow across the gathering. That day will come. I have no doubt about that."

"It's all about that, isn't it," she muttered. "You're doing all of this to get back at Shadow."

"No, I'm not! I'm doing this for us! I'm doing this because he never would have let me marry you! You were there! You heard him."

She shook the hair out of her eyes and got to her feet. "I'm tired. I'm going to go get some sleep."

He shot upright and grabbed her arm. Too many people sat up around the fires. They could all hear the conversation.

He steered her by the elbow and led her out of the ring of firelight. "What's the matter?" he whispered as soon as they got out of earshot. "I understand you were worried and upset when you found out I got captured, but I'm here now. I made it back. Can't you be happy about that?"

"I don't know. How can I be happy about it when all you can think about is Rosta?"

"Rosta! What about her?"

"You saw her in the Bounty Hunters' village."

"Yeah? So?"

"So you cooked up this whole mission to rescue her. How do I know something didn't happen between you?"

"Nothing happened!" he exclaimed and had to fight his voice under control. "Nothing could ever happen between me and Rosta. She's like a sister to me. We grew up together. You know that."

Vina evaluated him in the shadows. She evaluated him as closely as he evaluated any of his men. She measured whether she could trust him. How did it come to this?

"Maybe nothing happened between you physically," she murmured. "Maybe it only happened in your head."

"No! It wasn't like that. She's in trouble. Do you say I should just leave her there? I couldn't do that."

"You aren't talking about her like she's your sister."

"Why not? I would rescue my sister if she got trapped in that situation."

"Rosta is not your sister," Vina hissed. "You might have grown up with her, but she isn't your sister. Don't make it out like it's so far-fetched and I'm stupid for even considering it."

Hammer pulled his head in real quick. "I don't think you're stupid. Nothing happened between me and Rosta. I have no interest in her that way. I already would have wanted to rescue her and then she said she blames me for what happened to her. She blames all of us."

"So what?" Vina countered. "It isn't our fault she ran and hid when we escaped with the Godless. She could have come with us...."

"Exactly. So what's wrong with trying to balance the scales now?"

Vina's mouth tightened. "Not everyone sees it that way. Rosta did a lot of bad things to support her father and his men."

"So we should just leave her where she is? We should leave the Bounty Hunters in peace to do whatever they want with her? I can't believe you would even suggest that."

"I'm not suggesting it. I'm saying you can't blame me for questioning you about it when you disappeared and came back talking about another woman."

Hammer heard through that, too. He took a step closer and lowered his voice to a barely audible breath. "You are the only woman for me. You're weeks away from coming of age. Then we'll be together for real. No one will ever come between us then. I only want to rescue Rosta and bring her to a place of safety. Then one of the other men can marry her." She didn't answer, so he said, "Bugs, maybe."

She laughed the way he hoped she would. The faint light coming through the canopy glistened on her features.

He leaned and kissed her. One of these days.....

In a few weeks, a conversation like this would end with them going home to their own shelter and spending the night together. They would spend every night together for the rest of their lives.

He eased off just enough to see her eyes shining up at him. "You're the only woman I have ever wanted. I spent years with Rosta and never felt for her the way I feel for you. That won't change even if she comes to live here."

Chapter 12

H ammer lay on his stomach behind the ridge and peered over the side at the Ashtaws grazing in the grassy fields.

"Lead them into the jungle to the southeast—where we stashed the other pile of Fogpo," he ordered. "We'll lead them down the canyons from there."

"What if one of them tries to escape?" Ziti asked. "We won't be able to stop them."

"Then the best thing you can do is to get out of the way so they don't step on you," Scarecrow told him.

"That's what the Fogpo is for," Hammer added. "Keep them interested in following the Fogpo so the Ashtaws don't try to escape. Lead them into the canyons and we'll take it from there."

He pushed himself up on his arms, got to his feet, and picked up a branch. The others did the same thing, but Thuron stopped Hammer from going anywhere. "Look. The Renegades are back."

The men paused there and squinted across the valley. Another patrol of Renegades emerged from behind one of the western peaks just then and started migrating eastward to circle the valley.

Hammer threw down his branch. "Bear, Mammoth, Scarecrow, and Earthquake—you all come with me. We'll draw the Renegades back down the other side of the hills. The rest of you get as many of the creatures down into the jungle as you can. Don't worry about what size they are or how many you get. Just get them out of the valley and into the trees."

He waved to his men and they took off running around the valley rim. Hammer could run much better now. Just being back with his own people helped heal his injuries better than anything.

The Renegades saw the Godless coming. Hammer didn't try to pull a surprise on them. He wanted them to see him. He engaged them head on even though the Renegades outnumbered him and his men. They had eleven people. He only had five.

That didn't matter. He had learned a few things from the Bounty Hunters. He closed with the Renegades, traded a few strokes with those who surrounded and attacked his men, and then Hammer pivoted to the side.

He dropped back and let the Renegades take the high ground. His men did the same thing. They all retreated down the hill heading away from the valley.

He backed toward the east—the northeast. He let the Renegades believe that Hammer's band had a camp over there—or maybe that the rest of their band was over there.

Hammer didn't care what the Renegades did or thought as long as they didn't see anything going on in the valley right now.

He really hoped his men got a decent number of Ashtaws away. He didn't want to wait any longer to implement Mora's ideas for domesticating these creatures.

The Renegades doubled down on their attack. They drove the Godless all the way down the slope to the edge of the jungle.

Scarecrow reacted first, bellowed at his enemies, and lunged for them. The Godless retreat lulled the Renegades into overextending themselves. They didn't expect the Godless to retaliate.

Hammer wouldn't have counterattacked so soon, but he followed Scarecrow's lead. The five men surprised the Renegades and cut down three of them right away.

The Renegades braced themselves to fight back, but the Godless didn't back down a second time. Hammer had deliberately selected the biggest and strongest of his men for this fight so they would be able to stand up to the Renegades when it counted.

The skirmish wavered back and forth for a minute. Hammer and his men pushed the Renegades away from the tree line, but the Godless eased off and shrank back each time. Hammer didn't want the Renegades going anywhere near the valley.

The Godless men eased off a little too much. The Renegades made another push and finally pressed the men all the way into the trees.

One of the Renegades slashed Scarecrow across the bicep. The wound sent him into a rage. He hacked his axe at the Renegades circling him, but they dodged and he missed.

The axe thumped into a nearby tree and larval Abnormits poured from the crack.

"Look out!" Scarecrow roared and shot off the ground in a heartbeat. He grabbed a low-hanging branch and pulled his legs up before the larvae got near him.

The Renegades didn't see in time before the larvae flooded around their legs. Hammer, Earthquake, Bear, and Mammoth launched themselves into the branches just in time.

The Renegades couldn't follow. They had no choice but to scramble to get away from the larvae, but it was too late.

"I guess we don't have to worry about them telling anyone what we're doing," Earthquake remarked as the Renegades' screams started to fade.

"Let's get back up to the ridge and see how the others are doing," Hammer suggested. "They might need help."

The men set off through the branches. No one could go down to the ground with so many larvae around.

The men had to travel farther east before they could go south. Hammer got ready to leave the jungle when he saw Cross coming toward him carrying a Fogpo branch in his arms.

An absolutely gargantuan Ashtaw female followed him through the undergrowth. Her size and bulk snapped trees out of the way. Her enormous feet shook the ground each time she took a step.

The canopy thrashed and crashed around her massive body, but she didn't notice. She plowed her way through the trees and even stepped on and splintered whole trees in her effort to keep up with him.

Cross's face lit up when he saw Hammer. Now Hammer and his men were the ones who had to scamper to get out of the Ashtaws' way.

Cross grinned at Hammer when they drew level with each other. The creature lowered her head, snapped a bunch of tree limbs off, and chomped a mouthful from the Fogpo branches in his arms.

Cross kept walking and didn't stop. "We're going down to the canyon now!" he called over to Hammer. "No reason to stop."

Hammer opened his mouth to answer, but it was already too late. Cross passed out of sight. The Ashtaw's massive sides blocked Hammer from seeing anything else.

He could only stand and stare as three juveniles followed that one female. One of the juveniles was an older adolescent Ashtaw. The other two were newborn twins scuttling along the jungle floor trying to keep up with their mother.

The other men led more adults. Almost all of them had young Ashtaws at foot. The mothers rumbled deep in their chests. They kept plunging through the undergrowth to grab more mouthfuls of Fogpo from the men.

One of the Ashtaws yanked the branch so hard that she ripped Flawless completely off his feet. He dangled eight feet off the ground before the leaves tore and he fell down still holding his branch.

Cross stopped by the fresh stack of Fogpo branches the men had left there to keep the creatures passive and compliant.

He picked up a fresh branch, but the mother Ashtaw didn't follow him when he walked away. She stopped there, thrust her huge head down into the pile, and started eating.

Her young did exactly the same thing. Then all the Ashtaws did the same thing when they caught up with the pile.

Hammer and his men had to keep well out of the way. The men brought ten mothers down here with at least fifteen young.

The party didn't start moving again until all the men caught up, picked up the Fogpo branches, and carried all of them away.

Hammer and his men leapt in to help out. The project took all the men working together to carry all the Fogpo away. The Ashtaws wouldn't leave without that.

The men had to spread out so the procession didn't turn into another stampede. Cross went in front with his mother and three young Ashtaws. The other men spaced themselves out at a distance behind him. That isolated each family cluster together.

Hammer got stuck near the back of the line. The Ashtaw following him wasn't as big as the others. She looked barely full grown and she only had one young calf with her—also a female.

Hammer couldn't believe how well this worked out. He didn't expect to get this many Ashtaws on his very first attempt—or so many young ones.

Cross hiked down through the jungle and took a roundabout series of pathways before he entered the canyons. He had to choose his route so the Ashtaws could fit between the cliff walls.

He finally stopped in a wide, flat river bottom with a decent-sized stream running through it. Grass covered the banks. Trees hung from the surrounding stone walls.

The Ashtaws let out their deep, booming rumbles when they entered the canyon. Cross dropped what was left of his Fogpo branches on the flat riverbanks and stood there smiling at the Ashtaws when they bent down to eat.

He extended his hand and touched the side of the mother's head. She snorted at him, jerked her head away, and then studied him while she munched her mouthful of leaves.

He only smiled at her. Then she moved her head close enough to take another mouthful. She didn't react at all when he touched her the second time.

He stroked the young Ashtaws, too. They didn't startle. They barely noticed. They let him touch them all over—on their heads and faces, their necks, and their bodies.

The other men did the same thing. Hammer put his branches down at a distance from the others so the Asthaws wouldn't bump into each other or fight over the leaves.

The young female lowered her head to eat Hammer's offering. She didn't even blink when he stroked her neck.

Her young one bumped into Hammer in her haste to get closer to the branches. He stepped aside to let her in and then touched her all over, too. These creatures were so docile that they didn't care.

Cross, Bugs, and Omen made it to the valley first. They spent a few minutes getting familiar with their Ashtaws and then raced off into the nearby jungle to retrieve the band's third stash of Fogpo.

The men brought everything back, mounded the branches in front of the Ashtaws, and then Hammer and his men stood back to admire the creatures.

"It worked!" Omen breathed. "I can't believe it actually worked."

"Now we have to keep them here." Hammer turned away. "Let's go."

He and his men returned to the head of the canyon. The cliff walls widened there. The Ashtaws could fit into the canyon easily.

The men separated to either side of the canyon entrance and cut ropes tied there. The ropes whipped out of the men's hands, released counterweights strung up in the nearby trees, and four thick tree trunks dropped into place to block the canyon entrance.

The first trunk fell with one end on the ground. The other end crashed down onto a block of stone on the opposite wall. The block held the trunk up at an angle across the canyon entrance.

The second trunk fell straight across from the top of the first to another block on the opposite wall. The third angled in the opposite direction—just enough to create a barrier to keep the Ashtaws inside.

Hammer stood back and studied the blockade. "I guess we'll find out pretty soon if it's strong enough to hold them."

Lonion turned back to look at the Ashtaws. "They look pretty happy here. They don't act too anxious to leave."

Hammer and the others all turned around to follow Lonion's gaze. The mother Ashtaws finished eating as much Fogpo as they wanted. They wandered down the banks grazing and browsing.

The canyon was another box canyon big enough that no one could see the other end of it from here. The Ashtaws could wander around as much as they wanted. They just couldn't get out—not without ramming these trunks out of the way.

"Now what do we do with them?" Stray asked.

"Now we domesticate them," Hammer replied. "We already took the first step. Now we keep them docile and happy, bribe them with treats, and get them used to us. Let's go braid some more rope and get started working on our harnesses. We're going to need them."

Chapter 13

Hammer bent over, threw his leg over the lower angled tree trunk blocking the Ashtaws' canyon, and wedged his body through the gap to enter the canyon.

Vina and the other four girls had taken responsibility for cutting Fogpo branches every day, bringing the food down here, and spending time taming the Ashtaws to get them used to people.

The Ashtaws had no problem relaxing around the girls. Human beings were so small. The Ashtaws couldn't possibly see any of the Godless as a threat.

The Ashtaws learned in no time that people meant food—good food. The Ashtaws came right up to any person who entered the canyon now even if the person didn't bring food.

Hammer and his men stood off by the blockage and watched the girls petting and talking to the Ashtaws. The girls even played with the smallest creatures.

They scampered around, head-butted the girls, and tossed their heads to snort when the girls laughed. The girls accompanied the Ashtaws to the stream to drink and the girls even splashed water in the creatures' faces.

The creatures tolerated it all. Their passive nature made them perfect for domestication.

Hammer took a deep breath, murmured, "Here we go," and stepped out into the canyon.

The men's arrival produced an instant effect on the Ashtaws. They came toward the men and lowered their heads even though the girls had been giving the Ashtaws as much Fogpo as they wanted.

Hammer stopped halfway down the bank and took the bundle off his back. One of the enormous females lowered her head, rumbled, and sniffed him.

He petted her a few times and then, before she could move, he threw the bundle over her neck right behind her head. He raced to tie the rope tightly enough, but he didn't make it in time.

She reared away and shook the bundle off. The untied ropes fell loose and the bundle hit the ground. The other men had equally poor success.

"Why don't you wait until we bring them some more Fogpo?" Vina suggested.

"Why don't you just climb on instead of trying it with these bundles," Eleph asked. "Then you wouldn't have to worry about tying something around the Ashtaws' necks."

"The Ashtaws need to get used to having something tied around their necks," Hammer pointed out. "We might as well start now without someone getting thrown off to their death."

The girls laughed at him. "At least wait until they're eating," Vina went on. "Then you can tie the ropes as tightly as you want."

Hammer shrugged. "Okay. You might have a point there."

"You'll definitely have to tie the harnesses on while they're eating," Sema added. "You should hold a handful of Fogpo inside the harness so you can slip it over the Ashtaw's head."

"It sounds like I should leave this project to you girls," Hammer remarked.

The girls laughed again. "Maybe you should," Vina replied.

"Show me how you would do it," he told her. "Tie the bundle around one of their necks."

She smirked at him and explored around the canyon until she found a certain plant. The girls had discovered a second plant the Ashtaws considered a delicacy.

She brought some of the leaves back and handed them to Hammer. They attracted the Ashtaws with an irresistible pull.

Three mothers jostled and shoved to get near enough to him. He wound up dividing the leaves between the three of them.

Sure enough, they lowered their heads to eat the leaves. Vina took all the time she wanted to tie the bundle around one of their necks.

She tied it onto the Ashtaw female that Hammer had just been trying to tie the bundle onto. His first attempt accustomed the creature to the sensation.

The Ashtaw shook its head, but it didn't dislodge the bundle, not even when the Ashtaw straightened up all the way to its incredible height. The creature stood there chewing for a second, shook its head once more, and went back to grazing.

Omen burst out laughing. "I don't believe it! This is actually working!"

"We can expect more problems." Hammer glanced around. "See about tying the rest of these bundles to the other creatures—and tie the smaller bundles to the young ones. We need to get them used to it, too."

"What about the harnesses?" Vina asked.

"We'll wait like you said. We'll come with you the next time you feed. Then the creatures can start wearing the harnesses all the time."

She laughed at him. "I'm sure they'll love that."

"They might not love it at first, but they'll get used to it. They won't even notice it."

His men used a combination of bait to get the Ashtaws to lower their heads again. Then the men tied the bundles around each Ashtaw's neck. The creatures tolerated that, too.

"It really is amazing," Earthquake remarked as the creatures wandered back to their grazing. "I didn't want to believe it myself. It doesn't seem possible that we've been working with these creatures every day for over a week and we still haven't come up against any major roadblocks."

"It will happen. Don't you worry." Hammer turned his back on the Ashtaws. He couldn't stay here anymore. "I don't look forward to the day when someone actually tries to ride one of these creatures. Things will get dicey then if they don't get dicey before that."

Earthquake fell in next to him on their way back out of the canyon. The others took longer and stayed to socialize with the Ashtaws.

Earthquake and Hammer bent over to climb through the blockage of tree trunks. Hammer waited on the other side for Earthquake to catch up with him.

"Why do you keep doing it if you think it's so dangerous and doomed to failure?" Earthquake asked. "You're the one who has been the most enthusiastic and certain about this project."

"Not quite. I think Cross is the most enthusiastic and certain about this project. He's much more enthusiastic and certain about it than I am."

"Then why do you keep doing it?"

"I don't think it's doomed to failure. I just think it will take a long time. We're enjoying some early success right now, but we still haven't challenged these Asthaws—not really. Riding them will be the first major test. I'm sure things will go wrong at the most dangerous possible time."

Earthquake shot him a grin on the side. "So who do you have picked out for the maiden voyage?"

"Myself, of course. You don't really think I would send someone to do that in my place, do you? This whole thing was my idea. I wouldn't put one of the men in harm's way without at least trying it myself."

The two men paused under the trees to wait for Cross, Scarecrow, and the twins to catch up. The other men waited their turns to climb through the blockage.

All the men looked happy now. The Ashtaws had that effect on everyone. The whole band came out of the Ashtaws' canyon with smiles on their faces.

All of Hammer's people believed in the project now, including Omen and the twins. They never questioned Hammer's decisions anymore.

The party headed back to their camp. The place was turning into a real home the Godless could sink their roots into.

The snap of a twig ahead made Hammer freeze in his tracks. He recognized the sound of human footsteps. He wasn't the only man to move his hand to his weapon. Even some of the girls did the same thing.

They all stared when Stray staggered through the trees, stumbled, and went down on his knees. He clawed in the dirt trying to get to his feet so he could go on.

Blood saturated his hair, ran down his neck, and smeared on his skin when his friends tried to pick him up. Bruises and gashes cut his face and torso. He was unarmed.

The party surrounded him in seconds. Hammer got in Stray's face. "What happened?! Who did this to you?"

"Bounty Hunters...." Stray's eyes blurred out for a second before he hauled them back into focus. "Coming...."

"Where?!" Hammer demanded. "Where are they?!"

"The west.....west ridge....."

Hammer froze. "They attacked you on the west ridge?"

Stray nodded, but he couldn't focus his eyes. He couldn't even stand up straight.

Hammer got to his feet and stared down at Stray for a minute. Hammer's brain kicked into high gear. He barely remembered to tell the girls to take Stray back to camp and take care of his injuries.

Chapter 14

The girls helped Stray to his feet. He kept sagging and tripping over his own feet.

"We better go check the west ridge," Acrobat suggested. "The Bounty Hunters could have tracked us down the canyons."

Hammer didn't reply. He and his friends all took off up the steep defiles to the ridgetop. Hammer had plenty on his mind on the way up there. His band had a lot more to lose, now that they were actually succeeding in taming the Ashtaws.

He didn't stop running until he made it to the top of the ridge. Then he and his men tracked Stray's blood trail to the spot where the Bounty Hunters attacked him.

The men found blood splotches on the ground and nearby rocks. The party also found signs of a struggle, but the Godless didn't find any Bounty Hunters—or anyone else for that matter.

"What do you think?" Earthquake asked.

"I think Stray had no business coming up here." The words slipped out before Hammer thought to stop them. "I specifically ordered everyone to stay down in the canyon so no one would see what we were doing with the Ashtaws. He shouldn't have come up here at all."

"Do you want me to take a run around the valley?" Cross asked. "I won't engage anyone if I find them. I'll just come back and report it to you."

"Go west. Omen, you go east. That will cut the time in half. Meet back up and then return."

The two men ran off in opposite directions. Good old Cross.

There was nothing else to see here, so Hammer ordered everyone down the canyon to the camp. He went to visit Stray.

He lay on his back with his eyes closed in one of the men's open-sided shelters. Vina, Sema, and Daora worked over his injuries and brewed Gooji juice for him to prevent infection.

He didn't wake up when Hammer squatted down nearby to watch. Something weird was going on here. He could understand Stray getting irresistibly curious or maybe even worried because no one from the band was patrolling the valley anymore.

Maybe Stray just got anxious and paranoid. Maybe staying in the canyons for a week wore out his nerves so he felt he had to go up to the valley to take a look. Hammer would have believed almost anything at this point.

Hammer would not believe even for an instant that Stray went up there alone. No way. No one could be that stupid.

Stray didn't just wake up one morning and completely forget everything he'd learned in the last twenty years of his life.

Stray should have brought it to Hammer's attention if Stray really thought the danger was so severe. Stray should have told Hammer if Stray wanted to go check the valley.

Hammer gave that order for a reason. He brought all the Ashtaws down here for a reason. Neither of the enemy Clans knew the Godless were taking the Ashtaws. Hammer wanted to keep it that way.

"Maybe we shouldn't domesticate the Ashtaws after all," Bugs choked. "They'll only attract unwanted attention."

Hammer glared at the man. A thousand potential responses came to Hammer's mind for how he could address this latest wave of doubt.

Omen and the twins might have questioned at first, but they knew better by now. They believed in the project now.

"It won't take long before the other Clans find out we're keeping Ashtaws down here," Acrobat added. "They'll see the Ashtaws walking around with bundles tied to their necks. The enemy Clan will put the pieces together."

Hammer didn't answer. He could have pointed out that the enemy Clans wouldn't see that because they would never come down here. The enemy Clans wouldn't find out the Godless were keeping Ashtaws down in the canyons.

The enemy Clans didn't know enough about ancient ways to figure out that the Godless were trying to domesticate these creatures and train them to carry mounts in combat.

One thought kept coming back to Hammer's mind again and again. He couldn't get rid of it. The enemy Clans wouldn't find out what the Godless were doing unless someone in this group told the enemy what the Godless were doing.

The nightmare of Aster's betrayal flared to life with a vengeance. Hammer's own sister betrayed the band.

She got Alien killed, nearly got Mora and all the other women killed or recaptured—including Cheina—and would have gotten all the men and boys killed into the bargain.

No one was immune. Hammer learned that a long time ago. If Aster could betray her own family to the Renegades, then anyone else might do the same thing. He could count on one hand the number of people he didn't suspect. Cross. Lonion. Vina. That was it.

Which of these people was smiling in Hammer's face and pretending to care about him while they plotted his doom behind the scenes?

Was it Scarecrow? Hammer shivered at the thought. What about Ant? Hammer simply couldn't believe that.

He found it impossible to believe it of anyone, especially the men in his party. Hammer had grown up with these men since their earliest boyhood. Many shared his dream of killing their own fathers and freeing their mothers and younger siblings from captivity.

Earthquake came over to squat down next to Hammer just then. The men assembled the way they used to and kept watch over their wounded comrade.

Acrobat made eye contact with Hammer. Acrobat asked one more time, "Are you sure this is a good idea?"

Hammer didn't answer. Something broke inside him in that moment. He didn't have to answer. He never had to answer any of them—ever. They could doubt. They could question. They could even protest.

He didn't have to explain himself to them anymore. He decided. He ordered. They obeyed. That was the law.

None of these men had to stay in his band. They could all leave and go their own way whenever they wanted. He certainly wouldn't stop them if they did.

The band was already dangerously shorthanded. A few more men disappearing wouldn't make that much difference in the end.

The Ashtaws *would* make a difference—a big difference. How could these fools not see that—especially after the band's recent success?

Some of these men had actually ridden Ashtaws against the Bounty Hunters in the past. That was the weirdest past. These idiots did actually know it would work. Why did they doubt it now?

He could only think of one reason. These doubters must want him to fail. They wanted to prove him wrong—so why did they leave Shadow's band to come with him?

He refused to say another word about it to make it easier for them. They either stayed or they went. He didn't need to concern himself with any of that anymore.

He made a mental note to keep an eye on them. Acrobat. Bugs. How many others? They were too smart to open their mouths right now, but they would.

Acrobat was the one who suggested that the whole party go up to the main ridge to check if the Bounty Hunters were still there. Was that intended to lead the men into an ambush? Did the Bounty Hunters bloody Stray to lure the rest of the party up there?

It worked. Hammer and his men did go up there to check, but the Bounty Hunters weren't there.

It wasn't an ambush—not that time—but it was definitely something. Hammer just had to figure out what it was before his enemies led him into a real ambush.

Chapter 15

H ammer turned a hunk of Gorlock meat on the spit. A spurt of juice hissed into the flames and they flared higher before they died down.

Hammer burned his fingers, yanked his hand away, and sucked his fingertips before he tested the meat with his knife again.

Vina came over to him carrying a gourd of water. She put it down next to him and kept moving around the camp doing her work. Earthquake returned and sat down on Hammer's other side. "How is it coming along? Is any of it ready yet?"

"All you think about is food," Hammer teased.

Earthquake laughed. "It isn't my fault I got this big. I need a lot of fuel. I can't help it."

"We should organize a separate hunting party just for you. You could eat one Gorlock by yourself while the rest of us share the other."

Earthquake's cheeks colored. He lowered his eyes to accept the bowl of food Hammer passed him. Earthquake tipped up the bowl and made snarling and growling noises like he really planned to inhale the whole pile in one mouthful.

Hammer enjoyed the joke and laughed with his friend. They both laughed when Earthquake put the bowl down with only one piece of meat in his mouth.

"Seriously," Earthquake asked. "What are you going to do about *those* two?"

He nodded behind him toward one of the other three-sided shelters the men used. Bugs and Acrobat sat next to Stray.

He was awake, smiling up at them, and talking in a low voice. Hammer didn't listen to what the three men said to each other. He didn't need to.

They wouldn't be talking about him, the Ashtaw project, or anything else important—not where Hammer and the rest of the band could hear them. The men would do that in private.

"They'll cause you trouble," Earthquake muttered. "Mark my words."

"Not necessarily," Hammer replied "I don't see that I have to do anything about them. They might just be expressing doubt like Omen and Lucky did at the beginning. I don't have a problem with that."

Earthquake made a face. "Someone is always potting against every Kral. It's inevitable."

Hammer looked down at his hands cutting up the meat. "It doesn't matter. My friendships will keep falling away from now on. Everyone I once considered a friend will become a subordinate if they haven't already. That's the one thing that is inevitable."

"I'm still your friend," Earthquake pointed out. "I'm still here. You don't see me acting like a subordinate, do you?"

Hammer grinned at him. "Thanks. It's nice to know most of these people still want me as their leader."

"Of course they do. No one else is qualified."

"I'm not qualified, either," Hammer pointed out. "I'm the youngest man here. You, Scarecrow, and Mammoth are all bigger than me. I would be doomed without your support."

"Stop it!" Earthquake fired back. "As if we would do anything other than support you. You've been our Kral since we were boys. Who else would we take?"

Hammer shrugged. "Someone would have to take over. Why not you or Scarecrow? You would be great."

"We aren't talking about that!" Earthquake snapped. "You're here. That's the only thing anyone needs to know."

"You talked about it while I was gone."

"You aren't gone!" Earthquake countered. "Now drop it. You're it. You're the one. Get used to it."

Hammer didn't answer and Vina came back a second later. She sat down next to him and he served her next. The conversation shifted and Bugs and Acrobat returned to say that Stray was feeling better.

Hammer talked of other things, but his conversation with Earthquake stuck with him. Overwhelming gratitude gripped Hammer's heart that some or most of his men still supported him.

They did more than support him. They needed him. They demanded that he take charge of this band.

That position was his by right. They made him their leader when he was fourteen years old. He stayed their leader for almost ten years. That didn't change when the men left Shadow's band.

He didn't actually know for certain that these doubters were plotting against him. He really needed to stop seeing enemies everywhere. Heaven knew he had enough enemies already without fabricating new ones.

He stretched out on the ground and rested his head in Vina's lap. She ran her fingers through his hair and then started undoing some of his braids.

He let his eyes drift shut and swam in the sensation of her combing his hair and re-braiding it. Her touch felt incredible.

At least he would always have her. He never doubted her and....well, she did doubt him when he came back from the Bounty Hunters' village and told everyone about Rosta.

He could forgive that. Vina would come of age in a few weeks. She was bound to get nervous coming up to that.

He should have been a lot more nervous about it than he was. Keeping so few girls around all these single men should have concerned him more than it did.

He trusted them. None of them would step out to come between Hammer and Vina. He didn't worry about that.

What if he was wrong about that? What if whoever did it decided to step out for Vina *and* the band? Then Hammer would wind up dead.

He drifted off and fell asleep there before he figured it out or came to any conclusions.

He woke up lying in the same place, but Vina wasn't there anymore. She must have slipped away while he slept and gone to spend the night in her shelter where she belonged.

He got up, drank some water, and went down to the stream to wash his face. He wound up washing the rest of himself while he was at it. He felt better after that.

He returned to the camp and shared breakfast with his men and the girls. Stray woke up feeling better. He moaned and groaned a lot, but he got to his feet and limped around enough to get himself something to eat, too.

The men usually fell asleep wherever they happened to be lying down when they got tired enough to fall asleep. None of them had any assigned places or even any regular places. Only the girls had that.

The party rejoined and gathered up the harnesses the men constructed out of hides. Hammer planned to use pieces of bone as bits to go inside the Ashtaws' mouths, but he wasn't ready to go that far yet.

He planned to put these harnesses on the Ashtaws' heads and let the Ashtaws wear the harnesses around for at least a week before he took the next step.

He might even decide to use the eye-flap harnesses that Mora designed—at least at first until the Ashtaws got used to carrying riders.

The party stopped along the way and collected a hefty supply of Fogpo leaves. The band assembled in a different canyon and planned exactly how they would go about harnessing the creatures.

"Each of you will take a harness and a supply of leaves to lure the creatures' heads to the ground," Hammer instructed. "Place your hand with the leaves through the harness. As soon as the Ashtaw bites into the leaves, slip the harness over their head, drop the leaves, and they'll lower their heads the rest of the way to eat the leaves. That will leave your hands free to tie the ropes. It should be a simple matter after that."

"Here's hoping it works," Cross added.

The party left that canyon, turned a corner, and everyone skidded to a halt when they saw the Ashtaws' canyon. It was empty.

The tree trunks that formed the barricade lay on the ground with the ropes still tied around their middles. All three trunks had rolled away from the entrance. The Ashtaws must have hit the trunks with all their weight to knock those heavy trunks out of position.

Hammer's stomach dropped into his shoes. The grassy banks, winding stream, tall cliff walls dotted with trees growing out of clefts and cracks—it was all empty. Not a single Ashtaw remained inside the canyon.

"What do you want to do?" Vina's voice trembled. "What *can* we do?"

That strain in her voice brought Hammer back to his senses. He turned around and handed her the harness he was carrying. "You girls go back to the camp. Take the harnesses with you. We'll need those later."

"You mean we have to start all over again from the beginning?" Bugs countered. "You can't be serious."

"We don't have to start all over from the beginning because those Ashtaws are already used to us. The work we put in won't go to waste. Come on. Let's go see if they made it back to the herd."

The party split up. The girls went back to the camp. Hammer and his men returned to the valley.

He scanned the horizon first for any sign of invaders. Then he looked down into the valley. Three of the escaped Ashtaws still carried their bundles tied to their necks. That made them easy to pick out.

He also picked out the big female with twins and an adolescent juvenile. She was the only one with twins. He also spotted his young female with her little one.

"At least they're still here," Cross pointed out. "They'll definitely be used to the bundles by now."

"They'll be used to us, too," Hammer added. "They would come straight toward us if we went down there now."

"Do you still want to harness them?" Lonion asked. "It would probably be easier if we just left them here instead of trying to restrain them. They'll only escape again."

"You're right, but we can't run the risk of one of the enemy Clans finding out what we're doing. Let's go down there and cut those bundles free. We'll just have to come up here when we want to work with the Ashtaws."

"The girls won't be able to come up here to feed and tame them," Ant remarked. "It would be too dangerous to let the girls leave the canyon."

"Of course," Hammer agreed. "We'll just have to do it ourselves."

"Then how will we stop the enemy Clans from seeing what we're doing?" Earthquake asked.

"Maybe we won't have to," Hammer replied. "None of them knows about domestication. We only know it's possible because Mora told us it was. Maybe the enemy Clans will see us and not understand what we're doing. They won't be able to duplicate it anyway."

The party descended into the valley. Walking straight into a herd of thousands of these giant creatures felt a lot different from just handling the friendly Ashtaws the band had already tamed.

Hammer turned out to be right, though. The tame Ashtaws stopped what they were doing and walked right up to the men. The men didn't bring any Fogpo, so none of the other surrounding Ashtaws paid any attention to the men.

The Ashtaws lowered their heads and the men cut the bundles free. Now no one could tell those Ashtaws from all the others.

Hammer would have liked to mark these creatures with some way to distinguish them, but he couldn't do that without giving the game away. He would just have to work around that by taming as many other Ashtaws as possible as quickly as possible.

"Do you want to harness them now?" Cross asked. "We can do that here as easily as down the canyon."

"Not now," Hammer replied. "Take the men back to camp—all except Pitch and Lucky. You two patrol the ridgeline for any sign of intruders."

"Where are you going?" Earthquake asked.

"I need to take a walk by myself. I need to think."

No one argued. He headed east into the jungle, climbed into the canopy, and took off balancing through the branches for a long way before he stopped.

He hunkered in the canopy for a while and listened. He was alone. No one followed him. He waited a lot longer than he needed to before he continued on his way.

He kept going until he dropped out of the trees outside the Ashtaws' canyon. It looked as beautiful as ever, but the silence ruined the peaceful effect.

The canyon didn't mean the same thing now. It didn't mean the band would be safe from their enemies. It didn't mean he had vindicated himself in front of his men by showing them all a better way.

He advanced as far as the canyon entrance. No Ashtaws would ever stay here again. He made a mistake by trying to confine them. They belonged with their herd.

He even went inside the canyon and looked around at all the places the girls had been getting acquainted with the creatures this past week. Happy memories enlivened every corner of this canyon.

He eventually turned around, left the canyon, and stopped next to the fallen tree trunks. He took a deep breath, looked down at the ropes, and saw exactly what he knew he would see—exactly what he came here to find.

He picked up the end of one of the ropes. It hadn't frayed. None of the Ashtaws chewed through that rope. They didn't snap it when they charged the tree trunks to smash their way out of the canyon.

The end of the rope had been cut off perfectly cleanly with the sharp blade of a knife. Someone from the camp snuck down here in the middle of the night and let the Ashtaws go free. The only question was who did it.

Chapter 16

Hammer strolled into the camp, spotted Vina and Sema squatting by one of their fires, and he went over to sit down next to them.

Vina's eyes found his and bored into his soul. "Are you okay?" she asked.

He nodded and took a bowl of food out of her hands. "I'm fine."

"Pitch and Lucky came back an hour ago," Sema told him. "They found tracks of Renegades, but no people."

Hammer only nodded. Renegades or Bounty Hunters in the area—that was going to become his constant reality. He no longer held out any hope that he would ever eliminate them completely.

It might take him years to domesticate the Ashtaws—or at least to get them into some condition where he could use them against his enemies. He might never accomplish it in his lifetime.

He was still chewing his food when Earthquake, Cross, Pitch, Lucky, Omen, and Ant approached him from multiple sides of the camp.

His men gathered around him, squatted down, and Ant actually sprawled on his side on the ground. He propped himself on his elbow and looked up at the others while they talked.

"We scouted the ridgeline like you said," Lucky reported. "We found tracks of Renegades on the north side."

Hammer frowned. "That's strange. That's where the Bounty Hunters attacked Stray."

"Why would the Bounty Hunters and the Renegades be in the same place?" Ant asked. "Unless they're fighting each other."

"Do you want to go back over there and track them down?" Earthquake asked. "We should eliminate that patrol before they come back to haunt us."

"No, we won't go chasing a patrol that isn't bothering us," Hammer decided. "We know they're there and they know we're here. We can wait for them to actually come into the valley before we do anything."

"What if they bring back more men?" Omen asked.

"I want to get started harnessing the Ashtaws," Hammer replied. "That's more important."

He broke off when the rest of their men entered the camp from somewhere. The four uninitiated boys came from one side of the camp. They must have gone off over there by themselves.

Hammer didn't have a problem with the boys forming their own nucleus separate from the rest of the band. Hammer and his men had done the same thing. It was in the natural order of things.

Stray, Bugs, Bear, and Acrobat had been sitting around the shelter where Stray had been recovering. He had been lying down while they talked.

Eager, Falcon, and Flawless arrived from another direction. Flawless carried four dead Ridgebeak chicks in one hand. He carried them dangling by one foot each.

Blood oozed from a gash across Eager's chest. The three of them must have just come back from hunting.

Flawless squatted down next to Ant and started plucking the chicks to butcher them. He and his two companions didn't see anything unusual about anything going on in the camp right now.

Vina and Sema read Hammer's mind, got to their feet, and vanished.

"If we're going to harness the creatures, maybe we should make some more harnesses," Cross suggested. "If we're going to leave them in the valley and work with them there, why not work with as many as possible? The more Ashtaws get used to it, the more Ashtaws we'll be able to use."

"Do you remember what Mora said about the harnesses in the first place?" Thuron added. "She said the ancients used to leave the harnesses on all the time. Then a person just had to grab the harness and lead the creature around wherever he wanted to lead it."

"We couldn't do that," Scarecrow fired back. "We can't lead these creatures anywhere."

"Not with their harnesses, but we can lead them just fine with Fogpo," Ant pointed out.

"I think Thuron is trying to say that we wouldn't have to re-harness the creatures every time we wanted to ride them," Lonion added. "It would also help us identify the Ashtaws we've tamed and the ones that are ready to ride."

Earthquake turned back to Hammer. "What do you say? I guess we should probably wait to see if the Ashtaws even take their harnesses before we decide that."

"Actually, there is one other piece of business we have to settle before we do any of that." Hammer rummaged in his back. "A much more important piece of business."

"You're the one who is making the Ashtaws our most important business," Bugs pointed out. "Now you're changing it to something else. What's more important than defending ourselves against our enemies?"

"This." Hammer pulled out the ropes from the tree trunk barricade. He collected them all and held them up in a bouquet so the men could see. "Someone cut these with a knife—which means someone in this circle right now has a date with the ants."

Silence fell over the party when they saw the evidence right there in front of their eyes. Hammer didn't soften the blow. In fact, he made it worse by standing up.

He didn't let go of the ropes. He kept fiddling with them in his hands and then happening to look around at the people nearest him.

Everyone stiffened when he got to his feet. Ant did not get to his feet. He only raised his eyebrows. Of course he knew he was safe. Earthquake didn't get up, either. Flawless kept plucking his Gurlg chicks like he heard this conversation every day.

Everyone else was either already standing up or they got that way when he mentioned someone going on a date with the ants.

Hammer sauntered slowly and casually through the group looking everyone up and down. "What do you say, Omen?" he asked. "You thought taming the Ashtaws was a terrible idea."

"That was before!" Omen exclaimed. "I don't think that now! I told you that! We were so close! I wouldn't let them free! I swear it!"

Hammer stopped in front of Bugs and Acrobat. Acrobat squirmed. Bugs wrenched himself in all directions—not that that was anything unusual for him.

His eyes darted here, there, and everywhere. He only made eye contact with Hammer for a split second each time before Bugs looked away.

"I didn't do it, Hammer!" Bugs stammered. "You have to believe me!"

"Why do I have to believe you?" Hammer asked. "You just said I keep changing my mind about what's important. What could possibly be more important to any Kral than one of his men challenging him to his face like you just did?"

"I didn't....!" Bugs's voice rose to a shriek before he fought it under control.

He tried without success to control his body. Trying to control himself only made him squirm harder. His voice shook when he finally worked up the courage to speak again.

"I didn't challenge you, Hammer! I would never do that. I only meant....."

Now Hammer was the one who raised his eyebrows. "You don't think taming the Ashtaws is a good idea, do you? You don't think investing this time to train them for combat is worth it. You think like Omen did that we should pull out and go back to the northern valley. You think we should live there for the rest of our lives and forget about everything else."

Bugs writhed so furiously that he couldn't answer. Hammer stepped forward and stopped in front of Acrobat, but Hammer didn't address him directly.

Hammer strode down the line of men scrutinizing each one with intense concentration. "I'm going to find out who did this, and when I do, I will not be merciful. Whoever did this is a traitor to our band. Whoever did this wasted over a week of work by everyone in this band, including the girls. We don't need someone like that around."

He stopped at the other end of the row and came back. He took just as much time to skewer each person to the core.

"Each of you has a choice to make. You can follow my orders, you can step out and challenge me in the open, or you can start walking. You know the way back to Shadow's camp. I won't stop anyone from leaving, but this is the last time I will ever hear any of you contradict my orders or tell me that this project is a waste of time or that I don't know how to make up my mind. If I hear anything like that again, they'll be the last words I hear from that man's mouth. Is that perfectly clear to all of you? You wouldn't dare to talk this way to any other Kral and you won't talk that way to me."

His men nodded, but that didn't satisfy him.

He stopped in front of Omen. "Am I your Kral or not?" Hammer demanded.

"Yes, of course. Always," Omen stammered.

"Then act like it. We aren't friends anymore." Hammer raised his voice so they could all hear him. "We aren't friends anymore! We grew up as friends when we were boys, but we aren't anymore. I'm your Kral or you're on your way east to declare Shadow your Kral. Those are your only two choices."

Only Ant broke the silence. "Of course you're our Kral, brother," Ant called up from his place on the ground. "We don't have any other."

Hammer waited, but no one contradicted. Bugs, Acrobat, Omen, and the twins all remained silent.

Hammer crossed a line in that moment. He wouldn't listen to any more contradictions, protests, or anything intended as something other than a helpful suggestion.

It would take a lot from now on for him to listen to someone's suggestions. He would have to already trust the person. They would have to prove themselves to him before he took their input on anything.

He stepped back so he wouldn't confront them so aggressively. "We have a unique opportunity here. We might be the only people who are in a position to use these creatures against our enemies. Mora's information makes that possible. We won't run away to the northern mountains as long as we have a chance to make this a reality."

He paced back and forth a few more times to measure how everyone took his comments—and his demeanor. The people he already knew and trusted in his corner acted as casual as ever. They already knew everything he was saying.

The people who should have trembled in their shoes did tremble in their shoes. This little confrontation didn't solve anything. The same problems still existed beneath the surface whether these people challenged him or not.

He still didn't know the identity of the traitor who freed the Ashtaws. Nothing would ever settle down until he finished off the bastard for good.

Whoever the traitor was had grown up with Hammer and the others the same as everyone else. Whoever it was pretended to be one of his closest friends and allies.

The traitor wouldn't do anything so stupid as to contradict him in public. The traitor wouldn't openly question his authority or say or do anything to put him on his guard.

Was Cross the traitor—or Scarecrow or Earthquake or Lonion? Hammer shook those thoughts out of his head. He couldn't start thinking that—not after the whole Aster fiasco.

"It might take us a long time to master these Ashtaws," he went on. "We might have to spend our whole lives fighting to hold this territory while we work around the clock to accomplish it. I still say it's worth it even if you and I never reap the benefits from that. It would be worth it if we could hand down these Ashtaws to the next generation. A fighting force of trained Ashtaws would be the best way to ensure that the next generation actually survives. We would give them a land no one will ever be able to take away from them—a land where our children and grandchildren will actually be safe. I think it's worth it. If you're with me, you're welcome. If you don't think it's worth it to accomplish that, no one is making you stay. I'm sure you can travel around and find another band where you can spend the rest of your lives fighting to defend yourselves. You can come to the end of your lives with nothing to show for it and your descendants no safer than you were when you started. It's your choice. I've already made my choice. Now it's your turn."

He squatted back down in the same place. Flawless finished gutting his chicks. He didn't stop working through Hammer's whole speech.

Flawless scraped the offal out of the way, spiked three chicks onto the spit, and arranged them over the coals to cook. Then he stood up, scooped the offal into a bowl, and carried it away into the jungle to dispose of it.

Ant kept reclining on his elbow in the same position. Earthquake went back to eating.

Cross squatted down on Hammer's other side and pulled a piece of hide out of his shoulder bag. He had been working on a design for some kind of seat where the mounted Ashtaw rider could sit behind the creature's head.

Hammer changed the subject by turning to him. "How is it coming along?"

Cross shot Hammer a crazy grin. Cross got more excited about the Ashtaw project than anyone. He couldn't possibly be the traitor. "I think I finally figured it out. See?" He held up a piece of hide.

"It looks like a loincloth," Ant remarked.

A bunch of the other guys laughed. Hammer made a decision not to look up to see what all the others were doing. The people he had just reprimanded might slink away with their tails between their legs—and well they might.

He put the whole matter out of his mind—as far out of his mind as he could.

Cross pointed to the two leg holes in the loincloth. "The rider sits in this seat with their legs sticking through these holes. The seat positions the rider's legs around the Ashtaw's neck so the rider is comfortable. The rider is close enough to the creature's head that he can steer using the reins."

"That sounds like a good design," Hammer remarked. "How does the seat attach to the creature's neck?"

"That's what I need to figure out next. The problem is that the Ashtaws' heads are so high off the ground. When they're walking upright, their neck sticks straight up into the air like the trunk of a tree. Tying ropes around it will cause the seat to drift down the neck. Eventually, the rider will be too far away to hold onto the reins."

"So what's the solution?" Scarecrow asked.

Cross shrugged. "One solution is that we make the seat a part of the head harness. Then the seat can't fall down."

"Won't that put too much weight on the creature's head?" Thuron asked.

"It's the only solution I can think of right now." Cross turned to Hangman. "I want to talk to you about another idea I have. You might not like it....."

"Tell me what it is. I want to hear everything."

"Well, think about it. Whoever is riding in this seat will be too far off the ground for the enemy to hit them."

"That's the point," Ziti chimed in. "The rider will be safe from enemy attack."

"But it also means the rider won't be able to attack the enemy," Cross pointed out. "He'll be too high off the ground."

"Isn't that what the Ashtaw is for?" Flawless asked. "That's the whole reason we're training these creatures. They do our fighting for us."

"What if we could do one better?" Cross bent over and sketched with his forefinger in the dirt next to his feet. He drew an outline of an Ashtaw. "We could build some kind of platform. Mora said something about this before. The platform straps around the creature's back and people ride in it up here. We could attack our enemies from there."

"Attack them how?" Ant asked. "We wouldn't be within weapons range to attack them."

"She said those people used spears and arrows," Hammer added. "We don't have that and we don't have time to get proficient at it."

"Maybe that's something we could hand down to the next generation, too," Cross suggested. "We're already planning to invest years into this project. Why not learn how to do it? We could learn how to make our own arrows and we could learn how to shoot them."

"She said the ancients used stone to make arrowheads," Pitch pointed out. "We don't know how to do that. We would have to experiment for way too long before we figured it out."

"We have metal," Cross told him. "And we know where we can get more of it."

Hammer's mind shifted gears. The Bounty Hunters used spears. They also had metal.

The Bounty Hunters' spearheads were too big to use with arrows, but what about just using them with spears? The Godless could use them from the platform on an Ashtaws' back.

It would take planning and a whole lot of practice, but maybe Cross was right. Maybe it would be worth it to multiply the Godless force and overcome the disadvantage of their small numbers.

The conversation shifted back to other topics. Flawless kept working on his chicks to cook them. Then he passed around the meat to all his friends.

The men ate together. The girls mysteriously reappeared out of the woodwork as soon as the men stopped talking about anything serious.

Hammer didn't let himself think about the traitor problem for the rest of the evening. He enjoyed himself. The time would come to deal with the traitor. The bastard couldn't stay hidden forever.

The sun went down and the men drifted away to go to sleep somewhere. Hammer went out into the trees to relieve himself and to get a drink from the stream.

Vina had gone into her shelter hours ago. He would have liked to spend some time with her before he went to sleep, but he could wait. His time would come.

He turned around to return to the camp when he met up with Earthquake coming the other way. "We really have to stop reading each other's minds like this," Earthquake teased.

"You don't want to read my mind, brother. Believe me."

Earthquake laughed at him. "Why should you worry about it? You're the one who discovered this traitor. I'm sure whoever it is will be lying awake in a fit of anxiety tonight."

Hammer snorted. "Something tells me they won't be."

Earthquake got serious and studied him more closely in the dark. "Have you decided what you're going to do about that?"

"I already told you. I'm going to feed the bastard to the ants. That's the best a traitor deserves."

"You did the right thing with all your faint-of-heart cowards. You won them over."

Hammer made a face. "I should have punished them or outright eliminated them. I was too kind to them."

"No, not at all. A Kral has to be diplomatic sometimes. That's what makes a great Kral. He knows when to be diplomatic and when to be harsh."

Hammer didn't answer. He stood there and waited while Earthquake got himself a drink, splashed water on his face, neck, and arms to cool himself off, and the two friends fell in side by side on their way back to the camp.

Earthquake didn't know what made a good Kral any better than Hammer did. Hangman was the only Kral either of them ever had. Maybe he knew when to be kind and maybe he knew when to be harsh.

Hammer found it impossible to look back on Hangman as anything other than the perfect Kral. All his decisions—every word that came out of his mouth—they all seemed so perfect and infallible at the time.

Hammer already knew that wasn't the case. Hangman had his faults.....but Hammer couldn't think right now what they were.

Hangman probably would have let the doubters live. He would have let them off with a warning the way Hammer did. That was the best measure Hammer could come up with to decide if he did the right thing.

Hangman wouldn't eliminate or punish anyone for doubting. Hammer couldn't count the number of times Hangman had let his men contradict him in front of the whole band and even in front of Hangman's own children. He was hands down the most patient man Hammer had ever known.

Chapter 17

H ammer puffed out his cheeks. "All right. Here goes nothing. Remember. Just get the harnesses onto the creatures' heads and get away. Don't stick around to wait for their reaction—and if they start to struggle, pull away, drop the harness, and beat a hasty retreat. None of this is worth your lives."

"You got it, brother," Scarecrow growled.

Hammer made one last assessment of his men. Ten of them had harnesses and bunches of Fogpo leaves to lure the creatures' heads to the ground.

Hammer was one of the harnessing team—if he and his men actually succeeded in harnessing these creatures. They all had a long way to go before anyone actually mounted one of the Ashtaws.

He nodded to his men and they started down the hill. Hammer didn't send Bugs. The guy would have spooked the Ashtaws into a stampede even without a harness.

Bugs, Stray, Eager, Omen, and Acrobat stayed on the ridge with the uninitiated boys. All the rest of the men went down into the valley.

They spread out and each man headed for a different Ashtaw with which he was already on familiar, affectionate terms. Hammer had to hike a long way down the valley before he met up with the young female and her little juvenile.

They came right up to him. The female thrust her head into the Fogpo leaves and ripped off a mouthful.

Hammer took that opportunity to pull the harness over her head. He dropped the leaves and she bent down to eat the rest of them. She didn't even twitch when he tied the harness around the back of her skull.

She didn't notice that or when he touched her head, neck, and shoulder the way he used to. He didn't have to run away from either of these creatures. They stood next to him as placidly as ever.

He glanced around to see if the rest of his men were enjoying equally good success. He couldn't see any of the men through all the massive Ashtaw bodies grazing around him.

He started to turn away to go meet up with them. At that moment, a piercing scream echoed out of the distance. It came from the east—from the jungle right on the other side of the ridge.

He shouldn't have been able to hear a single human voice from that distance. He probably wouldn't have been able to hear it except that he recognized the voice instantly. It made the hair stand up on his scalp. It was Vina. She was there screaming in the jungle.

He whirled away and charged up the nearest slope to the ridgetop on the eastern side. She shouldn't have been over here. She should have been miles away in the canyon camp. She shouldn't have left it to come out here and put herself in danger. Something was seriously wrong.

He charged down the other side of the hill, plunged into the undergrowth, and followed the sounds of endless screams. They drove him ballistic. No one better be hurting her.

He made it half a mile from the valley before he burst in on four Bounty Hunters hauling Vina through the jungle. They headed north—which meant they had started farther south.

He already knew that because their village was in the northwest. They had to take her around the valley before they got her back to their village.

She struggled and kept tearing herself out of their grasp. They only laughed at her. Enough of them kept their hold on her to stop her from getting away.

Her long, loose hair got into her face and stuck to sweat and tears clinging to her cheeks. One of the Bounty Hunters grabbed for her chest and ripped the tie on her shoulder when she yanked away from him.

His fingers caught her top and the shoulder strap fell down to expose her chest. Hammer didn't wait around to see anything else. He drew his blades and stepped out into the open to confront them.

They all let go of her at the same time. That was his first clue. Three of them could have dragged her off while one Bounty Hunter stayed behind to fight him—or two of them could have taken her away while two of them ganged up on him.

They all backed away from him. She scampered behind him and huddled behind his back. He wouldn't be able to fight as well with her there, but he didn't have to fight at all in the end.

He pushed her behind him and rushed the Bounty Hunters. They broke away and ran for it toward the north.

He only ran a few dozen yards before he stopped and watched them out of sight. This was all wrong. Four Bounty Hunters didn't need to retreat from him. They definitely wouldn't let go of a female captive once they got their hands on her.

He didn't go after them. He turned back to Vina. Her panic set in, now that she got away from them. She panted and wheezed in half-choked sobs between ragged, gasps for breath.

"Are you okay?" he murmured. "Did they hurt you?"

She shook her head fast and folded her arms over her chest to hold her top on.

Hammer couldn't stand seeing her like this. He put his weapons away, took hold of her shoulder strap, and retied it on her shoulder. "How did you get here?" he asked. "You should have stayed in the camp. I told you girls not to come this close to the valley."

"I didn't, Hammer!" Her features wrenched and she grimaced to hold back sobs. "I would never do something you said was dangerous."

"Then what happened? You can't tell me the Bounty Hunters made it that far south without us finding out. We're running patrols around the valley three times a day as long as we're working with the Ashtaws there."

"They didn't....I mean.....the Bounty Hunters didn't come that far south. Some me n.....in black masks.....they captured me while I was getting water from the stream. They carried me away....."

"Didn't the other girls see or hear you yelling? Didn't you call out?"

Her face screwed up in anguish again. "I couldn't! They....I mean....the men....."

The sight of her twisted his guts into knots. He put his arms around her and pulled her in. "Never mind. It doesn't matter. You're safe now."

"It does matter!" she howled and shoved him away so she could stand upright. "They held their hands over my mouth to stop me from making any noise. They brought me up here. I fought them all the way, but they overpowered me. I tried to fight back, but....."

"Never mind," he repeated. "I'm sure you fought your hardest. They won't bother you anymore."

"You don't understand, Hammer!" she choked. "The men who took me.....they weren't Bounty Hunters. They left me here.....the men who took me from the camp left me here for the Bounty Hunters to find."

He blinked at her in stunned disbelief. Someone kidnapped her from the canyon camp—but no one knew about the canyon camp. No Bounty Hunters or Renegades knew the camp existed.......unless someone told them.

The Bounty Hunters didn't know about it. They might know it existed, but they didn't know where it was.

They didn't have to know where it was because the kidnappers brought Vina straight to them. They left her in the eastern forest—right where the Bounty Hunters would find her.

Who would do something like this? Whoever took Vina couldn't have been trying to steal unprotected women. The kidnappers would have taken all five women if that was the case.

No, the kidnappers only wanted Vina. Why? Because she was Hammer's sweetheart, of course. Whoever did this took Vina to get back at Hammer.

The picture became clearer by the second. The kidnappers didn't want Vina for themselves. They just wanted to get rid of her.

She fell apart as soon as she got the words out to tell him what he most needed to know. Her face convulsed and closed up the rest of the way. Her lips curled back from her teeth in a grimace of pure agony.

He pulled her into his arms and she broke down sobbing right there on his chest. He enveloped her in as much of his body as he could. He had saved her this time, but what about the next time?

They were still standing there when he heard footsteps coming from the west. She tore out of his embrace and wiped the tears off her cheeks before Earthquake ran up to them.

"I saw you run off," Earthquake looked back and forth between Hammer and Vina. "What happened?"

"I'll explain later." Hammer took Vina's hand and pulled her forward. "I need you to take Vina back to the canyon camp and stay with her there until I come back. Do everyone a favor and don't ask any questions about what happened. Just take her home. She's already upset enough."

Earthquake opened his mouth—no doubt to ask exactly that—but he stopped himself when he saw her crying. He finally nodded and said, "Sure, brother. No problem."

"Go with Earthquake," Hammer murmured to her. "I'll meet you back at the camp as soon as I can. Go on. Everything will be all right."

She wouldn't look at him when Earthquake put out his arm and steered her away into the jungle. She cast a wretched glance at Hammer over her shoulder. He watched her go with a sinking feeling in the pit of his stomach.

Whoever was doing this didn't just threaten him. They threatened Vina, too. That was unforgivable. He had to find out who this traitor was and pay the bastard back for his treachery.

He waited until Earthquake and Vina passed out of sight. Then Hammer spun the other way and took off running along the Bounty Hunters' trail.

Chapter 18

Hammer skimmed through the trees checking the ground for the smallest trace of the Bounty Hunters' tracks.

They left plenty of sign for him to follow. They didn't run very well. They definitely didn't run in a way to conceal their presence—not the way the Godless would.

Hammer could have climbed into the trees, but he wanted to stay on the ground so he could confront the Bounty Hunters when he finally overtook them.

They slowed down after a few miles and walked the rest of the way. He thought up all the ways he would capture them, dismember them, and torture them to make them tell him who the traitor was.

He didn't care at all for the lives of a few Bounty Hunters. They meant nothing to him.

He slowed to match their pace. Then he heard voices ahead. He snuck from one clump of foliage to another and almost didn't believe it when he came to a small clearing.

Stray, Bear, and Bugs stood there side by side having a perfectly civil conversation with the same four Bounty Hunters who had been trying to drag Vina off.

It took Hammer a minute to really, fully believe that his own men—the boys he'd grown up with—were actually behind this.

His brain finally kicked back into gear and he heard what they were talking about. They weren't having a civil conversation at all.

"You still owe us," one of the Bounty Hunters snapped. "We did what you asked. It isn't our fault it didn't work."

"We agreed to pay you to kill Hammer," Stray fired back. "You didn't. I bloodied myself and spent three days recovering to set this up. We won't let you screw us out of payment now for something you didn't even do."

"You agreed to pay us to set up an ambush so *you* could kill him," the same Bounty Hunter countered. "You said you would bring the girl to us and we would make it look like we were taking her off. You said we would let her go as soon as he came and you would take care of the rest."

"It isn't our fault!" Bugs interjected. "It took us too long to get down here from the ridge. You had him outnumbered. You could have killed him easily. Then we wouldn't be in this mess."

"That's your fault," the Bounty Hunter returned. "Pay up or we'll take payment out on one of yours. Maybe you have a girl down in the south country who needs a real man instead of a sniveling boy."

"Fine. Take it." Stray nodded at Bear. He took a package wrapped in hide out of one of his shoulder bags and shoved it at the Bounty Hunters.

The one guy doing all the talking took the package, peeked inside, and then grinned. "Perfect. See you boys around. Have a good one."

The four Bounty Hunters turned to leave. That was Hammer's cue. He stepped out into the open. "Don't leave yet!" he called out. "We haven't concluded our business."

The Bounty Hunters turned back. Their expressions changed instantly when they realized he was alone. "You're crazy, Hammer," Bear exclaimed. "You can't win against seven of us."

"You're the crazy ones for thinking you could cross me," Hammer returned. "Do you think I would let you get away with harming Vina—and putting all the rest of us in danger?" He sneered at his former friends. "All three of you deserve the ants for even associating with these freaks."

"You'll pay for that!" The first Bounty Hunter raised his spear.

Hammer tightened his grip on his weapons and braced himself for the fight he knew was coming. He actually looked forward to this. All seven of these bastards deserved to die.

The Bounty Hunters grinned and leered at him the way they usually grinned when they watched their captives fight each other.

Bear grinned, too. Bugs and Stray looked terrified. They knew better.

Hammer took one more step forward. Bear was right. Hammer couldn't fight seven of them, so he would have to make this count by taking down the most important traitors—his own.

He considered the Bounty Hunters something like animals. He put them in the same category as dangerous jungle creatures he could use to attack his enemies when he needed to.

All seven of them rushed him. They surrounded him in a ring. The Bounty Hunters used spears. They were the least dangerous weapons.

Bugs fought with two stolen Renegade blades. Stray used metal kukris he had taken from the first Bounty Hunter village that Hangman's band destroyed. Bear fought with two short stone axes, one in each hand.

Hammer understood every detail of his three comrades' fighting style. He could predict them all.

He couldn't predict the Bounty Hunters, so he swiveled in their direction and swung his blades. He hacked one of the spear shafts in half and disarmed its owner except for the wooden shaft in the guy's hands.

Hammer had to turn the other way to confront his three comrades—his three former comrades.

He smashed Bear's axes away. He was the biggest, strongest man here. He even outsized the Bounty Hunters.

The other two Bounty Hunters lunged for Hammer from behind. They would have impaled him with their spears and left him dead on the ground.

A high-pitched whistle interrupted the fight just then. Hammer spun around to defend himself—and stared in shock when one of the Bounty Hunters folded to the ground at his feet. A metal hunting knife stuck out of the guy's skull right behind his ear.

Another hurtling missile tumbled right in front of Hammer's eyes. A long, rectangular Renegade blade revolved past him, lodged in the second Bounty Hunter's head, and cracked the guy's skull in half. He buckled right next to his friend.

Hammer whirled one way and then the other. as Cross, Scarecrow, Flawless, Mammoth, Ant, Eager, and the four uninitiated boys advancing through the jungle toward him.

Cross flexed his knees into a crouch with his empty hand still extended in front of him after throwing the knife and blade to save Hammer's life. Bugs, Bear, and Stay spun around to confront their comrades—their former comrades. Now Hammer's allies outnumbered the traitors.

Hammer straightened up and lowered his weapons. He didn't have to fight anymore. It was all over.

His men surrounded the three traitors. They saw the writing on the wall and didn't raise their weapons to defend themselves. What cowards they were. They just gave up even knowing what would happen to them. They didn't die fighting.

The men surrounded the three traitors, disarmed them, and marched them away into the jungle to the south.

Hammer turned to Ziti. "Take you boys into the jungle and bring the ants down to the camp. Be careful and make sure you stay far enough ahead of them so you can get into the trees if they start to overtake you."

"You got it," Ziti replied. He waved to the other boys and they all took off running in the opposite direction.

Chapter 19

H ammer followed his friends down the hill heading south toward the canyons. Mammoth and Scarecrow flanked Bear on either side. Bear was the biggest of the three traitors, so the men assigned their two biggest members to guard him.

Eager and Flawless escorted Stray. He wasn't the biggest or the strongest. They outsized him by a long way.

Cross and Ant were the smallest, so they guarded Bugs. He squirmed and writhed worse than ever.

"You won't really feed us to the ants, will you, Hammer?" Bugs asked over his shoulder.

"Shut your mouth," Flawless snapped.

"You can't blame us for questioning your leadership," Bugs went on. "We all thought taming the Ashtaws was a bad idea. Ask anyone. They'll tell you the same thing." Bugs proved his own stupidity by turning to Cross. "Go on. You can admit it. He can't do anything to us if we all stand together."

"Be quiet, Bugs," Bear snapped over his shoulder. "Sniveling and whining won't make him change his mind."

"You have to listen to reason, Hammer," Bugs wheedled. "We can talk about this."

"There is nothing left to talk about," Scarecrow snarled. "He said he would feed you to the ants and that's what he'll do. If he doesn't, we'll do it ourselves."

"He said he would feed someone to the ants if he found out they freed the Ashtaws," Bugs insisted. "We never let the Ashtaws out of the canyon. I swear it."

Hammer perked up his ears, but he didn't get involved in the conversation. He didn't have to. His men handled that for him.

Ant slapped Bugs across the back of the head. "Did you just hear Flawless tell you to shut your mouth? Be grateful we don't attach an Abnormit larva to your crotch on the way down to the camp. We would be more than happy to start this party early if you want us to."

Bugs looked up at him and Bugs's lips quivered. "You wouldn't do that—not to me—would you? We're brothers. We've always been brothers."

"Brothers don't make deals with the Bounty Hunters," Scarecrow fired back. "You deserve to die a slow, painful death just for that."

"Brothers don't abduct their brothers' wives and sell them to the Bounty Hunters," Cross added. "None of you three are brothers to anyone anymore."

Bugs turned back to him. "Come on, Cross. You're Hangman's brother. You couldn't feed me to the ants. I know you couldn't."

"I would feed Hangman himself to the ants if he did that to Sema," Cross returned. "Your life isn't worth spit even if Hammer showed you mercy. You wouldn't last ten seconds in this band before one of us got to you."

Bugs looked all around him. "Aw, come on, man! You can't do this to us!"

"If you don't shut the hell up, Bugs, I swear to Almighty God I'll feed you to the ants myself," Bear barked over his shoulder. "Save your begging and pleading for the ants. Maybe they'll listen to you."

Bugs didn't say anything else, thank the stars. Stray didn't say anything, either, not even to tell Bugs to shut up.

Hammer took in every word, but he didn't get involved. So none of these three let the Ashtaws out of their canyon. Someone else did.

Bugs might have lied about that, but Hammer didn't think so. The Godless had these three worms dead to rights. They had no reason to lie about anything.

They disagreed with his plan to domesticate the Ashtaws. They would be the first to admit it if they did release the Ashtaws.

It didn't matter because Acrobat, Omen, Pitch, Lucky, and Falcon caught up with the group a few minutes later. Falcon reported that all ten Ashtaws had their harnesses on. None of the Ashtaws resisted that, either.

Their placid tolerance of this whole process gave Hammer a very bad feeling, but he couldn't think about that right now. He sent the rest of his men ahead to the camp while he pulled Acrobat aside.

"Tell me you didn't have anything to do with this."

Acrobat turned white. "I didn't have anything to do with what?" He shot a terrified glance at the men disappearing down the hill. "Where are they going?"

"They're going back to the camp. Are you telling me you don't know what Bugs, Bear, and Stray were doing in the jungle while we were harnessing the Ashtaws? Do you really expect me to believe that?"

Acrobat gulped. "What were they doing? I wasn't with them. I was in the valley."

"Why were you in the valley? I put you, Omen, and Eager on the ridge. Didn't you see Bugs and Stray leave?"

"No, of course not! We were up there when Omen saw Pitch in danger. He got the harness on his Ashtaw all right, but then he got flanked by three others who were all after his Fogpo leaves. They boxed him in and would have crushed him. Omen went down there to help him out. Eager and I went to back him up in case he needed help to lead the Ashtaws away. We didn't see what Bugs and Stray were doing. We thought they stayed on the ridge."

"They went down the canyon, kidnapped Vina while she was alone, and brought her up here. They left her in the Bounty Hunter's path for them to capture. Those three made a deal with the Bounty Hunters and paid them off to take Vina so those three could ambush me and kill me. Did you know about any of this? I swear to God, Acrobat, if I find out you're lying to me, I'll make you suffer a lot worse than the ants will. Now tell the truth. Were you involved in this?"

"No, Hammer! I swear I wasn't!" Acrobat's features quivered all over. "I would never do something like that! I would never sell a Godless woman to the Bounty Hunters! Are you crazy?"

"There are apparently a lot of people in this band who question my leadership. That's what Bugs says. Do you have anything to say about that? You, Bugs, and Stray have been getting awfully friendly lately, haven't you?"

Acrobat opened his mouth more than once before he mustered the courage to say a word. "I.....I'm sorry, Hammer. You're right. I spoke against you behind your back. I shouldn't have done that. That was wrong. I deserve to be punished for that. I'll accept it if you have to feed me to the ants for that."

"I won't feed you to the ants for speaking against me. I want to know if you conspired with these pieces of filth to kidnap Vina and kill me."

"No!" Acrobat's features twisted in a wretched sob, but he stopped short of actually falling apart right then and there. "I swear it, Hammer. I never knew anything about that. I would never conspire to do anything like that—and I certainly never thought we should kill you just because we disagreed with you."

"I expect you to do better from now on," Hammer told him. "Don't make me have to correct you again. Do you understand? Choose your friends a little more wisely in the future. You might want to associate yourself with people you know you can trust—people like Flawless, Eager, and Mammoth. Can you do that? I'm trusting you to pull yourself back from the brink."

"Of course, Hammer! I will! I swear it! I won't let you down again. I swear!"

Hammer compressed his lips to stop himself from tearing the guy apart all over again. Hammer didn't want to trust Acrobat, but Hammer had to start trusting someone.

Some people in this band deserved his trust. He shouldn't have trusted Acrobat, but anyone could make a mistake. Omen and the twins had spoken against Hammer. He wasn't sending them to the ants right now.

He sent Acrobat ahead to catch up with the others. They made it back to the camp as the sun slipped behind the canyon walls.

The commotion in the camp brought all the girls out of their shelters. Vina came out of hers. Her face had swollen up and she glared at everyone with bloodshot eyes. She must have been in there crying ever since Earthquake brought her back.

He stood guard outside her door. He didn't enter nor did he let anyone else enter, not even the other girls.

The girls gasped in horror behind their hands when the men brought in Bugs, Bear, and Stray.

"You girls come out with us into the jungle," Hammer ordered. "You should be here for this."

"What happened?" Sema gasped. "How did you find out they freed the Ashtaws?"

"We didn't! I swear we didn't!" Bugs turned to Hammer. "You can't do this! Give us another chance. Punish us any way you want, but don't execute us. Please. We'll do anything."

"Shut up, Bugs!" Bear roared. "Meet your death like a man instead of a whining coward!"

"Executed!" Daora exclaimed. "Why are they being executed if they didn't free the Ashtaws?"

"These men snuck back to camp a little while ago," Hammer replied. "They masked themselves and kidnapped Vina while she was separated from all of you. These men gagged her to stop her from screaming, carried her up to the eastern jungle, and left her in the path of four Bounty Hunters so they would capture her. They did it to stage an ambush so I would try to rescue her and they could kill me while I was distracted by the Bounty Hunters. The Bounty Hunters were supposed to back away so these three could hit me from behind, but circumstances worked against them and these three didn't show up in time. I told Earthquake to bring Vina back here and I followed the Bounty Hunters. I saw them meeting these three traitors. These traitors paid the Bounty Hunters to do all of this. They were in league with each other. If that doesn't deserve getting fed to the ants, I don't know what does."

The girls turned back to the three accused traitors. "Is that true, Bear?" Daora asked. "Did you really do all of that?"

Bear lowered his eyes to the ground. He didn't answer.

"If any of you has anything to say in your own defense, you better say it now," Hammer announced. "This is your last chance."

Everybody waited. No one said a word.

"What about it, Bugs?" Hammer asked. "You want a second chance. What do you have to say about anything I just said? Do you deny that you did any of this?"

Bugs opened his mouth and shut it. "No, I guess not."

"Then you admit you betrayed not just me but the entire band. You betrayed Vina. If you could do this to her, how do we know you won't do it to any of the other girls—or any of your so-called brothers here? How do we know you won't turn against any of us and try to kill us when it suits you?"

Bugs didn't answer. None of the traitors did. Bugs finally got it through his head that opening his mouth would only make matters worse.

Hammer made another decision in that moment, strode down the line, and stopped in front of Bear. He was the only one of the three who seemed to take any responsibility for his actions.

"I have one more question and then we'll wrap this up," Hammer went on. "Tell the truth. Was Acrobat involved in this plot at all?"

"Naw," Bear murmured. "He didn't know anything about it. It was just the three of us."

"Do any of you have any idea who let the Ashtaws go free?"

Stray and Bear shook their heads. Neither of them would raise their eyes to look at their former comrades.

Bugs actually said, "No," and immediately fell silent. That was a step in the right direction.

Hammer waved to his men. "Take them out of here."

Chapter 20

The three prisoners cooperated on their way out of the camp. Hammer didn't want to lead the ants into an enclosed box canyon where they might get trapped.

They would devour all the shelters that the girls had worked so hard to build. The band also had food supplies and other goods here—like the Ashtaw seat sling Cross was busy designing. Hammer didn't want the ants to eat that.

He led the way farther down the canyon to a spot where the walls split off into half a dozen different channels. The jungle widened there onto a sandy bank covered in grass. The overhanging trees made it a perfect location. Hammer nodded to his men.

The girls scrambled into the canopy. The men pulled the prisoners down on the ground and staked all three of them with their arms and legs splayed wide.

Bear and Stray went through the process silently. Bear slipped into a trance, stared up at the sky winking between the trees, and a peaceful expression came over his face.

He didn't look at any of the people around him while they tied him up, hammered the stakes into the ground, and left him there.

Stray started sniffling and whimpering the longer this went on, but he didn't lose his composure enough to plead for mercy or ask for another chance. He didn't say a word or look at any of his comrades.

Bugs made up for both of them by launching into a fresh tirade about how the three of them didn't deserve to die. Bugs kept jerking from Hammer to Cross to every other man in their party.

Bugs begged and pleaded. He promised all kinds of rewards and benefits if the band kept him alive. He tried again and again to get his former comrades to admit that they disagreed with the whole Ashtaw project, too.

None of them responded. Some refused even to look at him. They hammered in their stakes and climbed up into the branches with the girls.

They didn't have to wait long. Thousands of scratching feet announced the ants' arrival long before the four boys backed into the clearing scattering pollen in front of them.

The ants marched straight for the prisoners. Bugs went nuts, fought the ropes, and screamed out to his friends not to do this to him. He kept begging for his life right up until the very last second.

Bear didn't move. He stared straight up. His features never twitched even once even when he heard the ants coming.

Stray whined and sobbed in a steady stream of pathetic terror as the ants closed in. The boys stepped sideways to avoid the prisoners, tossed a few more handfuls of pollen over them, and bolted.

The boys charged for the nearest trees and launched into the branches just as the ants made it to the prisoners' feet.

Hammer jumped up into the branches. He stayed there a safe distance off the ground and watched the ants crawl the rest of the way up the prisoners' bodies.

Bugs started screaming the minute the ants touched him. He didn't even wait for them to take the first bite.

Stray held out longer. He burst out in loud sobs when they started on his legs and then he broke out in full-throated screams when they got to his face.

Bear didn't make a sound. Hammer found himself admiring the guy. Bear knew he deserved it and he took it bravely. Hammer had to give Bear credit for that even if Hammer couldn't respect anything else about the guy.

The ants left nothing behind. The boys waited until the ants started licking the blood out of the dirt. Then the boys sprang down, scattered pollen in front of the ants, and led them out into the jungle.

Hammer and the others waited until the last ants left the area. "Everybody go home," he ordered when the group climbed down to the ground. "We're all done here."

"But.....we still don't know who let the Ashtaws go free," Sema pointed out. "We still have a traitor among us."

"I know, but standing around staring at each other won't tell us who it is. Let's go. I'm sure it will come to light sooner or later."

The party returned to their camp in the box canyon. People tried to resume their normal activities, but a cloud hung over the band.

The four boys returned in a little while. Hangman thanked them and told them they had done a great job. "You should get ready for your initiation, Vuco," Hammer told him. "Start thinking about which creature you want to fight."

"I already know which creature I want to fight," Vuco replied.

Hammer looked up at him. "You do? What do you want to fight?"

"A Ridgebeak," Vuco replied.

Thuron buckled at the knees with a heavy sigh of relief. "Phew! I thought you were going to say something crazy like you wanted to fight a Krakelow."

"I was planning to," Vuco replied. "Then I thought I probably shouldn't, so I chose a Ridgebeak."

"Good for you," Hammer told him. "Daora comes of age next month. She and Earthquake will be getting married, so we'll do your initiation after that. You're the next oldest, Ziti. We have to wait three months before you can initiate, but you won't turn fourteen before then anyway. Do you know what you want to fight?"

"I'm still deciding between the Cursed Sand and a Stalkion."

Hammer nodded again. "Good for you. I'm glad to see you all thinking big. That's excellent. Keep me posted if you come to a decision. We would all love to welcome you as men of the Godless Clan."

The boys fell over themselves congratulating themselves on his praise. He left them to themselves and crossed the camp to the fire in front of Vina's shelter.

She didn't look up at him when he sat down next to her. He put his arm around her shoulders, kissed the side of her head, and she sank against him. She didn't look up. She stared into the fire in miserable silence.

He didn't break it. The kidnappers and the Bounty Hunters didn't hurt her—not on the outside. They did hurt her on the inside. They scared the crap out of her—and then she found out it was three of her own people who did it to her. That had to sting.

One of those traitors was still right here in this camp right now. Hammer studied each person in turn. Who was it? Who was the hidden traitor? The ants had missed out on part of their meal tonight. Hammer would have to change that.

The rest of the band kept quieter than usual. The men sat close to their sweethearts near the girls' shelters. That left the single men out in the cold. The men didn't mix as much.

Hammer prepared himself to spend the rest of the evening in silence and to sleep alone that night.

His driving need to be near Vina both compelled him with an irresistible force to move in with her for good at the same time that it gave him the inner peace not to.

He needed her like he needed to breathe—and yet he felt in moments like these that he could wait forever. He didn't need to sleep with her or to experience her body or even to kiss her.

He could feel perfectly satisfied just to sit here with his arm around her or maybe not even that. Just knowing she was his to protect and care for—he didn't need anything more than that.

The others drifted off to sleep. Cross and Sema got to their feet and stood inches apart for a long time holding hands, kissing, and whispering to each other in an undertone.

How did Hammer get so lucky to have Cross leave his family to come with Hammer's band? Hammer couldn't imagine what he would have done without Cross.

Earthquake and Daora went inside Daora's shelter together. Earthquake didn't come out of it. Hammer really hoped Earthquake wasn't in there doing anything illegal. Hammer didn't need to come down on any of his men after what just happened tonight.

Cross and Sema kissed one more time. She broke away, let her fingertips trail out of his hands, and she ducked inside her shelter. He stood there for a minute staring at the door before he walked off into the darkness.

Hammer took the hint, leaned in to kiss Vina on the side of the head, and took his arm off her shoulders. "You probably want to go to sleep. I better go. It's getting late. I'll see you tomorrow, okay? Are you going to be able to sleep tonight?"

Her head shot up and her eyes overflowed with emotion when she looked into his soul. "Don't go, Hammer!" Her voice cracked. "Please...."

His eyebrows shot up. "I have to. I can't stay with you."

"Just......" Her eyes darted to the shelter and then out to the camp. "We don't have to go inside if you don't want to. I just.....don't leave....please. I...I don't want to sleep alone tonight. I don't even care if we sleep out here...."

"Okay," he breathed. "You don't have to sleep alone. I'll stay with you. Come on."

He stood up, took her hand, and helped her up before he led her inside her shelter. Her features convulsed all over the place. She barely held it together that long.

He pushed her down on her bed, sat down next to her, and put both his arms around her this time. He kissed the side of her head and murmured in her ear at close range.

"I'm proud of the way you held yourself today," he breathed. "You alerted me in time to get to you before they could take you anywhere. It could have been much worse and it wasn't thanks to you. You're the reason we caught those traitors. Now we don't have to think about them anymore."

"I'm sorry, Hammer!" she husked. "I'm sorry about all of this!"

"Why are you sorry? I love you. I would never want anything to happen to you. I wish I could have stopped it, but it worked out in the end because I got there in time. You're safe now. No one will harm you. We'll get married in a few weeks and then we'll stay together all the time."

She nodded fast, but she clamped her lips too tightly together. She couldn't speak. He didn't need her to.

"Lie down," he told her. "You're exhausted. You need rest."

He steered her down onto the bed, clasped her hand, and stretched out on the floor next to the bed. He rolled onto his side so he could look up at her while they both drifted off.

"I love you," he breathed. "I'm going to marry you."

Her eyes shone down at him out of the dark. She looked calmer and more settled now. "I love you. Thank you so much for today. I don't know how to thank you enough."

"This is all the thanks I need." He squeezed her hand. "Being here with you is all I could ever ask."

She didn't answer. The silence deepened between them and then her eyes closed.

He watched her sleep for a long time before he shut his eyes and drifted off. He didn't let go of her hand.

Chapter 21

H ammer drifted out of a sound sleep. He didn't know what woke him.

He took a second to realize why it was so dark. He couldn't see anything. Then he smelled Vina nearby. He was in her shelter still holding her hand while they slept.

He started to settle back down to sleep, but movement caught the corner of his eye right at that moment. He glanced up and turned onto his back just as someone lunged for him and stabbed down with a knife.

The knife would have gone straight into his chest if he hadn't turned right at that instant. The darkness hid his assailant's features. He only saw and felt that it was a man.

The night slashed across the side of his ribs. He winced, roared out in pain, and the surprise made him let go of Vina's hand more roughly than he should have. He accidentally pulled her arm.

That noise and movement woke her up, but he didn't have time to think about that. The attacker pounced on top of him, pinned Hammer down, and drove down with the knife a second time.

The first strike woke Hammer all the way up. He reacted on high alert, blocked the second attack, and the knife embedded in the dirt next to his head.

Adrenaline torched through his veins. He couldn't go down like this. Would the attacker go after Vina next? Why not? Everyone else was doing it. Why not this attacker, too?

Hammer struck out, punched the assailant across the jaw, and then seized the bastard by the hair. The attacker was a Godless man with long hair done up in braids. Hammer knew the instant he touched his attacker's hair that it was Earthquake.

Hammer couldn't tell how he knew this because Earthquake didn't wear his hair much differently from every other man in their band.

Hammer knew, and once he made that connection, he really knew. He didn't need to see more than an outline to recognize Earthquake. His size, bulk, and smell gave him away.

Hammer also recognized Earthquake's breathing. Hammer had spent too much time around this man not to know exactly who he was dealing with.

Hammer couldn't overpower Earthquake, so Hammer went with the next best thing. He pried Earthquake's head back as far as Hammer could get it. Earthquake tried to draw his knife out of the dirt. Hammer controlled Earthquake's movements using his hair.

Earthquake bellowed loud enough to wake up the whole camp. Vina shot off the bed and screamed when she realized what was going on. Earthquake raised his knife, but he couldn't see where he was striking. He tried to stab down a third time.

Hammer took advantage of that moment, rocked Earthquake up just enough for Hammer to get one of his hands free, and flailed one arm toward Vina's bed.

His hand slapped down on her hip. She carried a hunting knife there that she used for skinning and butchering whatever kills the men brought back to camp.

Hammer's fingers closed on the hilt. He pulled the knife and plunged it into Earthquake's side just below his arm.

Hammer's desperation and rage exploded. He stabbed again and again bellowing in lunatic fury. Blood sprayed all over the place and even spattered Vina.

Hammer would have kept stabbing until he bled Earthquake dry, but Earthquake groaned just then. He started to wilt on top of Hammer. That gave Hammer an idea—a grizzly idea.

He shoved Earthquake off. The guy crashed down on the floor and let out another agonized groan when he rolled onto his uninjured side.

"Oh, my God!" Vina exclaimed. "Are you okay?"

Hammer was too furious to answer. He shot off the ground, seized Earthquake by his hair again, and dragged him outside. Half a dozen fires lit up the camp. Hammer could see so much more here.

He saw all his men coming toward him with their weapons drawn. He also saw the blood pouring down Earthquake's side.

"What the hell is going on?" Ant demanded.

"This son of a bitch just tried to kill me!" Hammer spun around and kicked Earthquake hard in the ribs. Hammer made sure to do it on the injured place where Hammer stabbed Earthquake. "You're a traitor, aren't you, you rotten, filthy, stinking bastard?!

You're the one who has been working against us all this time, aren't you?! You're the one who let the Ashtaws out of the canyon. AREN'T YOU?!!"

Earthquake yelled out in pain each time Hammer kicked him, but Hammer didn't let up—not until Earthquake reared off the ground and screamed out in broken agony. "YES!! I DID IT!! Stop!!"

Hammer would have liked to keep going just because Earthquake said that, but Hammer's energy died in that moment.

"You're bleeding, Hammer," Cross murmured.

Hammer looked down at his side. Blood poured from the cut on his ribs, but it didn't go deeper than the bone.

"He tried to kill me. He snuck into Vina's shelter and attacked me in my sleep. I barely woke up in time to save myself." Hammer's temper flared and he kicked Earthquake again. "Didn't you?! You attacked me in my sleep, you stinking coward?!"

"YES!!" Earthquake burst into sobs. "Just let me die, Hammer!"

"You're gonna die, you piece of filth!" Hammer spat. "You're lucky you're going to die—and you pretended to be my friend! You traitorous, lying scum!"

Earthquake huddled on the ground choking down sobs. He turned his face into the dirt to hide from all his comrades looking at him.

They didn't let him off easily. "How could you do this, Earthquake?" Omen murmured. "We looked up to you."

"I never thought it would be him," Lonion murmured. "I thought it could be a lot of people, but not him."

Their comments crushed Earthquake even more. "I'm sorry....." he choked. "I'm sorry....."

"You're sorry because you got caught." Hammer lunged for him, grabbed Earthquake by the hair, and yanked his head up. "Look at us! Look at the men who called you a friend. You betrayed them! You betrayed everything it means to be Godless—which means you betrayed everything we've spent the last ten years working for!"

Earthquake only answered with another pathetic moan. Hammer didn't want to listen to that.

He lowered the knife to Earthquake's throat. Killing Earthquake now would be too kind compared to what he deserved. Hammer should have dragged it out and made it more of a torture to pay Earthquake back.

Hammer couldn't bring in the ants at this time of night. Earthquake would bleed to death before that.

Hammer should have let Earthquake bleed out on the ground right here in front of everyone. That would have been a fitting death for him.

Cutting his throat felt more satisfying. It fed this enraged need for revenge to pay Earthquake back for his betrayal and cowardly assault.

The girls gathered in the background to watch. What Hammer did with Earthquake would decide the rest of the band's future. Everything would rest on the authority Hammer established for himself right here—tonight.

He tightened his fist on the knife to make the stroke, but one voice interrupted him. "No, brother. Don't do it this way."

Hammer's eyes snapped up. The person speaking to him was Mammoth.

Hammer saw it all in that moment. Mammoth must have been in on this. He must have been behind this attack together with Earthquake.

"Don't kill him like that," Mammoth went on. "He's already dying. Just leave him alone and let him die."

"Are you saying.....?" Hammer struggled through volcanic fury to form any words at all. "Are you saying.....I should show mercy.....to a man who tried to kill his own Kral......who snuck into his house under cover of darkness......and tried to stab his Kral in his sleep? Are you really saying.....a man like this deserves mercy?"

Mammoth held Hammer's eye contact no matter what. Mammoth didn't look away.

That on its own told Hammer loud and clear that Mammoth supported Earthquake's efforts. Did they draw straws to decide which of them would attack Hammer?

"You think I should let him bleed?" Hammer threw Earthquake down on the ground and stepped sideways. Hammer already knew what was coming.

"He's suffered enough," Mammoth went on. "Don't make it worse. You already killed him. Do you really need to make him suffer?"

Hammer's mind clicked again. He held out the knife—Vina's knife. Blood saturated the handle, the blade, and Hammer's arm up to the elbow.

"Take this knife, Mammoth," Hammer told him. "I'm ordering you as your Kral to execute this man right now in front of all of us. If you don't, I'll know you're a traitor, too. You've been conspiring with Earthquake behind my back, haven't you?"

Mammoth shuffled his feet for the first time. "I never said that."

"Then I order you to execute this man as a traitor. Do you care about a traitor more than your own Clan?"

"Of course not."

"Then do it." Hammer turned the knife backward and held it farther out to Mammoth. "What are you waiting for?"

Mammoth squared his shoulders. "I won't do that."

"You're either refusing a direct order from your Kral—in which case you deserve to be executed, too—or you're challenging me as Kral." Hammer hesitated. "*Are* you challenging me as Kral."

Mammoth squared his shoulders, took his huge axe off his back, and gripped it in front of him in both hands. "Yes. I am challenging you. You aren't fit to be Kral."

Earthquake groaned out, "No, Mammoth," but it was too late. Mammoth had already said those fateful words.

He tightened his grip on his axe handle and swelled up his shoulders to brace himself for a fight to end all fights.

Hammer saw the truth written all over Mammoth's face and his bulky body. He thought he could beat Hammer with strength. That was Mammoth's fatal flaw. He didn't see anything else.

He probably thought he deserved to be Kral because of his strength—or at least that he deserved to decide who should be Kral.

Hammer walked away to the other side of the camp. Cross, Ant, Scarecrow, and Flawless went with him.

Mammoth retreated to the far end of the camp. Hammer didn't see if anyone went with him or who went with him.

"All you have to do is stay out of range of his axe," Ant murmured under his breath. "Every time he swings, you dodge, get behind his stroke, and hit him from the sides, below, or behind. Understand?"

Hammer nodded. He already knew all of that.

Cross glanced behind him. "Who's over there?" Hammer asked. "Who's with him?"

"Omen, Pitch, Lucky, Acrobat, Eager, and Falcon are all still standing in the middle of the camp with the four boys," Cross replied. "No one is with him."

Hammer nodded again—more to himself this time. "That's good. Then it's just him and Earthquake."

Cross's eyes darted down to Hammer's side, but none of his men mentioned the wound that Earthquake had given him. Hammer didn't even feel it. He would have to block it out of his mind if he hoped to survive against Mammoth.

One hit from Mammoth's axe would finish Hammer for good. Everyone knew it. Mammoth knew it. He would rely on that.

"Wear him down," Flawless added. "He doesn't have good stamina. He's too big and too heavy. Keep moving around. Make him work for every stroke."

"And when you hit, hit hard," Scarecrow chimed in. "Don't toy with him. Just finish him and be done with it."

Hammer nodded again. He didn't seem to be able to do anything else. "I will. I know. Thank you."

"He's coming back," Cross remarked and looked down at the knife in Hammer's hands. "That should be enough as long as you stay away from his axe. Don't try to block it. Just avoid it."

Hammer nodded for the fourth time. He already felt his mind shutting down. He'd been Kral of this band for less than a month and he was already facing his first challenge. That didn't bode well for his future career.

Then again, maybe he was facing his first challenge because he'd been Kral for less than a month.

He would have liked to talk to Hangman right now, but Hangman couldn't help him. Hangman had never faced any challenges—from anyone. Everyone respected him too much.

He showed up in Ceon with his brother and his cousins. They already considered him their leader. Then Red and his men had put themselves under Hangman's leadership without a squeak of protest.

He made it sound like he was the one who protested Red's men subordinating themselves to him. Hammer and his men had certainly never challenged Hangman. They worshipped the ground he walked on.

Hammer didn't even regret losing these men. Bugs. Stray. Bear. Earthquake. Mammoth. Five men down. Hammer had ten men left, but at least they were the right ten.

He would rather do this with ten men and five girls than fifteen men when a third of them would be willing to betray the rest of their comrades. The band would get stronger because of this.

Chapter 22

Hammer's friends parted and he saw Mammoth coming back to the middle of the camp. Hammer strode forward to meet him.

Hammer and Mammoth met in the center of the camp. The boys and other men pulled back to give the combatants room. One of them would walk away as Kral. The other wouldn't walk away at all.

Mammoth almost checked himself when he saw Hammer approaching carrying only the one knife. He wouldn't need any other weapon if he played this right.

Mammoth took one look at Hammer's facial expression and braced himself for the first swing. Mammoth planted himself there in the middle of the camp. He couldn't move around while he was swinging his axe.

He wound back for the first stroke. Hammer stayed inside the axe's radius just long enough for Mammoth to commit himself to the stroke.

He put all his weight and strength behind it and hacked down from top to bottom and left to right. He would have chopped Hammer in half, but Hammer sprang back just in time.

The axe whistled past him and he dove in. He had to thrust with all his strength to break through the solid wall of muscle on Mammoth's chest and stomach.

Hammer lunged inward, grabbed Mammoth by the shoulder, and Hammer wedged his body there to hold both of Mammoth's arms to one side.

Mammoth couldn't correct until the weight of his axe stopped swinging. Hammer drove in and stabbed up and under Mammoth's arm.

The blade penetrated through the top of Mammoth's abdomen. Hammer tried to angle the knife upward to impale Mammoth's lungs, but Hammer couldn't be sure if he succeeded.

He had to leap away just as fast when Mammoth straightened up and took a fresh grip on his axe. No blood came from Hammer's first stab wound.

The wound infuriated Mammoth. He bellowed in rage, raised his axe, and hacked straight down right on top of the spot where Hammer stood.

Hammer veered, pivoted behind Mammoth, and stuck him in the ribs right where Hammer stabbed Earthquake. This hit definitely weakened Mammoth. He doubled over and groaned before he reacted much faster this time.

He spun around and swung his axe extra hard. Hammer actually staggered in his haste to get back in time.

He almost didn't make it. The axe would have lodged in his neck and probably taken his head off, but he stumbled and actually tripped and pitched onto his backside.

He sprawled and stared up in horror as Mammoth stormed toward him, raised the axe one more time, and hacked it down with all his immense power right on top of Hammer.

Hammer rolled sideways, reared off the ground, and stabbed Mammoth on the other side of the ribs. It was the only place Hammer could get to any vulnerabilities. Mammoth had too much bulk and padding everywhere else.

Mammoth took longer to recover this time. He stayed there, bent over, with his axe driven five inches into the dirt. He gave Hammer all the time he needed to scramble to his feet, dart behind Mammoth, and stab him again through the back.

Mammoth had to use every ounce of his strength to pry his axe out of the ground. He staggered a few steps, turned around, and faced Hammer. Mammoth's eyes bleared for a second before he hauled his vision into focus.

Hammer stayed out of Mammoth's range until Mammoth steadied himself. How much longer could Mammoth keep going?

Facing this man reminded Hammer of his initiation. Maybe challenges were a man's initiation into being Kral. Maybe he had to go through this before all the remaining survivors fully recognized him as Kral.

He knew that wasn't true because all the remaining survivors already considered him Kral. He didn't have to prove anything to them.

He had to prove it to himself. That's what this was. He had to become Kral in his own mind. He couldn't doubt himself anymore—not that he ever did—or maybe he did. Maybe he let people like Bugs and Earthquake get inside his head.

That didn't matter right now because Mammoth was the last man standing. Mammoth heaved his axe up, wound it back, and swung.

He must have already been losing his senses because he swung without coming inside the axe's radius. The weapon zinged six inches past Hammer's chest and just kept on going.

Mammoth lost his grip on the handle. The axe went sailing off into the darkness and left Mammoth standing there empty-handed.

He didn't seem to register what had just happened. He didn't seem to be aware of very much, not even Hammer standing right in front of him. The fight was over. Mammoth wasn't even here anymore.

Only one thing remained for Hammer to do. He had to get rid of these two traitors. How he did it no longer mattered anymore.

He lunged for Mammoth, tackled him, and drove the knife hard up under Mammoth's chin. Hammer angled the blade and drove it into the fleshy underside of Mammoth's jaw.

The blade impaled his skull up to the hilt. Hammer heard the skull crack deep inside Mammoth's head, but the two men were already falling backward together.

Mammoth thumped down hard on the ground with Hammer right on top of him. Hammer couldn't loosen his fingers from around the knife hilt.

The impact jolted Hammer hard. He took a few seconds to realize where he was and that the fight was really over now.

Mammoth lay under him with his eyes fixed wide open and locked on the starry sky overhead. Mammoth didn't move again.

Hammer had to think about it before he commanded his fingers to loosen. He should have pulled the knife out and given it back to Vina. She needed it to protect herself and to do her work.

He didn't think of that until later. Just loosening his fingers took every ounce of mental focus he had left.

He dragged himself to his feet and almost fell over when he turned around to survey the rest of the camp. His men and the four boys stood off to one side.

He didn't see anyone over there who would cause him any problems. Not even Acrobat would cause Hammer any problems anymore.

The boys and the four men who supported Hammer right before the challenge—they all smiled at him.

The boys couldn't keep still. They practically jumped up and down in delight that Mammoth was dead. Hammer was the undisputed Kral of their band now. No one would ever question him again.

He remembered to turn around, pull the knife out of Mammoth's skull, and Hammer wiped the blood off on Mammoth's arm. Then Hammer stumbled over to Earthquake.

He lay unconscious on the ground where Hammer had left him. Earthquake might have been unconscious for the whole fight. Hammer couldn't bring himself to do anything about Earthquake—not now. He would be dead soon if he wasn't already.

Hammer waved at nothing. "Get them out of here. Someone can take them into the jungle and feed them to the ants as soon as the sun comes up."

Eager and Scarecrow both came forward. They were the biggest men in the band now, but Hangman didn't give a crap about anyone's size. He had his people.

He could almost wish that Bugs, Stray, Bear, Earthquake, and Mammoth had stayed behind with Shadow's band, but not even that mattered anymore.

Hammer didn't even care that Acrobat *should* have stayed behind with Shadow's band. Hammer had become the Kral he was supposed to be because of these traitors. They had made him what he was.

They had finally made him into the Kral who could carry this band into their future. He hadn't been that Kral when he left Shadow's band. He still followed Hangman's lead all the time. He was that Kral now. He could thank these traitors for that.

Eager picked up Mammoth. Scarecrow picked up Earthquake. The two men carried the bodies out into the jungle. Hammer never saw them again.

Eager and Scarecrow came back just a few minutes later. They must have just dumped the bodies out there beyond the trees. Any creature could come along and devour Mammoth and Earthquake before morning. Hammer really just didn't care.

He stumbled back to Vina's shelter and buckled onto the ground by the fire. He couldn't hold himself up a second longer.

She sat down next to him, rested her hand on his shoulder, and leaned in to kiss him on the side of the neck. "I love you," she murmured.

He glanced over. "You aren't hurt, are you? He didn't get you, did he?"

She burst into a beautiful glowing smile. "Of course not. You woke me up before he could do anything."

Hammer looked down at the knife in his hand. Every ounce of his being told him to give it back to her, but his mind refused again to connect to his hand.

He stared at the knife for a long time. "I should probably give this back to you. Just...just let me clean it for you first."

Her eyes twinkled. She pulled a water gourd toward herself, dampened a piece of furry hide, and started sponging the blood off his side.

She started low down on his waist and worked her way up getting closer to the cut. He couldn't move even when she washed the cut itself. He kept staring down at the knife in his hand. His brain took extra time to catch up with everything that just happened.

The other men and girls went through an identical process of winding down for the night. The men returned to their sweethearts. Cross reassured Sema, hugged her, and held another whispered conversation with her before she went back inside her own shelter alone.

Ant and Eleph stood outside her shelter and held each other for a long time. Neither of them let go until she broke away to go inside.

Masha and Lucky went inside her shelter together. Hammer didn't wonder if Lucky was doing anything illegal with Masha. Hammer couldn't explain to himself why he suspected Earthquake of this but not Lucky.

Only one person stayed outside alone. Daora glanced back and forth across the camp like she was looking around for Earthquake.

Vina's eyes darted to Daora. "I feel sorry for her."

"If she was part of their scheme, then no one should feel sorry for her. If she wasn't part of it, then she has nothing to worry about and she should be happy Earthquake is gone. She can marry a good man now."

She bent over his side and smeared leaf paste on the wound. Then she got busy cleaning the spattered blood off herself. There was a lot of it.

"It might take her a while to get over him and understand that," Vina murmured. "I don't envy her that process. It would be terrible if the man you loved turned out to be a traitor."

Hammer had a flashback to his mother throwing herself into the ants at Aster's execution. Cheina just couldn't live without Alien. The blow must have hurt a hundred times worse when Cheina found out her own daughter was the one who did all that.

Hammer shook himself, kissed Vina on the cheek, and stood up. "I'll be right back. Then we can go back to sleep the way we were when this whole thing started."

She smiled up at him. "I don't mind as long as we sleep—nothing else."

He laughed, but he had to get serious when he crossed the camp and straightened up in front of Daora.

She went through a dozen different facial expressions from terror to defiance to confusion. "I had nothing to do with any of this!" she snapped. "Don't think you're going to accuse me of anything!"

"I wasn't going to accuse you of anything. I don't suspect you of anything. I only came over here to check and find out if you're okay with what just happened. I won't blame you for hating me."

"Why would I hate you for executing a traitor to our Clan? That's your job as Kral."

Hammer nodded at nothing. "I don't mean to insult you, Daora. I'm sorry if this offends you, but I have to ask—also as part of my job as Kral."

She turned white. "What is it?"

"I've seen Earthquake coming into your shelter and even spending the night there."

"Yeah? So? You spend the night with Vina. Lucky spends the night with Masha."

"I just want to make sure Earthquake didn't break the law before he died. He broke so many others. I want to make sure he didn't violate any with you."

"Of course he didn't!" she snapped. "Do you think I would sell myself for something like that?! What do you take me for?"

"I don't take you for anything. I'm just asking. It would have been his crime—not yours. You're still underage."

She looked away. "He didn't do anything. I never let him."

Hammer hesitated. "Are you saying he wanted to?"

She waved to one side. "He wanted to, but I never let him. That's all you need to know."

Hammer winced. "Then your virtue is intact and you're a better person than he is. I understand if you need to take some time to get over all of this. You have my permission to marry any man in the band if you wish."

Her head snapped around. "You mean....you aren't going to take me to the gathering?"

"Vina, Masha, Sema, and Eleph won't be going to the gathering, either. If you want to go to the gathering, you can—in which case we'll all go and we'll all choose each other. We're all within one year of coming of age, so it will still be valid. If you choose a husband from this band, then none of us will go. We'll start with the five of us and take it from there when the boys come of age. I know it isn't totally official, but it's as good as it gets under the circumstances. It's my decision as Kral how to handle exceptional circumstances and this is my ruling. You can let me know if you decide to marry someone else or if you want to go to the gathering."

He turned to walk away. "Hammer!" she blurted out. "Thank you."

He only nodded at her. He had said what he came here to say. Now he needed to go fall over somewhere—somewhere no one but Vina could see him.

He returned to her shelter. He really didn't want to sit down by the fire again. He didn't trust himself to stand up again if he did that.

She got up when he approached her. She didn't ask any questions. She held the door open for him to go inside.

His eyes closed even before he collapsed on the floor by her bed. He didn't even have the strength to lift his hand to hold onto hers.

He followed her movements with his ears while she shut the door, crossed the room to his side, and stretched out on the bed next to him.

Her hand appeared on his forehead. She stroked his cheeks and ran her fingers through his hair. He drifted off to that blissful sensation finally relaxing him in the knowledge that everything was going to be okay now.

Chapter 23

Hammer lay flat on his stomach behind the ridgeline and peered over the side at the Ashtaws grazing. One month had passed since Mammoth challenged Hammer as Kral.

The band was a lot smaller now, but they worked cohesively as one unit. No one had to worry anymore about anyone sneaking around behind anyone's back.

The remaining men dedicated all their energy and free time to domesticating the Ashtaws. The band had made incredible progress and finally succeeded in riding the creatures.

The ten mothers the Godless first took down to the canyon had become the men's mounts. The Godless could walk out into that valley, approach any of the ten, mount up, and ride them around. The men didn't even have to tempt the Ashtaws with Fogpo leaves anymore.

The young Ashtaws kept growing. Hammer and his men handled them and constructed miniature head harnesses and weighted neck harnesses to get the little creatures used to carrying a rider.

The young ones treated this as normal now. Hammer had even started to branch out and tame other mothers and their young.

Scarecrow's low, murderous growl brought Hammer back to reality. Scarecrow had married Daora only a week after Earthquake's death. Daora was of age and Scarecrow was of age. They were the first married couple in the band.

Ant and Eleph had married one week after them. Hammer and Vina had to wait another month—just like Cross and Sema. Masha and Lucky had to wait another four months before they both came of age.

Getting married had made Scarecrow a thousand times more dangerous than he had been before. He glared so much more fiercely at everything and fought a hundred times more venomously when he faced an enemy who threatened Daora.

"What are we waiting for?" Scarecrow snarled. "We have the Ashtaws. We should obliterate these bastards. Isn't that why we did all this—to fight our enemies?"

"We don't know how the Ashtaws will act in combat," Omen pointed out.

"Yes, we do," Scarecrow fired back. "We've already used the Ashtaws against our enemies once. They're more obedient now than they were back then."

"The Bounty Hunters might turn their weapons on the Ashtaws," Lucky interjected. "The Ashtaws could get injured and run out of control."

"Are you trying to insult my intelligence?" Scarecrow snapped. "A Bounty Hunter spear couldn't penetrate the hide on an Ashtaw's legs. The Bounty Hunters wouldn't be able to stick the Ashtaw any higher than that. Using the Ashtaws to attack the Bounty Hunters is totally risk-free."

Hammer snorted. "I think you might be taking it a little too far there, brother. Nothing is risk-free—especially not when it comes to the Ashtaws."

Scarecrow made a face. "Fine. So it isn't risk-free, but it's a lot more risk-free than fighting the Bounty Hunters on the ground. We put a lot of work into training these Ashtaws. When are we going to start using them?"

Hammer stared across the valley at a tiny Bounty Hunter patrol working its way eastward from the northern end of the valley.

"They're coming from the north again," Cross pointed out.

"They always come from the north," Ant replied. "The Bounty Hunters and the Renegades come from the same place. I don't know about you, but where I come from, that usually means something."

"And they always travel east," Flawless added. "East and south—almost like they know something we don't want them to know."

"Of course they know," Eager countered. "Bugs and the others must have blabbed all our secrets to them. The traitors probably drew the enemy a map of how to get to our camp."

"Scarecrow is right," Hammer decided. "We have to do something about them and doing something about them with the Ashtaws will be better than doing it on foot."

Scarecrow clapped his hands. "That's what I'm talking about! It's about time."

"Let's go," Hammer ordered. "Mount up and we'll intercept the Bounty Hunters over there—at the Broken Tooth gap."

He pointed at a spot on the eastern ridge. The Godless men had spent every day up here. It was only a matter of time before they named every feature of the landscape.

The men retreated down the hill behind them so the ridge hid them from the Bounty Hunters. Hammer used hand signals to send his men down the ridge toward the west.

They skirted the valley on the opposite side and dropped in where the Ashtaws would hide the men from any prying Bounty Hunter eyes.

The men had to make their way through the herd of Ashtaws the men hadn't gotten around to taming yet. The men had spent so much time in the valley that none of these creatures reacted to the men's arrival. The Ashtaws just kept grazing.

The men could even hide behind the Ashtaws' legs and peer out to find out where the Bounty Hunters were. The Ashtaws didn't adjust their footing when the men touched them.

Hammer spotted his mount ahead. The young mother he had befriended early on had grown considerably in the short time since he first met her. Her young female juvenile had also developed into a thriving adolescent.

They both adored Hammer. The mother nuzzled him and rumbled at him when he approached her. She kept her head down so he could strap the neck seat around her neck. He slipped the bridle over her head.

The men didn't use bits. The head harnesses worked perfectly well the way they were without training the Ashtaws to take anything into their mouth.

Hammer's heart started racing when he swung up into his seat sling. He stuck his feet through the holes and his mount raised her head.

She carried him up, up, up to a massive height. He glanced across the valley toward the eastern ridge. He looked at the Bounty Hunters from their level now.

They didn't see the men mounting up all over the valley. The Godless attacking while mounted on Ashtaws would be the absolute last thing the Bounty Hunters expected.

Hammer tugged the reins to his left and kicked his left heel against the Ashtaw's neck. Their skin was so tough that he could kick his hardest. The Ashtaws only felt it as a light tap.

"Go! Go! Go!" he called into her ear. The men used a combination of foot signals, rein pulls, and word commands to signal the Ashtaws to turn, stop, or go.

He also swatted her neck with the long end of his braided hide reins. Swatting her didn't hurt her, either. She barely felt it.

She wheeled at that command and took off stomping across the valley. Her young juvenile trotted along at the mother's heel. The other Godless broke out of the herd at the same time.

Those ten Ashtaws cut sideways and set off at a right angle from the rest of the herd. The surrounding Ashtaws paid no attention to this, either. The Godless rode their Ashtaws around the valley all the time nowadays.

Hammer's heart leapt when the Bounty Hunters passed behind some rocks. They would never see the Ashtaws coming. He kicked both heels against the creature's neck and swatted her again. "Go! Go!"

The other men did the same thing. The Ashtaws responded perfectly, stormed up the hill, and clambered all the way up the ridge until they came out at the Broken Tooth. It was a gap between the rocks where the ridge flattened out into a wider area.

Hammer's mount made it to the gap first. He encouraged her one more time and she lumbered up there just as the Bounty Hunters came out from behind the rocks. She stopped in the middle of the gap and looked around trying to decide what to do next.

The ridgetop footpath surrounding the valley passed through rocky defiles not big enough for any Ashtaw to set foot in. The Bounty Hunters were traveling too fast to stop. They sure were in a big rush to get south. Hammer didn't have to ask why.

They blundered straight into Hammer's mount and then the other ten Ashtaws stomped up the hill and entered the gap, too.

The Bounty Hunters skidded to a halt and stared in horror at the Ashtaws in front of them. Hammer couldn't be sure if they even saw the Godless mounted in their seats. He wheeled his mount toward them and kicked her hard. "GO!!" he roared. "GO!!"

She lunged forward. He couldn't be sure if she saw the Bounty Hunters, either. She just responded to his command the way he trained her to. She stormed toward the defile. Hammer didn't have a clue what she would do when she got there.

The Bounty Hunters hustled to back off. Some of them tried to look up at the Ashtaws instead of watching where they were going. Four Bounty Hunters tripped over themselves, fell, and met their end under the Ashtaws' giant feet.

The rest of the Bounty Hunters blundered toward the defile in a desperate hope that the rocks would protect them. Hammer actually thought the Bounty Hunters had a decent chance once they got inside the defile, but no such luck.

His mount bellowed out and charged straight into the defile. He never dreamed one of these creatures could be so strong, but he should have realized. They were so big and unbelievably powerful.

His mount crushed rocks underfoot and smashed the defile apart with her enormous shoulders. She barged straight through it and trampled a dozen Bounty Hunters in her path.

She burst out the other side still roaring in confusion. She had no idea what she was even doing up here.

Hammer leaned back in his seat and pulled on the reins. "Easy!" he yelled. "Easy!"

She slowed down the way he'd trained her to. She stopped there and her young juvenile caught up a minute later.

The other riders steered their Ashtaws in different directions, tracked down the rest of the Bounty Hunters, and trampled them into the dirt. The Godless didn't leave a single Bounty Hunter alive.

Scarecrow raised his fist in triumph and whooped across the ridge. "Whoo!"

His outburst startled his mouth. She roared out loud, reared on her hind legs, and made the ground shake when she landed hard on her front feet.

Hammer circled his hand above his head to signal his men to take the Ashtaws back to the valley.

The men used a different signal to get the Ashtaws to lower their heads so the men could dismount. The Ashtaws stood in passive silence or grazed while the men removed the harnesses.

The men attacked each other, hugged, and whooped in triumph once they dismounted.

"We did it!" Lucky yelled. He actually cupped his hands to his mouth and bellowed across the valley for all the world to hear. "We did it!! Do you hear that?! We did it!"

Hammer laughed with his friends. He couldn't help feeling pretty smug. His experiment worked. The men had just run their first successful operation to defeat their enemies using the Ashtaws as mounts.

The men got serious on their way back up to the ridge. "What are we going to do with them next?" Flawless asked. "We should strike a decisive blow to stop these Clans from invading our territory."

"I agree with Flawless," Cross added. "We should get a lot more aggressive in retaliating against intruders. This is our territory. We should control it for ourselves and not allow anyone else to invade no matter who they are."

Hammer paused on the ridgetop and squinted toward the east. "I've been thinking the same thing. These invaders are obviously trying to get to our camp. The traitors must have told them that we have women there. These enemy Clans will keep coming until we stop them."

"So what are we going to do about that?"

"I have an idea, but you men aren't going to like it."

Ant howled. "Oh-ho! Listen to this, brothers! You know it's bad when he starts off by saying we won't like it."

"You might as well tell us," Scarecrow added. "How can it be bad if it gets rid of the enemy Clans?"

"Okay, you asked for it," Hammer replied. "These invaders are so hot to find our camp. I say we let them find it."

Eager gasped. "You can't be serious! You would put all our women in danger? Why?"

"They're already in danger. They're in danger as long as the enemy Clans are trying to get to the camp. The enemy Clans are going to find the camp sooner or later because they already know it's there. The only way to get around that is to make them think they have found the camp when what they've really found is an ambush."

Scarecrow burst into a grin and rubbed his hands together. "I like the sound of this more and more the longer you talk. How do we spring this ambush?"

"It's simple. We move the camp to a location where the Ashtaws can get to it—I mean a location where the Ashtaws will be able to attack the invaders when they come."

"You're talking about using our wives as bait," Ant pointed out.

"Yeah? Where's the problem with that?" Hammer asked. "The women already are bait. They're the ones attracting these marauders. The Bounty Hunters and the Renegades wouldn't care less about finding our camp if the women weren't there. The only difference is how well we can defend the camp when it happens."

"Don't you think it would be better if we defended the camp where it is?" Ziti asked. "Is that why we put the camp down in that box canyon—so it would be more defensible?"

"It is defensible down there, but we have five fewer men and we have the Ashtaws. We can't defend the box canyon with the men we have and we can't use the Ashtaws down there, either. I say we move the women up here, build a dummy camp....over there on that flat spot in the jungle, and watch and wait for the Bounty Hunters to come for the women. Then we'll roll in with our Ashtaws and send the Bounty Hunters where they belong."

"It will be harder to track down the Bounty Hunters when they're in the jungle," Ant pointed out.

Hammer shrugged. "That's true, but there is no ideal scenario for any of this. The alternative is to set up the dummy camp out here in the open where the Ashtaws will be able to track the enemy down."

"I think that's a better plan," Cross replied. "We can set up this dummy camp close to the valley. Then we can hide the mounted Ashtaws inside the valley until the Bounty Hunters show themselves. They'll probably hide in the trees and use the jungle as cover so they can get close to the camp. They'll see that the place is undefended, come out of hiding, and then we'll come out of hiding with our Ashtaws."

Scarecrow burst out laughing. "That will be great! Let's do it."

Hammer didn't answer. He could see a lot of flaws in this plan, but he could see a lot of flaws in every plan. There was no perfect plan.

Chapter 24

H ammer and the men took their time returning to camp. "I don't look forward to explaining this to Eleph," Ant murmured when they got near the canyon.

"I'll explain it to all the women at once," Hammer told him. "If they want to get mad and attack someone, they can attack me."

Scarecrow laughed. "You're a braver man than I am. I'll hide behind you and let Daora go after you instead."

The others joined in the joke. They were all in a good mood by the time they met up with their wives and sweethearts.

Hammer returned to Vina's shelter. The other men who had wives and sweethearts made some excuse to bring them over there, too. That was Hammer's cue. "I want you women to pack up the camp and get ready to move tomorrow morning," he announced.

Eleph's head shot up. "We're moving? Why?"

"Because it's too dangerous here," Hammer replied. "The traitors must have told the Bounty Hunters and the Renegades that we're here. Both Clans have been trying to make their way south and around the valley ever since we moved here. This canyon isn't a secret anymore."

"So where are we moving instead?" Sema asked. "Are we going back north to the mountains?"

"No, not at all. We're staying here in this territory. We've worked too hard to win it. We won't give it up without a fight."

"I don't understand," Eleph interjected. "Where are we going instead if we don't stay here and we don't leave the territory?"

"I want you all to move your camp up onto the flats outside the valley. The Bounty Hunters are already looking for the camp. Moving there will make it easier for them to find you."

"You want us to set up camp......right where the Bounty Hunters are certain to find us?!" Eleph countered. "You want us to deliberately put ourselves in harm's way—so they'll attack us?"

"Yes," Hammer replied. "I mean....I'm hoping we get to them first before they attack you, but yes, I want them to find you and get ready to attack you. Then the men and I will bring in our Ashtaws and destroy the enemy Clans."

The women exchanged glances. "I don't like this," Daora murmured.

"I don't like it, either," Hammer replied. "The alternative is that you stay here. Just understand that we can't defend the camp here. We don't have enough men and we can't bring in the Ashtaws. They're our one real advantage and we've put in all this effort to train them to defeat our enemies. That's what we plan to do, but we can't do it down here. This canyon is too narrow and too isolated."

Another tense silence fell over the group. None of the men got involved to back Hammer's order. He said he would break the news and he did.

Vina came to his rescue. "Well, I guess we better start packing up the camp bright and early tomorrow morning."

"Just get out of the camp as soon as the Ashtaws show up," Hammer went on. "We'll try to take out the Bounty Hunters before they get inside the camp, but we might not be able to. Some of them might get inside the camp before we get there or they may run into the camp when they see the Ashtaws coming."

"What will you do then?" Sema asked.

"That's what I'm telling you. If that happens, we'll have no choice but to take the Ashtaws into the camp. So I want all five of you to get out of the camp as soon as you can as soon as the attack starts. Don't flee the camp until after the Bounty Hunters and the Ashtaws show themselves. You can pretend to be running away from the Ashtaws. Then we can ride the Ashtaws into the camp and finish off the Bounty Hunters without worrying about stepping on one of you."

Eleph laughed. "We wouldn't want that."

Hammer smiled at her. "No, we wouldn't. So are you all ready for that?"

The women looked at each other again. "I suppose it's the best course considering everything," Sema remarked.

Her practical sense swayed everyone else who needed to be swayed. The women started talking about dismantling their shelters and which parts they would take up to the valley instead of reconstructing everything from scratch there.

None of them questioned the move after that.

"How long will we stay up there?" Vina asked. "Will we stay only for this attack or will we move there permanently?"

"I think we should come back down here afterward," Ant chimed in. "This place is so much better protected—and better concealed. Why waste that? Maybe we can get rid of all the Bounty Hunters who know about this place. Then we can go back to being invisible and the Bounty Hunters won't know where to find us. We can keep them isolated around the valley where they already know they can find us."

"I was thinking the same thing," Hammer replied. "I think it should just be this one time."

"Then we shouldn't take anything," Masha pointed out. "We should leave all our shelters here and construct new ones up there."

"They don't have to be permanent shelters," Eleph told her. "We don't have to construct anything that will stand the test of time."

"It would be better if you didn't," Hammer replied. "The Ashtaws might step on one of the shelters and break it. Don't build anything you aren't ready to lose in the battle."

That settled it. The women went back to talking about all their plans and how they were going to do everything. Sema wanted to know everything about the location to make sure it was close enough to the jungle for the women to find building materials.

"You're a genius," Scarecrow murmured to Hammer after the women went off to start packing up their possessions. "I'm going to tell Daora to come talk to you anytime she gets mad at me."

"That might not be such a great idea," Hammer replied. "I might make it worse."

The women spent the rest of the day packing up the few possessions they wanted to take with them. They finished by the middle of the afternoon and announced to Hammer that they were ready to move now. They didn't want to wait until tomorrow.

The whole band climbed out of the canyons. Pitch and Lucky ran a patrol around the valley to make sure the coast was clear. The rest of the men stood guard while the women made camp.

Scarecrow kept shooting murderous glances in all directions. "This must be the first Godless camp in history ever constructed out in the open like this," he snarled.

"Let's hope it's the last," Hammer replied. "We'll need to run continual patrols around the valley after this. We'll need to take it in shifts so someone is always on watch for the enemy to approach."

"Technically, we should only need to patrol this side of the valley," Flawless pointed out. "We don't need to care about anyone moving on the west side. The Bounty Hunters will have to come over here just to get near the camp. We only need to patrol the northern and eastern sides."

"We should still patrol everything," Thuron interjected. "The enemy Clans might anticipate us and come at us from the west and south. Then we would get caught unawares and the women would be defenseless."

Flawless shrugged. "Okay. I see your point."

"It's too bad we can't keep the Ashtaws in readiness the whole time," Omen remarked. "I don't like having any delay between when we spot the enemy moving in and when we mount up for the assault."

"We'll have enough time," Cross told him. "Think about it. If our scouts do their jobs, we should have plenty of advanced warning when the Bounty Hunters start moving in. Then we'll have to wait until they get close enough for us to attack and destroy. We don't need to keep the Ashtaws in readiness. We could be waiting for days if we did that."

Pitch and Lucky came back and reported that the valley was secure for now. Hammer held a conference with his men. They agreed to patrol the valley in pairs the same way with two men each running around the valley in opposite directions to cover the whole ridgeline.

A third man would stand guard on the east side to watch for the Bounty Hunters' most frequent line of approach.

The women listened until the men made that decision. Then the five women went back to building their shelters. They finished by the end of the day.

The friends sat around their fires talking and sharing their food as usual. "I suppose these fires will help attract the Bounty Hunters' attention," Eleph remarked.

"What if the Bounty Hunters attack at night?" Vuco asked.

"Our scouts should still pick them up before they get here," Hammer replied. "They shouldn't be able to surprise us."

"We won't be able to use the Ashtaws at night," Ant pointed out.

"If one of our scouts reports that the Bounty Hunters are moving in at night, then we'll evacuate the camp and take refuge in the jungle until morning," Hammer decided. "We'll try another time. We won't try to fight the Bounty Hunters at night. That's too dangerous."

The band drifted off to go to sleep. Hammer returned to Vina's shelter. He stayed with her every night now, but he always slept on the floor and held her hand in his sleep. That was their routine until she came of age. Only a few weeks to go.

Chapter 25

H ammer woke up in darkness when he felt someone shaking him awake. "Hammer—wake up!" someone hissed in his ear.

He startled upright trying to blink the fog out of his head. "Huh? What's happening?"

"The Bounty Hunters are moving in! They're on their way past the eastern ridge right now!"

Hammer sat the rest of the way up. His brain cleared enough for him to recognize Acrobat bending over him.

Acrobat had laid all of Hammer's doubts to rest by behaving perfectly over the last month. Acrobat had never given Hammer any cause to question Acrobat's loyalty or commitment to this band.

Acrobat had been posted on the western ridgeline patrol with Eager last night. Hammer didn't have to suspect Acrobat of coming to warn Hammer if the Bounty Hunters weren't really there.

Vina stirred when Hammer took his hand out of hers. He shook her awake next. "Wake up, Vina," he whispered. "The Bounty Hunters are coming in. I need you to go wake up the other women and get everyone ready to move when the time comes."

She woke up instantly and left the shelter with Hammer and Acrobat. Hammer got confirmation when he and Acrobat met up with Eager outside. Flawless was still on the eastern ridge watch. He must be up there monitoring the Bounty Hunters' progress.

Hammer, Eager, and Acrobat went through the camp in a whirlwind waking up everyone else. The men gathered their harnesses and hustled up the hills to the ridgeline.

They found Flawless crouching between the rocks on the northeast side. The sun was just coming up over the jungle.

Hammer and his men squatted down near Flawless. They all watched a sizeable party of Bounty Hunters trekking down the countryside on a dead course for the Godless camp.

"I guess they won't have to look too hard to find the camp," Ant pointed out.

"They certainly brought a lot more men this time," Lonion added. "There must be fifty of them down there."

Hammer didn't gloat over the Bounty Hunters proving him right. The Godless never would have been able to defend the canyon camp against this many attackers.

"How long do you want to wait?" Scarecrow asked.

"We'll wait at least until they get into position to attack the camp. They should slow down and maybe try to conceal themselves before they make their move. They'll expect to meet Godless men defending the camp. We'll strike then."

The men kept watching. The hours dragged past. The Bounty Hunters did slow their approach. They slowed it long before they got anywhere near the Godless camp.

The women moved back and forth between their shelters. Anyone watching from a distance would see normal activity there—except that there were no men in the camp.

The Bounty Hunters took refuge in the jungle to conceal their approach. The Godless men lost sight of the enemy.

"Now what do we do?" Lucky asked. "We can't send scouts over there. We wouldn't be able to signal each other."

"The Bounty Hunters are close enough." Hammer stood up. "Go mount your Ashtaws and bring them up to the Broken Tooth. We'll be able to wait there until the Bounty Hunters make their move."

The men took off running down the hill. Flawless went with them. Staying on watch wouldn't tell the Godless anything.

The men only ran halfway down the hill before they slowed to a walk. Hammer had to concentrate extra hard to calm himself down so he wouldn't spook the Ashtaws.

This moment would make or break Hammer's band. This moment would be the ultimate test to find out if all their hard work paid off or came to nothing.

The tension and agitation in the men would determine how the Ashtaws responded. Hammer stopped at the edge of the herd just to make absolutely certain he approached them calmly—as calmly as he approached them yesterday.

The rest of his men halted with him. Hammer had to fight his every instinct not to rush out there and charge his Ashtaw in a blur of confusion.

The Ashtaws saw the men coming. Hammer's female studied him from a distance. He had never hesitated to approach her before. She came toward him. The other mounts did the same thing. The men had trained the Ashtaws too well.

Hammer's female lowered her head and butted him. She saw him holding his seat harness. It was time. He didn't need to wait any longer.

He buckled it on and mounted up. She swung her head up high and he kicked his heels against her neck. He didn't yell the command. He just said it on a calm undertone. "Go!"

She took off walking up the hill to the Broken Tooth. He let her walk slowly and calmly. He didn't need to hurry.

She stopped in the open place. He could see so much more from up here, but he didn't see any Bounty Hunters. They must still be hiding in the jungle. They must be sneaking into position over there where they could attack the women without warning.

The women still moved around camp as usual. Their talking voices and laughter drifted on the breeze.

Hammer couldn't recognize any of the women from this height, but one of them stopped in the middle of the camp to look up at him. The Ashtaws' presence should alert the women that the attack was about to start.

The other mounts pulled into the gap alongside Hammer. No one moved for a second. This scene didn't give Hammer any pause at all. The Bounty Hunters had played right into his hands when they decided to hide in the jungle.

They would all attack the camp from the east. That would give the women a perfect line of escape to evacuate the camp and flee to the ridge. The Bounty Hunters would invade the camp—right where the Ashtaws could trample all the Bounty Hunters to death.

Hammer saw the whole scenario play out in his mind before it happened. He only had to execute it.

The whole area looked and sounded perfectly peaceful right up until the moment when the Bounty Hunters flooded out of the trees. They came in force, swarmed outward from the tree line in a black wave, and surrounded the camp instantly—or they tried to.

The distance between the ridge and the camp gave the Bounty Hunters all the time they needed to cross the gap and invade the camp by the dozen.

The women would have been defenseless, but they must have been watching and waiting for that moment. All five dropped what they were doing and ran for it.

Hammer kicked his mount and swatted her hard. "Go! Go! Go!" he yelled.

She lunged forward with a roar and took off barreling down the other side of the ridge with all the other mounts right with her.

Their pounding feet quaked the ground, but the Bounty Hunters were too busy running down the five women. The Bounty Hunters didn't notice or hear a thing.

The Bounty Hunters rampaged through the camp tearing into all the shelters looking for the men.

Eleph, Masha, and Daora escaped to the west and raced up the slope heading for the ridge. All three had the presence of mind to run far enough away from the Ashtaws to stay out of the way of the stampede.

Vina and Sema ran off in opposite directions, but they didn't get away in time. The Bounty Hunters caught both women, dragged them screaming to the ground, and started muscling them backward toward the jungle.

Hammer narrowed his eyes in fury at the tiny figures in front of his mount. She thundered down the slope to level ground, crossed the fields in a few seconds, and charged straight into the camp.

The vibration translating through the ground finally got the Bounty Hunters' attention. They turned around and then bolted when they saw the Ashtaws coming.

The twelve who had caught Vina and Sema hesitated a second too long. These men got distracted by the women's struggling. The Bounty Hunters had to work hard to control the women.

The Bounty Hunters finally looked up and behind them to see what was making all the noise. They froze and then let go of the women to spin around and face the Ashtaws, but no army of Bounty Hunters could fight these huge creatures.

The two women launched to their feet and sprinted out of the way in time to clear the area. Hammer didn't have to worry about the women anymore. He urged his mount forward. Now the Ashtaws were the ones marauding and rampaging through the camp.

Hammer steered his mount this way and that to squash as many Bounty Hunters as possible. Some of the fools actually stood their ground and hurled their spears at the creatures, but the weapons only bounced off the Ashtaws' enormous tree-trunk legs.

These idiots put themselves right in line to fall under the Ashtaws' feet. Half the Bounty Hunters charged away to the north to escape the slaughter.

They ran straight into another ambush when the four uninitiated boys leapt out of hiding and attacked the Bounty Hunters one or two at a time.

Some of the fleeing Bounty Hunters tried to turn back only to fall to the Ashtaws after all. Another battle broke out as more Bounty Hunters tried to break away, but the Godless cut their number down to less than twenty.

The boys pursued them for half a mile and brought the number down to fifteen before Ziti ordered them all to fall back and rejoin the band.

Shouts, yells, and triumphant laughter rang out over the countryside once the last Bounty Hunters disappeared behind the hills.

"And don't come back or you'll get the same thing!" Scarecrow roared across the fields.

"And tell all your friends what they can expect if they ever come back!" Flawless added.

Hammer couldn't help but laugh when he saw the Bounty Hunters fleeing—the ones still left alive. The dead scattered the destroyed camp. Others dotted the fields all around.

Most of the Bounty Hunters had gotten absolutely flattened or even liquified when the Ashtaws stepped on them. The Ashtaws didn't even notice when they stepped on a person, shelter, or anything else.

Hammer's mount looked around, now that he wasn't giving her any commands. She rumbled in her chest, lowered her head to the ground, and started grazing right there in front of the trees.

He had no reason to stay mounted, so he slipped out of his seat harness, untied it and the harness around her head, and patted the side of her neck. "Great work today, beautiful," he murmured in her ear. "You're a treasure. You deserve a reward for that."

He pulled a handful of Fogpo leaves out of his bag and dropped them on the ground for her to eat. She rumbled at him again and he scratched the corner of her skull where it met up with her long neck. She especially liked it when he scratched that spot.

Ant's and Eager's mounts decided that this was as good a place to graze as any. Both men dismounted. The others returned their mounts to the valley.

Chapter 26

The men burst into celebration when they met back up on the ridge after the battle. Hammer laughed and hugged his comrades.

Scarecrow cupped his hands around his mouth and bellowed out across the valley. "This territory is ours! Take a warning, all you invaders! This land is ours and always will be!!"

Then he burst out laughing. All the men flushed with the pleasure of their victory. Their eyes shone and they wouldn't stop grabbing each other, shaking each other, and even bouncing up and down in delighted triumph.

The men were still slapping each other on the back and grinning like lunatics when Daora, Eleph, and Masha rushed around the rocks all out of breath.

"Is it done?" Daora gasped. "Are they all gone?"

"Yeah!" Hammer replied. "It's over."

Scarecrow rushed her and scooped her up in a huge hug. The men surrounded the three women all laughing.

Hammer had to yell to make himself heard. "Let's get back down there and find Sema and Vina! We can go down the canyons before anyone else comes along."

No one could stop smiling and laughing on the way back down the hill. Sema and Vina returned to the destroyed camp where the whole band reunited.

Hammer couldn't contain his laughter when he hugged Vina. "We did it!"

"Those Ashtaws are scary when you see them from the ground!" she gasped. "I thought I was dead for sure."

The party didn't stop talking all the way back down to their former camp in the canyon. The atmosphere of celebration didn't stop, not even when Hammer posted patrols to continue making circuits of the valley.

No one bothered to go hunting that night even though the band only had dried food to eat. No one cared.

The friends built up their bonfire extra big and bright. No one tried to keep their voices down. The men kept bursting into excited hoots and laughter for no apparent reason.

"Enjoy it while it lasts," Hammer told them. "We're going for the Bounty Hunters' village next."

He expected that to throw a dose of cold water over the men's excitement, but it only fueled it. They laughed louder and shook each other harder.

"This is going to be great!" Pitch gloated. "I can't wait to see the Ashtaws flatten all their houses. This is going to be better than Kuvik setting their houses on fire."

"We'll be able to bring back women from there, too," Eager added.

"We're Godless," Hammer cut in. "We don't take captives, especially not women."

"What will we do with any women who are left alive?" Omen asked. "Most of them are captives anyway. They'll just be roaming around free with no protection."

"If they join us willingly, they're welcome and so are any male slaves we free." Hammer replied. "No one will come back a captive."

His mind immediately switched to Rosta. He didn't know if he would be able to find her, much less convince her to come back to the Godless with him. He had to try, though.

Using the Ashtaws to assault the Bounty Hunters' village would present a whole new range of problems. He wouldn't be able to warn the captives ahead of time to flee as soon as the killing started.

He and his men would have to dismount to tell the captives that they were free to join Hammer's band or return to their own people as they chose.

That would take time—and what would he do with his mount in the meantime? She would be roaming around free while he stayed on the ground.

He didn't voice his concerns to his men—or to anyone else. He already knew he would carry out this operation one way or the other. He'd already delayed too long.

He lay awake thinking about it until long after Vina and the others fell asleep. He fell asleep late and woke up early. His mind wouldn't shut off.

He left Vina's shelter before daylight, wandered up to the valley, and met up with Cross and Falcon. They were just coming back from their patrol.

"Go down to the village and get some sleep," he told them. "We'll be leaving for the Bounty Hunters' village soon."

"I don't think I could sleep now if I tried," Cross replied.

Hammer understood too well to argue. He called back Lucky who was on guard to the east. The men returned to the camp.

Hammer left the four boys to guard the women while the men collected their comrades and their harnesses, said goodbye to the women, and mounted their Ashtaws.

The Ashtaws didn't balk at all when the men rode all the way up the valley to the northern end, over the ridge, and descended into the jungle. The Ashtaws' long legs covered the miles in no time. Hammer spotted the Bounty Hunters' village a long way off.

He didn't try to slow his mount. He encouraged her. The Ashtaws crashed through the jungle with all their power, smashed trees out of the way, and scattered all kinds of dangerous creatures. Even Krakelows fled from the Ashtaws.

Hammer's heart started racing when he saw people moving from building to building in the village. He didn't even really care anymore if he hurt some of the captives. They were the ones who beat him up and got him caught last time.

The other Ashtaws responded to their riders' encouragement. The Ashtaws drew level with Hammer's mount and overtook her. Their movements spurred her into a run and she charged. Hammer didn't slow her down or try to calm her. He loosened the reins.

The thunder of Ashtaw feet rocked the jungle. Some of the Bounty Hunters looked up from their work—or were they captives?

They screamed and ran when they saw ten full-sized Ashtaws bearing down on their village with a vengeance. Hammer couldn't tell from here if these people even realized people were riding and steering these Ashtaws.

Hammer's mount bellowed out, lowered her head, and stormed into the village. So many people scurrying around her feet sent her into a rage. She stomped straight into a row of houses and smashed them out of the way the same way she smashed trees in the jungle.

Splinters and shattered boards twirled everywhere. People caught inside scrambled to get away only to fall under the Ashtaws' feet.

Hammer's mount came to the end of the row. He wheeled her back the other way to make another pass.

The Bounty Hunters played right into his hands again by assembling at the edge of the village. They made a stand there, brandished their spears, and formed a barricade to meet the Ashtaws.

Hammer's men marauded through the village destroying every house. Cross kicked his mount into a run and obliterated the big meeting house with a whole crowd of Bounty Hunters still in there.

The Godless noticed one by one that the Bounty Hunters were gathering to confront them. A hundred Bounty Hunters stood over there. Their spears glistened in the sunlight. They formed a bristling forest of sharp, deadly weaponry.

All those men and all those spears would have sent Hammer fleeing if he had to face them on the ground. Now he and Eager pulled their mounts shoulder to shoulder and advanced on the Bounty Hunters' formation.

The Bounty Hunter line wavered and then stood firm. They didn't back down.

Their position made them perfect targets. They didn't even realize their own error until Cross and Omen angled their mounts from the left and Pitch and Scarecrow moved in from the right.

The Bounty Hunters cast glances around them on all sides. Their hesitation gave Ant and Flawless all the time in the world to maneuver their mounts from behind.

The Bounty Hunters adjusted their position again. They pulled into a circle with all their spears pointed outward at the Ashtaws. The Ashtaws didn't even understand that these toothpicks were actually weapons.

None of those spears could harm an Ashtaw. The creatures were just too big and their hide was too tough. Hammer didn't know of any weapon that could penetrate an Ashtaws' hide. Bounty Hunter spears certainly wouldn't do it.

He didn't get a chance to give the order. A scream echoed out of the jungle somewhere behind him. That sound sent a shockwave through the whole battlefield. The Ashtaws reacted out of control for the first time since the Godless had started taming them.

He expected the Ashtaws' first scare to send them into another stampede. It did, but they stampeded in the direction they were all facing—inward.

The Ashtaws charged the Bounty Hunters, trapped them in the center, and the Ashtaws went into a confused turmoil when they found themselves standing too close to each other.

They stamped their feet and crushed the Bounty Hunters into the ground while the mounts and their riders tried to untangle the chaos.

Hammer's mount didn't respond to his signals, commands, or the reins. She roared at the other Ashtaws, crashed into them, and eventually broke apart and barreled out of the village.

She calmed down as soon as she got into the jungle and realized she wasn't with the other Ashtaws anymore. She turned around.....and stopped there to think about it.

The other Ashtaws reacted the same way. They scattered and then calmed down as soon as they realized they were safe and out of the confusion.

Hammer rode back into the village—what was left of it. The men rode from building to building destroying everything in sight. Of course no more Bounty Hunters came out to confront the Ashtaws.

Hammer gave the order for his men to retreat into the jungle. They had to retreat a long way to put enough distance between them and the destruction.

"Stay here," he told his men. "The captives will return to the site the way they did last time. I'll go talk to them, tell them they're free and they're welcome to join us, and then we'll travel back to the valley on foot."

"Let me come with you, brother," Cross called down. "Don't go alone."

Hammer didn't want to take anyone with him, but some of the problems he foresaw would definitely make the process riskier if he went alone.

"All right. You can come. The rest of you take the Ashtaws back to the valley. We'll catch up with you later."

Hammer and Cross gave the commands for their mounts to lower their heads. Hammer took the two harnesses off his mount, patted her, gave her a reward, and watched her follow the other Ashtaws back into the jungle.

"You really conquered this one," Cross murmured under his breath. "I never thought the Ashtaws would work out this well."

Hammer turned away. He felt weak and vulnerable on the ground—not invincible the way he felt mounted on his Ashtaw. "Let's get back over there. I don't want to hang around any longer than we have to."

The men took a long time to walk back to the village. Dead Bounty Hunters and a few dead captives covered the ground in between all the wrecked houses.

The survivors started to assemble there by the time Cross and Hammer showed up. Some of the freed captives brandished weapons at the two men.

Hammer raised both hands to show he was harmless. "We're the men who freed you," he told the captives. "You're all free to return to your own Clans."

"We don't have Clans anymore," one woman told him. "The Bounty Hunters wiped them all out."

"You're welcome to come with us if you don't mind becoming Godless," Hammer replied. "My mother was a captive of the Renegade Clan and I was born in captivity. The Godless freed us and we joined them. The Godless don't take captives or enslave anyone. We welcome anyone who sincerely wishes to join us and we protect all women and children. You're all welcome to come with us or you can go your own way and fend for yourselves. It's up to you."

His story swayed them. They exchanged glances. "We'll come with you," the same woman replied.

"I'm coming, too," a man chimed in.

Other voices rose out of the crowd. The freed captives discussed it amongst themselves.

Hammer raised his voice again. "I'm sure you all know where the Bounty Hunters stashed their weapons. You all need to arm yourselves and be ready to defend yourselves in case any surviving Bounty Hunters come back." He cast one look around. "Where's Rosta?"

"Who?" the man asked.

"She was a captive in this village. She has long hair and she wore clothes from the Renegade Clan. She was here before. She served drink to the men in the meeting house."

"I know who you mean," a different woman replied. "She isn't here."

"Where is she?" Hammer heard his voice rising. He couldn't have come all this way not to rescue Rosta.

The freed captives looked around in all directions again. No one offered any answer.

Hammer turned to Cross. "Take them out into the jungle and get them traveling back to the valley. I'm going to look around and see if I can find her. I'll catch up with you."

Chapter 27

C ross took command of the freed captives and gave them orders to organize themselves. They scattered and came back with stacks of stolen weapons from nearly every other Clan.

The party assembled there in the middle of the village. Cross went through the group to make sure all the adults armed themselves. He even armed some of the older children.

He ordered the freed captives to scavenge the village for any extra food, blankets, clothes, and supplies they could find.

Hammer didn't stick around long enough to get involved. He paced through the village and examined every dead body, including the dead captives. None of the dead was Rosta.

He went through the village a second time just to make sure he didn't miss her. She wasn't here.

He gave it up, left the village on the western side, scaled into the canopy, and scouted the terrain for a mile around. He thought at first that this village might have a second satellite village next to it like the one where Kuvik had rescued Yoa.

This one didn't have a satellite village next to it or anywhere in the area. He skimmed through the branches searching everywhere, but he still saw no sign of Rosta.

He returned to the village, but he didn't descend from the trees. Cross and the freed captives were already five miles away and heading farther east. Hammer could hear their voices from here.

He didn't follow them. He stayed in the branches where he could see the flattened village site. It looked awfully forlorn with all those ruined houses and dead bodies lying around.

He waited a long time. She didn't show herself until after sunset.

She crept out of the undergrowth without a sound. She must have been hiding in the jungle—or maybe she ran away and only came back now.

She didn't act like she knew about the freed captives leaving to become Godless. She didn't glance in the direction they traveled to leave this place. She started rummaging in the debris and hunting around for something—food, probably. She was unarmed.

She had never learned to hunt when she and Hammer were growing up together. All the Renegades had treated her like the princess she was. She barely had to do any work except to please and flatter her father.

She lifted broken boards to look under them, let them fall, and moved on. She would be the very first person someone recaptured after this disaster.

Hammer lowered himself to the ground and advanced to the edge of the trees. He would have to be careful so he didn't offend her or frighten her off. She would probably die out here if he didn't convince her to come back with him.

He took a few steps into the open. She shot upright, spun around, and stared at him across the village. He took a chance and crossed the rest of the way to stop in front of her.

"Kalo...." She choked and her eyes darted all around him. "What are you doing here?"

"I came back to free you like I said I would. Those are our Ashtaws. We domesticated them....."

"You what? What does that mean?"

"We trained them to ride and carry us in combat. We use them to defeat our enemies—and we used them to destroy these Bounty Hunters. I did it to get you out. You don't have to stay here. You can come to the Godless. You'll be free and safe to live your life. No one will harm you or take you captive again. I swear it."

She blinked at him. "You....you did this....for me?"

"Of course. I told you I would come back for you and here I am. Come on. Let's go. Come with me and I'll take you to our camp."

She didn't move. She looked everywhere but at him. "You.....you're Godless.....but why?"

"We joined the Godless when we left Ceon. Don't you remember? Cheina married a Godless man and we all grew up in the Godless Clan. We all initiated with them. They're good people. Now we have our own band. Do you remember Vina, Sema, and Eleph? They're all with us. You won't be alone. We're your people. You can come back with us."

He took a chance, slipped his hand into hers, and pulled her forward. Her resistance evaporated once she started moving. She followed him into the jungle on the eastern side.

He didn't try to hurry her along to catch up with Cross and the others. Hammer would have plenty of time for that.

He also didn't ask her to climb into the trees even though traveling on the ground was so much more dangerous. Any stray Bounty Hunters who might have escaped the Ashtaws could be out here.

They wouldn't be traveling in groups of more than two or three. Hammer could handle that at least until he met back up with Cross and the other captives.

They were all armed now. They would defend themselves once they understood that their freedom and probably their lives were at stake.

Hammer stopped after two hours of walking. He steered Rosta to a stream, sat her down, and used his bowl to serve her some water. Then he gave her some food out of his bag.

"I can't believe you're really Godless," she exclaimed once she started eating. "That's the last thing I expected you to be."

"It's the best thing to be. The Godless are strong and resourceful. They're the best people I've ever known. They're one of the few Clans that doesn't attack others to steal their women and goods." He looked away. "The man who married Cheina became a father to me. I wish he had lived long enough to see me become Kral of my own band. He might even have joined me—but that's the way it goes, I guess."

She gaped at him with her mouth hanging open. "You're Kral....of your own band?!"

"Yes. All the boys from Ceon joined my band—and Cross is from the band that freed us. He's a good man. He's a good friend."

She gulped and remembered to start chewing. "That's amazing."

He stopped himself from asking about everything that had happened to her after she left Ceon. He could guess and he didn't want to know the details.

"We have a bunch of single men," he told her. "You would be free to marry any of them if you chose to. No one will make you marry someone you don't like."

She looked away. "I don't know about that. No man would want to marry a woman who had been a captive."

"Why not? I just told you my adoptive father Alien married Cheina after Darso fathered three children with her. Alien didn't think anything of it and I'm certain no one would think it of you."

"Alien?!" she gasped. "His name was Alien?! What kind of a name is that?"

"All the Godless men take new names when they initiate. Cross isn't his childhood name. Only the uninitiated boys use their childhood names. My name is Hammer. No one calls me Kalo anymore."

"Hammer?!" she exclaimed. "That's a silly name."

He compressed his lips. "That is my name whether you like it or not. You would have to call me that if you came to the Godless. You would have to call all the men by their real names—their initiated names. Using a man's childhood name is considered an insult to a Godless man."

She laughed. "I couldn't call you that! You'll always be Kalo."

"Then I guess you can go out into the jungle alone with your Kalo and I'll go back to my people."

Her smile drained away. "I didn't mean that."

"I just told you it's an insult for you to call me Kalo. Is that what you're trying to do—insult me—after I just freed you from the Bounty Hunters and offered you a life you could only dream about before?"

"No, of course not....."

"I'm telling you right now that you will never—EVER—refer to any of the men by their childhood names—not unless you want to leave the Godless and go out alone. That's the condition of me rescuing you. I don't think it's asking too much that you treat us all with the respect we deserve, is it?"

She looked away. "No, of course not."

He took a few seconds to get his temper under control. She didn't know. He had to remind himself of that. She didn't understand the Godless way. She knew absolutely nothing about the Godless except that they had been enemies of her father's people.

She had grown up every day of her childhood hearing about the Godless as her enemies. She had helped her father and his men defeat and subdue the Godless as much as possible.

Hammer would have to be patient with her. He would have to make the rules clear to her and he would have to enforce them.

She would probably take a while to find a way to fit in with his band. At least she wouldn't be alone. The other captives would go through the same process before they became as fully Godless as Hammer and his original party.

Chapter 28

H ammer and Rosta met up with Cross's group that night. Hammer knew Cross would stop for the night eventually. Hammer kept Rosta moving until they overtook the freed captives.

Cross went from person to person making sure everyone had food, a place to sleep, and he treated any of their more serious injuries. Gashes, bruises, the scars and damage of old injuries from past beatings, and some even worse treatment covered every person.

The sixteen captives included eight women, six children of varying ages, and two men The men and children had suffered the worst—on the outside, at least.

The women showed more signs of internal, mental damage. One skeletal woman simply refused to look at anyone. She kept her head down and turned away while she crushed her two young daughters against her sides.

All three of them had sustained heavy bruises, but that didn't explain their skittish behavior. Hammer didn't go near them.

Cross tried once when he offered the woman some food, but the woman recoiled from him and almost yanked her daughters off their feet when she pulled them away.

The first woman who had spoken to Hammer intervened and took the food out of Cross's hands. "I'll give it to her. Don't take it personally. She acts that way around all the men—ever since the Bounty Hunters killed her husband."

"I don't take it personally." Cross handed the woman a bowl of leaf paste. "Please take care of them and find out how injured they are—if they're injured at all. Assure them that they're safe now and no one in our Clan will harm them."

The woman only nodded. Hammer and Cross retreated.

The other captives took to freedom much more readily. They came to life, helped each other, and both men and women offered to help stand guard overnight.

The two freed men presented a study in contrast. One was a young, strong, alert man with his hair cut off at the shoulders. He wore ragged clothes barely held together by rough, hand-sewn patches, but he looked by far the healthiest of the whole group.

He even still had good muscle tone around his shoulders. The Bounty Hunters must have fed him well during his captivity. Maybe they used him for heavy labor. Hammer didn't know.

The other man was old and so broken he could barely walk, but he pushed himself to keep up with the others. He walked with a stoop and had to look up to make eye contact with Hammer.

He introduced himself as Enzi. The younger man was Seron.

"Any help you need from us we're happy to give, young man," he told Hammer. "We're grateful for your intervention."

"Don't mention it," Hammer replied. "We're glad you're here and that you're willing to stand up for yourselves."

The old man looked around. "What would you like us to do? I can't fight as well as I could when I was younger, but I'll do my best."

"I don't think that will be necessary, but I appreciate the offer. Maybe you can help me. Do you know everyone here?"

Enzi nodded. "Sure. I was in that village when the Bounty Hunters brought all these people in."

Hammer gaped at him. "You were a captive for that long?! When did they take you?"

"They took me and my family when I was a boy. I've been with the Bounty Hunters ever since."

Hammer gulped. This was so much worse than he expected.

Enzi eyed him. "What is it you want to know?"

"Do you....you know everyone here. Maybe you can tell me their names."

"That's Loza." Enzi indicated the first woman who had spoken to Hammer—the one who offered to help her shocked companion. Then Enzi nodded at the woman and the two girls. "That's Dura. The older girl is Fama. The younger one is Volura. They were Abbalo's slaves. He was a fiend."

Enzi snarled these last words and then spat on the ground. Hammer didn't ask any other questions.

Enzi and Seron went through the group of captives introducing Hammer to everyone. He explained the basics of Godless culture to them so they knew what to expect once they made it back to the valley.

"So will we learn how to ride the Ashtaws, too?" Seron asked.

"If you want to help us defend our territory, then we would be happy for your help," Hammer replied. "The Ashtaws take some getting used to. No one will make you go near them if you don't want to."

"What about when our children get old enough to go to the gathering?" Loza asked. "How will that work?"

"If you stay with the Godless that long, then you'll all follow Godless law. I'll take you to the gatherings as soon as your children get old enough." Hammer surveyed the group again. "Your sons will initiate into the Clan when they come of age—or you can decide to return to your original Clans. It's up to you."

Murmured conversation broke out. Everyone discussed the pros and cons of his comments.

He retreated and sat down next to Rosta. "You're serious, aren't you?" she asked. "You would really initiate these boys into the Godless Clan to become your warriors."

"Why not? It happened that way for me. My men and I were never happier than when we became Godless. We worked hard for our Kral and earned his respect. We earned the respect of all the older men."

"I don't know if I could ever be anything other than a Renegade."

"You would have to be." He turned to face her. "Do you still blame me for leaving you behind?"

"I suppose I shouldn't. It isn't as though I asked you to take me with you and you turned me down."

"I didn't know where you were or even if you were still alive. We had to withdraw from Renegade country before anyone found out we had escaped. I didn't have time to look for you."

She nodded. "I understand that now."

He hesitated and then launched into the other thing that was on his mind. "Some of the women in our band remember you. They don't remember you fondly if you know what I mean."

Her head shot up. "What do you mean?"

"I mean they remember you as someone who helped your father subdue captives. The women remember you as one of the people who subjugated them and kept them as prisoners and slaves. I just want to warn you ahead of time before we get back to the band."

She looked away. "Maybe I shouldn't go there, then."

"I think you should. The women all understand that you grew up under different circumstances. You need to show them that you're ready to turn over a new leaf and start being a cooperative member of our band. You need to show them that you're willing to let go of the past and start over if you expect them to let go of the past and start over."

"I will," she replied. "I don't expect to treat anyone in your band that way now."

"I hope not. Let's go to sleep. We have another long day of travel tomorrow."

He found her a blanket and bedded her down by one of the fires. He stayed up and stood guard with Cross and Seron.

The three men talked late into the night. Seron told Cross and Hammer about where he'd come from, what he could remember from his original Clan, and how things were in the Bounty Hunter world.

Seron interrogated Cross and Hammer about everything Godless, especially the initiations. Hammer saw shades of his former self in Seron even though Seron was already a fully grown man.

His questions reminded Hammer so clearly of the questions he used to ask Hangman, Alien, and Viking about the Godless, the initiations, and everything else.

Hammer read Seron's mind. The guy was preparing himself to initiate into the Godless Clan. Seron must have already made up his mind about that.

Hammer could respect that. He and Cross both started treating Seron as one of their own. Hammer respected Enzi, too, even if he wasn't exactly a fighter anymore. He had the heart of a fighter and it showed.

Loza took extra special care of Dura and the girls for the rest of the evening. Hammer didn't know what would happen to those three, but at least they would be safe with the Godless now.

Chapter 29

Hammer climbed up the steep hill and let out a sigh of relief when he looked down at the Ashtaw Valley. He was home.

"This is it," he breathed to the people around him. "This is our territory. We're safe now."

The freed captives gathered around looking down at the sun shining on the flat grasslands dotted with huge creatures.

"It's beautiful," Loza murmured. "I never thought I would see anything like this again."

Hammer turned away. "We can follow the ridge from here. Then it's all downhill into the canyons to our camp."

He led the way along the ridge heading east and south. The freed captives formed a single file line. Hammer's spirits lifted when he thought about getting back to the canyon and his home camp. Vina would be thrilled to see him.

His band was about to start looking awfully different from now on. Some of these women might pair off with his single men. That would definitely lighten the mood after more than half his men had been alone all this time with no way to look forward to anything else.

Hammer had noticed Seron getting close to Loza during the two days it took the party to travel back to Hammer's territory. Hammer didn't intervene. He pretended not to notice, but he couldn't be happier for both of them.

They both struck him as practical, determined, and resilient—more so than the other freed captives.

Dura didn't slacken her vigilance even once when it came to keeping her distance from everyone, including the other women. Hammer couldn't remember her ever letting go of her daughters except when they ate.

Even then, she kept a sharp eye on them every second of the day. She refused to make eye contact with anyone else.

Hammer put Dura and her daughters out of his mind. They would either integrate into his band or they wouldn't. He really just didn't care anymore if they ever spoke to, made eye contact, or interacted with anyone other than Loza.

As far as he was concerned, Dura and her daughters could live apart in their own shelter and never participate in the band. He didn't care what they did as long as they found some safety with his people.

He made it halfway around the ridgeline before a shout startled him from somewhere. He looked and spotted Ant standing on a high rock on one of the ridge peaks.

Ant raised his weapon above his head. The next instant, all the rest of Hammer's men and the four boys rushed around a corner. All of them came armed and ready to attack.

Hammer's hand flew instinctively to his weapon, but he didn't draw it. Seron *did* draw his weapon. He even leapt forward to protect the party, but Cross held him back.

The men slowed and then stopped when they saw who was invading their territory.

"You scared the crap out of us, Hammer!" Lucky gasped.

"It's all right. These are the freed captives from the Bounty Hunter village." Seron still didn't stand down until Hammer pulled him away. "These are my men. These people are coming back to the camp with us. This is Seron, Enzi, Loza, and you all know Rosta."

Rosta held herself back. She didn't open her mouth to greet the men even though she knew every single one of them.

She didn't say a word while Hammer introduced them all to the newcomers. Then they all caught up on their way down the ridge to the southern canyons.

"Did my mount behave herself on the way back?" he asked Ant.

"She didn't even notice that you were missing. She's a fickle little thing. She'll do anything for a handful of Fogpo."

The men laughed. Then they started exchanging stories with the freed captives. Seron got all mixed up with the group when he realized these men were the ones who had brought the Ashtaws into the Bounty Hunters' village.

He grilled them all on their early life, Hangman and his men rescuing everyone from Ceon, and everything Hangman's band had been going through between then and now.

The rest of the party fell silent to listen in awe when they heard about Cross, Hangman, Viking, and Alien attacking the Renegades to free Mora.

None of the freed captives said a word to interrupt when the men talked about their adventures in the artillery battery and the northern mountains.

The party made it back to the canyon camp before anyone could get into the story about what happened with Aster, Cheina, and Alien's death.

Vina rushed out and threw herself into Hammer's arms as soon as the party entered the camp. She clasped his hand and beamed up at him. "I knew you could do it!"

"You weren't worried about me when I didn't come back? Tell the truth."

She laughed—and then her smile vanished when she turned around and saw all the captives. The other women advanced slowly and stopped. The two groups faced each other.

Hammer took over. "I want each of you women to take responsibility for some of these new people. Make shelters for them. Make sure they have everything they need. Ant, I want you to take Eager, Flawless, and the four boys and go out hunting. We're going to need food for tonight and as much as you can get for the coming days."

"I want to go hunting, too," Seron interjected.

"Okay, go ahead." Hammer opened his mouth to say something else.

That was the moment when he noticed Eleph glaring at Rosta. Eleph had said she would kill Rosta.

Hammer stepped between the two women and directed Eleph to take Dura and two other women to the other side of the camp. "Make sure they have a comfortable place to sleep tonight—and make sure Dura's shelter is away from everyone else's."

He gave Eleph a pointed look and sent her on her way. She cast a few backward glares at Rosta before Eleph led the new people out of sight.

All the Godless women split up and got busy helping the new people settle in. The women took food out of their own supplies to feed everyone.

A few of the freed captives went with the women to gather building materials from the forest. Loza and Sema hit it off right away. They talked all the way out of the canyon.

Most of the freed captives sank into a shocked daze, now that they knew they were finally safe. Hammer turned around. Vina was already helping two other women and their children. That left him alone with Rosta.

He got busy cutting branches and tree limbs from the surrounding jungle. She went with him and talked to him the whole time about people they knew back in Ceon. She didn't help him.

He explained that away. She didn't know how to build a Godless shelter and she was his guest. He just hoped she understood her situation well enough to be polite to the other women.

He didn't know what went down between Eleph and Rosta, but it must have been something pretty bad to make Eleph hate Rosta so much.

Chapter 30

H ammer was too busy working on the shelter to talk to Rosta very much. She did all the talking until he finally stepped back and dusted off his hands.

"There you go," he told her. "That should take care of it for tonight. You can modify it and make it your own. I'm sure you'll find plenty to improve on it."

She beamed at him. "You're so generous. I love that about you."

She threw herself at him, flung her arms around his neck, and planted her lips right on his mouth.

He reared back in horror and wound up pushing her away too hard. "Hey! Stop!" he yelled. "What are you doing?"

"What's wrong?" She waved toward the shelter and then eased up close to him, slipped her arm around his waist, and pressed her body against his. He would have had to be dead not to feel her rippling her body all the way down to his hips.

She burst into a big, suggestive grin. "Do you want to go inside?"

He raised his hands one more time to shove her away, but right at that moment, at the worst possible time, Vina walked around the next shelter and stopped there where she could see everything Rosta was doing.

"What the hell is going on?!" Vina snapped.

Rosta's head snapped around and she glared at Vina. "Mind your own business and go back to work."

Vina's jaw dropped. Hammer saw the situation disintegrating before his eyes.

He pushed Rosta away for the second time, but he managed to do it gently enough not to hurt her this time. "Rosta....you don't understand. Vina.....she's my intended. We're going to be married in less than a month when she comes of age...."

Rosta spun around the other way and glared at him instead. "You what?! You brought me here to be with you! Don't you dare say you're dumping me for someone else."

"I did not bring you here to be with you!" He fought his voice under control, but he still heard it shaking. "I brought you here to save you from the Bounty Hunters like I promised. You said you blamed me for them capturing you in the first place. I brought you here to rectify that—not to be with you. I'm already promised to someone else."

"I don't believe you." She took a step forward and raised both arms.

He saw her about to try to embrace him again. He raised his hands to stop her, but Vina reacted first.

She dodged between Hammer and Rosta, shoved Rosta away, and slotted between them. "Keep your hands off him," Vina snapped. "You're the outsider here. If you don't stop throwing your weight around, you'll be the first to go. Don't think we don't remember everything you did back to Ceon. You better pull your head in if you want to stay here in that nice, fancy new shelter of yours."

Rosta recovered instantly and stormed right back up to Vina. "How dare you?!" Rosta snapped. "You have no right....."

Hammer had heard enough. He cut around Vina, pushed her behind him, and confronted Rosta himself. "I told you once if I've told you a thousand times, Rosta. You'll accept our ways or you'll go right back out into the jungle on your own. Vina is my intended. We're going to be married as soon as she comes of age. You accept that along with everything else or you won't have a place here. I'm Kral of this band and my word is law with everyone, including you. You can go straight back to the Bounty Hunters for all I care. You can spend the rest of your life with them and enjoy yourself. I expect you to treat Vina and all the other women with respect. They're as responsible for saving your life as I am. If I hear anything else, you will be the first to go. I promise you that."

"You want *that* instead of me?" Rosta sneered at Vina peeking out from behind his shoulder. "You're soft in the head. You deserve each other."

She stormed off, passed the shelter he had worked so hard to build for her, and disappeared around another shelter. Hammer didn't see whose it was.

Vina threw up her hands and spun away, but at least she didn't leave. "I don't believe this!" she muttered. "After all you're doing for her, she has to bring her poison around here."

He eased up behind her and rested both hands on her shoulders. "Don't listen to her. You're the only woman I will ever marry. She can't say anything to drive us apart."

"She shouldn't even be here," Vina muttered over her shoulder. "You never should have brought her here. She isn't like us. She doesn't belong here. You'll see I'm right."

"If you're right, then she'll leave or I'll drive her out. Consider these growing pains. We can expect more of the same from all the other new people. Give her a chance to learn our ways. She's never been Godless before."

"The others are all so nice," she murmured. "They're all so grateful and they can't stop talking about how kind you and Cross were on the journey here."

"Then stay with them." He bent in and nuzzled into her hair. "Don't go near Rosta. She'll come or go—one way or the other."

"And what should I do if she mouths off to me again—sometime when you aren't around to correct her?"

"Then come and tell me and I will correct her. I won't tolerate anyone insulting you. I told her my decision. She either accepts it or she leaves. That's all anyone needs to know."

She snorted. "I better get back to work. We have a lot to do before the sun goes down."

She walked away and the hunters came back a few minutes later. They had killed three adult Gorlocks.

Hammer mobilized everyone to help bring in the meat. Rosta and Dura didn't want to leave the camp. He left Dura alone, but he told Rosta she wouldn't eat tonight if she didn't help out.

He caught Eleph, Vina, and Masha shooting death glares at Rosta on the side, but none of the three women went near enough to talk to her.

They studiously avoided her through the whole process of butchering the Gorlocks, carrying the haunches back to the camp, and processing the meat.

The women worked together to build frames over the fires to dry all the food for later. Rosta worked well as long as she stayed with the other freed captives.

Ant, Eager, and Flawless all reported to Hammer that Seron was a brave and enthusiastic hunter. They all praised him and exclaimed over what an asset he was.

The men helped cut up the meat and hang it up to dry in the smoke over the fires. Hammer noticed Pitch, Omen, and Eager all getting friendly with the new women. An air of excitement and new possibilities pulsed through the camp.

Hammer had to take his turn patrolling the ridge that night. He took Acrobat and Scarecrow with him, posted Scarecrow on the eastern side, and Hammer and Acrobat split up to run in opposite directions around the ridge.

The stars were already coming out by the time they met back up on the north end of the valley. "Do you think I could marry someone?" Acrobat asked on the way back.

"Why not?" Hammer asked. "Do you have someone in mind?"

"No, not like that. I just wondered."

"Pick out someone you like—someone who isn't already taken by someone else. Then start talking to her and see if you hit it off. You have no reason to live alone. Look at Scarecrow. He didn't wait around for lightning to strike before he got friendly with Daora."

"I never thought I would get married," Acrobat murmured. "I always thought I would stay alone for life. We spent all that time in the north country and then traveling south. I thought I would be too old to marry by the time we came back to any territory where we could go to the gatherings."

"Well, these women aren't Godless and you're over the age of gathering. I'm your Kral, so it's my decision if you marry someone who happens to enter our band. You couldn't go to the gathering now. If you like someone and she accepts you, you can marry her."

"What about Rosta?" Acrobat asked.

Hammer's head shot up. Every nerve tensed. "What about her?"

"She's pretty. She seems friendly enough."

Hammer looked away. "If you make friends with Rosta and you both want to get married, I'll be happy for you both."

"So.....you don't think.....?"

"I don't think what? Just say it, brother."

"I wasn't sure if you were still planning to marry Vina. You and Rosta seem awfully close."

"We were close growing up. I couldn't leave her to the Bounty Hunters, but Vina is the only woman I will ever marry. Rosta is like my sister. I feel responsible for her, but I'll never marry her."

"Oh, okay." Acrobat's tone softened. "That's good."

Hammer let himself relax. "You should talk to her. She needs a husband."

"Are you sure? Sometimes I think she would make a domineering wife. She needs a strong man like you who will tell her what to do."

"Then you be the strong man who will tell her what to do. Don't be soft and don't let her domineer you. If she acts that way before you get married, tell her you won't tolerate it."

"Then she won't marry me."

"You already know what it's like to live alone. You said you thought you would stay alone for life. What's so bad about that? That would be better than being made a fool of by your own wife."

Acrobat fell silent. Hammer really started to hope Acrobat would marry Rosta. That would take her mind off of Hammer.

How many other members of his band assumed he was throwing Vina away in favor of Rosta? He had to change that. The only question was how to change it.

Chapter 31

H ammer's eyes floated open in a peaceful haze. He gazed up at Vina's face. She was just waking up, too.

He loved waking up and seeing her face first thing in the morning. She would come of age in one more week. Then nothing would stop him from seeing her face first thing every morning.

Yelling voices startled him out of his daydream. One of the men yelled. "Hey! Get your hands off!"

He scrambled to his feet and rushed outside in time to see Eager and Acrobat shoving and bumping each other's chests. "I told you to back off!" Acrobat stormed.

"Back off yourself!" Eager countered. "You don't own this. Get the hell out of my way!"

Hammer barged over there and shoved them apart. "What the hell are you fighting over?"

"I came out here and saw this bastard sitting next to Rosta," Acrobat fired back. "I told you to stay away from her."

"She isn't your wife, you stupid twerp!" Eager countered. "I can sit next to any woman I want as long as she isn't married."

"You knew I was interested in her because I told you last night!" Acrobat fumed. "You deliberately got near here to push me out."

Rosta stood off to one side watching. She didn't outright smirk, but something in her twinkling eyes told Hammer she was enjoying having two men fight over her.

Hammer had to struggle to push the two men apart a second time. "How would you both like me to forbid either of you to marry her? Back off, Acrobat. Go sit over there before I have to get harsh with you. Go over there, Eager—NOW!!"

Hammer stood his ground and glared at both men until they backed off and then stormed away to opposite sides of the camp.

He cast a glance around. All the other members of his band, both old and new, watched the altercation from a distance. How many others would come to similar conflicts before they all settled in?

Hammer sighed and turned around. He stiffened all over again when he saw Rosta's expression. "Go back to your shelter and stay there," he told her. "You shouldn't be over here."

"Why not? Is there a rule about where women can go and where men can go?"

"This has nothing to do with men and women. There is no rule about where men and women can go. I'm talking about you. You're the problem here."

"Why am I the problem? I came over here to help cure the Gorlock meat and pack it away."

"This is Ant's shelter," Hammer replied. "Just do me a favor and go back to your own shelter. Don't make me tell you again."

"I don't see why I should."

"You don't see a problem with the fact that you've been here less than a day and you're already causing problems for multiple people? Did you deliberately lead Eager on when you knew Acrobat was interested in?"

"All I did was talk to him. You said yourself I don't belong to anyone. I can talk to whoever I want."

He glared at her, but. He didn't have time to deal with her—not right now. He had to go deal with Eager and Acrobat.

"I told you to go back to your shelter," Hammer snapped again. That's all you need to know about it." He turned and walked away toward the spot where he sent Acrobat.

Talking to Acrobat about Rosta would be much easier than talking to Eager about her. Hammer didn't look forward to either conversation, so he went with the easier one first.

She tagged after him. "I'm not interested in either of them." She darted forward and slipped her hand into his. "I want you."

He spun around fast and yanked his hand away. "I already told you not to do that. I'm as good as married already."

"You aren't married at all. Vina is underage. You could enjoy yourself with me in the meantime. Every man needs a woman."

She took a few sauntering steps closer to him. She wasn't seriously trying to pull this on him again, was she?

Apparently, she was. She turned on all the charm and seductive power in her eyes as she eased in closer to him.

He planted his hands on her shoulders and straight-armed her back to get her away from him. "I told you not to do that. I told you before that you could accept my ruling or leave the band and go your own way. If you ever suggest that again, I'll drive you out of the valley at the point of my blade. Is that clear? I'm your Kral. That's all I will ever be to you. You either accept my ruling on that and everything else, or I can send you to the ants if you prefer. Is that clear enough for you to understand?"

She made a face. "You're a fool."

"I wouldn't touch you if you were the last woman alive on the planet. Vina has been with me and supported me for years. There is nothing now or ever that you can do to come between us. Don't make me ever tell you again or I'll consider you a traitor to our Clan. You can choose anyone else in the band to marry, but don't let me catch you playing one against the other again. The cohesion of this band is too important to waste it on any woman, especially a traitor who would deliberately undermine my authority and turn me and my men against each other—or would you rather just turn around and start walking right now? I'm sure Eleph would be very happy to escort you back to the northern jungle and point you in the right direction so you can return to the Bounty Hunters."

Hammer took his hands off her shoulders and took a step back. He left her standing there alone.

Dead silence hung over the camp. Her expression changed at those words and she glanced around.

He became aware of everyone watching and listening to his every word. His people knew better than to doubt his threat. He had already fed three people to the ants and killed two others for not bowing to his authority.

He had never done it to a woman before, but he knew the story about Butcher and Shadow feeding Zyria and Boxer to the ants. A woman couldn't get away with treachery and betrayal just because she was a woman.

Another shout burst out at that moment. It broke the silence and startled everyone into spinning the other way. Hammer followed the sound and stood back to stare at Dura hustling her daughters across the camp. Loza almost had to run to keep up with them.

"No!" Dura snapped over her shoulder. "I've already made up my mind! Leave me alone! Get away from me!"

"You don't have to do this, Dura!" Loza exclaimed. "I'm sure it's all a misunderstanding!"

"Get your hands off me!" Dura fired back. "Get out of my way!"

"What's going on?" Ant asked from a few feet to Hammer's right.

Another commotion broke out on Hammer's left. "I didn't do anything!" Flawless's voice cracked. He stepped forward, but Seron and Scarecrow grabbed him and held him back. "I didn't do anything! I swear it!"

Loza tried one last time to stop Dura. "You'll die out there, Dura!" Loza exclaimed. "Your daughters will die! Don't do this!"

Dura reared back, threw her elbow at Loza, seized her daughters under each arm, and marched out of the canyon into the jungle.

"NO!!" Flawless choked. "I didn't do anything! I wouldn't! I swear it!"

Dura didn't look back. She vanished into the trees. "Should we go after her?" Ant murmured.

"Who do you mean by 'we'?" Hammer asked. "*We* couldn't go. If Loza can't convince her, what hope do we have?"

Flawless kept calling out louder and louder as Dura disappeared. He yelled at the top of his lungs that he didn't do anything, but she didn't stay long enough to hear him.

Hammer went over to him. "What happened? What do you say you didn't do?"

Flawless was too upset to answer. He whirled away, pressed the back of his wrist to his mouth, and took off running into the trees in a different direction.

"What happened?" Hammer asked the men around him.

"Nothing happened," Enzi interjected. "He asked me last night how long it had been since Dura's husband died. Some of the other women must have heard him and told her he was asking about her."

"He never approached her?" Hammer asked.

"Never," Enzi replied. "I can't even be sure he asked because he was interested. He was just curious."

Hammer looked around. Dura was gone along with her daughters.

"Are you sure we shouldn't go after her?" Scarecrow asked. "She can't survive out there. Even if she does, one of the other Clans will take her back."

"We would only scare her more if we went after her. Let her go." Hammer checked the surroundings. No one else moved a muscle. "The rest of you can go on with your own business. Get some breakfast. We have a lot of work to do today."

He waited until everyone went back to their own tasks. They formed clusters to work together. Rosta actually did what Hammer told her to do and went back to her own shelter away from everyone else.

Hammer slipped out of camp and tracked Flawless through the jungle. He ran a long way south before he climbed up into the canopy.

Hammer slowed when he saw Flawless perched in the branches at a distance. He sat high enough in the treetops to see out over the countryside to the south. He sat with his back facing the direction Dura had gone.

Hammer squatted down next to him. Hammer didn't break the silence.

"I didn't mean for her to leave!" Flawless's voice broke in a high-pitched whine. "I swear I never meant for her to leave!"

"I know you didn't, brother," Hammer murmured. "It isn't your fault. She probably would have left eventually anyway. She wouldn't stay with us. She was too hurt already."

"She could have stayed!" Flawless choked. "She could have been safe here—and the girls! She didn't have to leave!"

Hammer glanced over at his friend. Flawless's features spasmed all over the place. He struggled to hold himself together.

"We did everything anyone could do for her," Hammer murmured. "You can't blame yourself for this."

Flawless turned his head away and clamped his eyes shut. "I could have protected them! I could have taken care of them! I could have shown them what it was like for someone to care for them!"

Hammer rested his hand on Flawless's shoulder. So it was true. Flawless asked one basic innocent question about Dura and her past. He was too polite ever to intrude on her when he knew she wasn't ready.

Dura's decision stabbed Hammer in the guts. He would have liked to protect Dura and her daughters. He would have liked for his band to be the place where they found rest and solace from their ordeal. That would never happen now.

"You would have been perfect for them, brother," Hammer murmured. "They could have really used a man like you. You did everything you could. We all did. What Dura does is out of our hands now."

Flawless didn't answer. Hammer felt Flawless trembling where Hammer's hand rested on Flawless's shoulder.

Hammer got to his feet and headed back to camp. He didn't want to make it harder for Flawless than it already was. No one could help Dura. She just had to figure it out for herself. Hammer and his people couldn't save everyone.

He made it back to camp and spotted Omen sitting next to one of the new women. Her toddler son wobbled around while Omen and the woman talked in low tones with their faces inches apart.

Half the new women paired off with Hammer's men right away. Hammer didn't see anyone going near Rosta.

Acrobat and Eager both went about their own work. They didn't go near each other.

Acrobat saw Hammer coming and Acrobat lowered his eyes to the ground. "I'm sorry," Acrobat mumbled. "I know I messed up. It won't happen again."

"You aren't married to Rosta," Hammer snapped. "Expressing an interest to me or her or anyone else doesn't make you married. Understand? You don't lay any claim to her until you are married."

"I understand," Acrobat mumbled. "I won't let it happen again."

"That's good because it's my decision if you marry at all. If you can't conduct yourself with some dignity and maturity, I might decide you shouldn't marry anyone. Do I make myself perfectly clear?"

Acrobat stiffened, but he didn't raise his head. "Yes, perfectly clear."

"Don't let me see you near Rosta for the rest of the day," Hammer ordered. "And I'm forbidding you to go anywhere near her as long as you see her talking to or associating with any other man in the band. If you see her talking to someone else, you turn around and walk off in the other direction. Got that?"

Acrobat nodded. "I got it."

Hammer stormed off and tracked down Eager. He saw Hammer coming, too. "I know what you're going to say—and you're right. I'm sorry," Eager blurted out. "I only talked to her because he said he was interested in her."

"Did you talk to her to steal her from him? Is that it?" Hammer demanded. "Did you do this deliberately to hurt him and push him out?"

"No, nothing like that!" Eager insisted. "I just never thought about her before he mentioned her."

"And then? What happened once you did start thinking about her?"

"I thought she was pretty nice. She's good-looking. I thought maybe, you know?"

"Maybe what? Maybe you could get her interested in you instead?"

"No, no!" Eager insisted. "I just got curious....so I talked to her. That's all. He went completely over the edge. That's what happened."

"I'm going to give you the same order I gave him. Don't go near her if you see her talking to another man—any other man. If you see someone else near her, walk away in the other direction. Pull it in real quick or I might decide neither of you should marry anyone. Got that?"

Eager dipped his chin. "I got it. You won't have any more problems from me."

Hammer snorted. He would definitely have more problems from someone. The only question was who it would be next time.

Chapter 32

Hammer ducked under the door frame to enter Vina's shelter and looked around for his harnesses. He froze when he discovered Vina in there sobbing her eyes out.

"Hey! What's wrong?!" Hammer sat down next to her and put his arm around her shoulders. "What happened? Did Rosta say something to you again?"

"No!" She covered her face and broke down. "It's....I'm just going out of my mind, Hammer! I don't know what's wrong with me!"

"Can you talk to me about it? Did I do something to upset you? Please tell me if I did."

"No, you didn't do anything!"

"What's making you go out of your mind?" He hesitated. "Is it all the strain of the new people coming to live here?"

"No! It's nothing like that! I just.... I'm three days away from coming of age! I keep dreading that something will happen...."

Hammer wilted. Oh, that.

Things around the camp had been so chaotic lately with all the problems, conflicts, and difficulties. The new people tried their hardest to do everything right, but their presence put everyone on edge.

The camp wasn't the calm, peaceful, happy, humming place of cohesive cooperation that it used to be. Hammer and his solid core of friends—they all understood each other. They went through the worst together and built a life they all believed in.

He never had to question any of them—not the men or the women.

He sometimes worried in his private hours if the single men would be able to handle the loneliness of not marrying. Now all these new women had come into their lives—for good or bad.

Hammer winced again when he remembered Flawless's heartbreak. He had come back to camp hours after Dura's departure.

He went straight back to helping out with whatever anyone needed, but he kept more to himself now. He didn't try so hard to socialize with anyone, not even his old closest friends. Would he ever find someone?

Hammer hadn't had the time to think about Vina's coming of age. He had slipped into a deep, dark, solid place where he already thought of her as his wife. He could wait forever and never cross that line.

He leaned in, kissed the side of her temple, and rested his forehead against her. "Your coming of age doesn't mean anything. It's just another day in the rest of our lives. We're already married. You're already my wife in every way that counts. Everyone knows it. Everyone sees us together. No one thinks anything will change in a few days' time—because nothing will change. So I'll start sleeping on the bed. That's the only thing that will be different."

He leaned back and looked down at her tear-stained face. "You're a Kral's wife. You're the leader of the women in this band. You know you are. They all know it. You're already mine."

"What if something happens to you?"

"Something could happen to me tomorrow. Something could happen to me next year. Something could happen to me ten years from now. Everyone lives with that. I live with worrying that something will happen to you. That doesn't mean I'm not going to marry you. Nothing will stop me from marrying you—unless you tell me not to."

"I would never do that!" she blurted out.

He cupped her cheeks and raised her face to kiss her. "You're all mine. No one will ever come near you again—except our children."

Her face screwed up in misery. "I want that more than anything."

"You'll have it. It will happen. You'll see. Now I have to go. I have to meet up with the men on the ridge and get their report. I'll see you when I get back."

He kissed her on the forehead, took his harnesses, and went outside. He met up with Falcon coming to get him.

Hammer looked around. "Where's Lucky? He's on the next shift with us."

"I thought he was with you," Falcon replied.

The men searched the camp, but Hammer stopped in his tracks when he spotted Pitch, Ant, and Cross running into the camp just then.

"What are you doing back?" Hammer demanded. "You're all still supposed to be up on watch."

"They're up there!" The three men staggered to a halt. Ant doubled over and rested his hands on his knees to catch his breath. "They're up there!" he gasped. "The Renegades ....they're staking out the valley. We came as quick as we could!"

A prickle went up Hammer's scalp. "What do you mean by, 'staking it out'?"

"You better come and see," Cross replied.

Hammer didn't ask any other questions. He spotted Lucky heading toward where he and the men stood talking.

All six turned back and sprinted up the canyons to the ridgeline. Hammer got all his questions answered once he got there.

A crowd of thirty Renegades worked down on the valley floor within a hundred yards of the Ashtaw herd. Another line of what looked like a couple hundred Renegades filed down from the northern end of the valley to meet up with the first group.

The Renegades carried boards, tools, and who knew what else. The men already inside the valley constructed huts and houses, pitched tents, and some returned along the same line to bring in more stuff.

"Well, what do you know?" Hammer muttered to himself. "It looks like they actually think they're going to keep this area for themselves."

"What do you want to do?" Lucky asked.

"Fall back to the camp," Hammer ordered. "We won't do anything right now."

The men retreated in silence. No one said anything on their way back to the camp. Hammer's mind went into a tailspin in that silence.

This was the last straw. He had to stop this invasion in its tracks. He had sworn that he would destroy anyone who invaded his territory. Now these rotten bastards actually thought they were going to construct their own camp right there in the Ashtaw Valley.

Did the Renegades even realize the Godless were using the Ashtaws as mounts? Did the Renegades plan to do the same thing?

That didn't matter because he would never let them near the Ashtaws. The Renegades must know the Godless were moving back into this area.

The valley used to be Godless territory before Shadow's time. Then the Renegade Clan drove the Godless out. Now the Godless were retaking the valley as their own, so of course the Renegades had to show up to stake their claim.

No Kral could let something like this stand. No one was going to build an enemy camp on Hammer's land. No chance.

The problem would be mounting the Ashtaws within sight of the enemies he planned to attack. That would be difficult or maybe even impossible.

The other problem would be wiping out all the Renegades—and that meant literally all of them. He couldn't leave any of them alive.

"What do you want to do about this?" Ant asked when the men returned to the camp.

Hammer sank down on the ground outside Vina's shelter. "We won't do anything about it."

Cross jolted. "You mean....you're just going to let them build their camp there—right in the middle of our land?!"

"Yes, that's exactly what I'm going to do. I'm not going to let them know I'm even aware that they're doing it. In fact, I'm cancelling the patrols for tonight. No one will go up to the valley or run the patrol. Stay home tonight."

His men gaped at him in slack-jawed horror. "You can't be serious!" Lucky exclaimed.

Hammer leaned back on his arm. "I'm very serious. We don't need to patrol because we already know the Renegades are there."

"But...you saw how many of them are there!" Pitch fired back. "They could be bringing in five hundred men for all we know!"

Hammer nodded. "It sure looked that way, didn't it?"

Flawless and Eager came over just then. "What's going on?" Flawless asked.

"The Renegades are invading the valley," Ant replied. "They're building a little village on the valley floor right next to the Ashtaw herd."

"And Hammer says we're going to stay home and let them do it!" Lucky finished.

Eager raised his eyebrows. "Shouldn't we be trying to stop them from invading our land?"

"Haven't you men learned even one thing from using the Ashtaws against our enemies?" Hammer interjected. "They work best when our enemies are all concentrated in one place, especially if they're inside some structure like a house or a shelter. All we have to do is wait for the Renegades to build this little village or whatever it is. We'll let them finish all their construction. All the Renegades who are staying here will stay and all the others will leave. We won't have to worry about more of them coming into the valley in the middle of our assault. We'll wait for the Renegades to get comfortable and settle into their houses for the night. We'll strike at sunset when we and the Ashtaws can still see what we're doing. We'll ride our mounts around the herd, get them all spooked and agitated, and build up a stampede to trample the village. It's that simple. All we have to do is wait for our enemies to gather in one place."

His men stared down at him in shock. "You're serious," Cross blurted out.

"Yes! Did you really think I would just let them move in and not do anything about it?"

The men exchanged glances. "I thought you would want to do something now," Lucky murmured.

"Why would I want to do that when the bulk of the Renegade force is still outside the valley? They know we're here, but they don't know where. They probably think they'll establish themselves and use their camp or village or whatever it is as a base to hunt around until they find us. We'll let them think that and then we'll strike when they least expect it. We'll approach our mounts from the west side—opposite the Renegade camp. The Renegades won't see us or even understand that we're riding the Ashtaws. Any surviving Renegades will think the Ashtaws stampeded for some other reason. Then we'll track down the survivors and put them in the ground, too. We'll probably just have to keep doing this for the rest of eternity. We'll have to fight for your territory just like every other Clan already has to do."

Pitch threw himself down on the ground next to Hammer. "It's a brilliant plan. Thank Heaven we don't have to do anything right now. I'm exhausted."

"You three should go to bed," Hammer ordered. "You did right to alert me early on. We'll keep an eye on them from a distance. Something tells me we won't have to wait very long."

Chapter 33

"Three days," Scarecrow snarled under his breath. "They built the rotten thing in three days. It isn't fair."

"That's the power of manpower," Ant told him.

"You used the word, 'power' twice," Vuco told him.

"Do I look like I care how often I used a word?" Ant turned back to the view across the valley. "It does seem a shameful waste that they put so much effort into building those sturdy houses only for them to get destroyed so quickly."

"Don't feel too bad for them," Hammer replied. "They won't feel a thing once it happens. They won't have time to regret that they spent their last days alive building a village that will never exist."

"They'll feel the ground shaking," Cross pointed out. "Should we plan for the contingency that some of the Renegades might come out of their houses to see what's making the noise?"

"I already have planned for it," Hammer replied. "Seron and the boys will sneak into the valley with us and pin the doors shut while we mount up. The Renegades won't be able to come out. We just have to get our Ashtaws to step on the houses. Then we need to dismount as quickly as possible and hunt down the survivors so no one makes it back to their Clan alive. The Renegades will come to check on their new camp, find the place razed to the ground, and grass growing up through their comrades' skeletons."

Scarecrow gave a low chuckle. "You are so devious. I love it."

"I'm warning you now. We're going to have to continually pull these maneuvers on everyone who comes into the valley. No one will ever leave us alone. That's the price we pay for living this close to the gatherings. This country is too desirable. Everyone wants a piece of it. It's up to us to hold it for ourselves."

"Will fighting them actually work?" Ziti asked. "Isn't there any way to stake out this territory so everyone knows to stay away from it?"

"It will work. It will just take time," Hammer replied. "We have to turn this land into a black hole where people fall in and never come out. They come to take the valley and wind up vanishing without a trace. No one will ever find out what happened to them. Eventually, this country will develop a reputation and no one will come around trying to build villages here anymore."

The party fell silent. The sun was already going down on the peaceful Ashtaw herds.

The Renegades had built a sizable village in the valley. Hammer and his men no longer called it a camp because it wasn't one.

The Renegades had constructed the houses as sturdy as the houses in Ceon. The Renegades must have been planning to set up shop here for a long time. A lot of Renegades stayed. About a hundred men lived in the houses. Another fifty lived in tents.

No more Renegades carried lumber or supplies down from the north end of the valley. All of that had stopped yesterday after three days of solid construction. The Renegades who planned to stay had moved into the tents and houses. The rest had left.

Hammer and his men had been watching the place around the clock ever since the Renegades finished their construction. None of the Godless men or boys had gone back to their camp or seen their wives since this whole thing started.

Ant rolled onto his back, scooted down the hill out of sight, pulled a piece of dried meat out of his bag, and stuck it in his mouth. He shut his eyes and chewed while he waited for Hammer to give the word to act.

Scarecrow and Seron turned away and relaxed, too. Seron had become a regular fixture in all the men's patrols and maneuvers. Hammer really needed to think about initiating the guy, but Hammer had to initiate the boys first.

Vuco came first. He had worked too hard for too long to make himself as useful and valuable as possible to Hammer and the others. All four boys did. Hammer would never make them wait so he could elevate some stranger ahead of them.

Hammer found it hard not to initiate Seron, though. The guy was an absolute machine. He went on every patrol, every hunting party, worked on every project, and volunteered every time any of the men needed anything done.

He built structures for the women. He butchered any kills anyone brought anything back to camp. He even helped the women cook. There was no job he wouldn't do. He did everything with all his energy.

Hammer turned away to relax down the back of the hill, too. It was still too light to launch his assault on the Renegades. He planned to wait until dusk and maybe even nightfall.

Cross got his attention by bumping Hammer's arm. Cross waved Hammer back up to the ridge just as a bunch of Renegades came out of their houses. Lucky and Acrobat got Ant's, Seron's, and Scarecrow's attention. All the men climbed back into position to watch.

The Renegades came out of their houses, assembled from all over their village, and assembled at one particular house on one side of the village.

All the Renegades packed into that one house. Hammer didn't think it was possible for so many people to fit inside one house. The Renegades even closed the door behind them.

"Go!" Hammer whispered. "Go! Go! Go!"

The men launched to their feet without a word, charged down the hill, and skimmed west to approach the herd on that side. Hammer changed his mind when he spotted his mount nearby. She raised her head to look at him.

He slowed to a walk, but he couldn't stop his heart from pounding. He had to catch his breath while he strapped on her harnesses.

He climbed on board and she swung her head up. He scanned the Renegade village and spotted Seron and the four boys just bolting away from that one house.

Seron and the boys carried a heavy log with them from the Godless' hiding place on the ridge. Seron and the boys laid the log across the lower edge of the door and braced it with two big piles of rocks. That would slow the Renegades down enough for the Ashtaws to get there.

Ten more Ashtaw heads swept up high above the ground on all sides. The men sat in their harnesses from every mount's neck. Hammer kicked his mount, swatted her with the reins, and whispered, "Go! Go! Go!"

She took off running and he veered the reins hard to his right. He plunged his mount through the herd heading north—straight through the thickest groups of Ashtaws.

His men followed him every step of the way. Their speed set off a chain reaction in the herd. The other Ashtaws wheeled into line behind the mounted men.

Hammer drew level with the Renegade village, reined his mount hard to the right again, and cut a wide circle. All the Ashtaws charged away northward to follow the rest of the stampede. They left the valley clear.

Hammer carved a tight corner and urged his mount to run faster in a headlong charge for the village. The door trembled, but Hammer wouldn't have been able to do anything to stop the Ashtaws now even if the Renegades escaped.

They did escape. He made it halfway across the valley before the trapped Renegades succeeded in shoving the log and the rocks away from the door.

The door swung open and a dozen Renegades burst out into the night. They froze on the threshold and stared in disbelief at the Ashtaws bearing down on them.

Hammer didn't even try to rein his mount. He let her run and she charged straight into the Renegades. His plan had been to wheel her around and use the Ashtaws to trample the rest of the village in case he missed anyone in the first pass.

He didn't have to do that. His mount barreled through and over those Renegades at the front, smashed the house to kingdom come, and kept right on going.

So many Ashtaws thundered across the valley that they forced each other to separate. They had to cover the whole area and even spread wider than the village itself.

All of the Ashtaws ran so fast that they couldn't stop. Their weight and momentum kept the whole herd running its fastest right up until the moment when the entire massive body of Ashtaws plowed over the village.

The Ashtaws' giant feet and legs pulverized the Renegades, the houses, and everything in the herd's path. Nothing could stand against them.

Hammer relaxed into the inevitable. He wouldn't have been able to stop his mount—not with all the kicks, hits, and commands in his arsenal. He let her run with the herd.

The Ashtaws came to the hillsides rising to the ridge on the opposite side of the valley. The herd wheeled and stampeded all the way to the head of the valley before any of them started to slow down.

Hammer's mount turned south and happened to notice that she wasn't really running from anything or doing anything other than running around for no reason.

All the Ashtaws seemed to come to the same conclusion at the same time. They glanced around and slowed, but they still ran a long, long way before they decided they could walk instead.

They paced south and the herd spread out to go back to grazing. They wound up back where they started—where the Renegade village used to be.

No one would ever find that village. A giant swath of churned-up soil cut through the whole valley. Not a trace remained of any boards, bones, blood, or even a stain on the grass.

The grass would grow over the broken sod. The land would swallow this village as if it had never been there. It would vanish into the black hole of this territory. The village would become a legend and a story the Renegades told their children.

Hammer didn't have to give the command for his mount to lower her head. She did it herself and tore off a mouthful of grass. He climbed down, untied his harnesses, and met up with his men. They ran up the ridge and found Seron and the boys waiting in the same spot.

The men stashed their harnesses and the whole party set off at a dead run for the eastern jungle. Their work was just beginning.

Chapter 34

H ammer clambered into the treetops and took a position where the canopy overgrowth hid him from view. He looked down at the bodies of five Renegades lying dismembered and in some cases beheaded beneath him.

He held his breath to listen. The sounds of jungle creatures filled the canopy and spread through the jungle for miles all around him.

He didn't tense when he heard people running through the branches coming toward him. He recognized the sounds of Godless traveling off the ground for safety.

Cross, Ant, Scarecrow, and Flawless dropped out of the canopy and assembled on branches around Hammer's hiding place. "Did you find them?" he whispered.

Cross nodded. "Seven of them on their way back north. We heard them talking. They're trying to clear all of Godless territory."

"We should pull back to our own country," Scarecrow suggested. "We've been out here for five days."

"Wait a little while," Hammer replied. "We haven't found them all."

"We'll never find them *all*," Ant pointed out. "We could stay out here for years and never kill the whole Clan. You would have to wage war inside their territory if you really wanted to accomplish that."

Hammer looked down at the ground. "Not yet."

"You're inside Shadow's territory. Did you know that?" Cross whispered. "He would consider it an act of war if he knew you were hunting on his land—even if you were hunting Renegades."

Hammer didn't answer at all. He already knew he was inside Shadow's territory. Hammer had seen Shadow's nephews patrolling the area. They hadn't seen Hammer. He made sure they didn't see him.

They did find the dead Renegades he had left for them to find. They didn't know who killed these Renegades. Then the Godless men had left to go report the situation to Shadow.

He must know by now that another group was inside his territory hunting Renegades. Shadow would stop at nothing to find out who was doing it, but Hammer still hesitated to leave. Why?

He got his answer in a few minutes when another five Renegades came out of the bushes from the south. They were traveling north, too. All the Renegades traveled north.

Hammer remembered Hangman talking to his men about that. None of the men could explain it. Hangman had thought the Renegades must be amassing some overpowering invasion force to make an incursion into Godless country.

Hammer straightened up on his branch and tightened his grip on his weapon. The Renegades didn't look up. They didn't search the surrounding jungle at all. They just walked straight ahead without looking at anything. No Godless would have done that.

Hammer's men drew their weapons and sat up straighter on their branches, too. Cross and Flawless spread out.

The Renegades slowed and then stopped when they discovered the dead bodies Hammer had left for them to find. The Renegades studied the corpses. One Renegade turned to another and opened his mouth to say something.

Cross's movements disturbed the leaves in the high canopy. One of the Renegades noticed and looked up—just in time for Ant to drop right on top of the guy.

Hammer, Flawless, Scarecrow, and Cross dropped at the same instant, landed on top of the Renegades, cut down all five, and left all the bodies right there alongside the others.

"Now we can go," Hammer announced as soon as the men wiped the blood off their weapons.

Scarecrow snorted. "I swear you would stay out here all year if you knew you could kill a few more of your enemies."

"No, I wouldn't. I have a wife at home now, remember?"

Cross clapped Hammer on the shoulder. "You're right. You do. Congratulations. Come on. We better take you home to her before she decides to throw you out."

The men laughed, vaulted back into the canopy, and took off at high speed back toward the west.

Hammer never looked back even once. More Renegades and Bounty Hunters would keep invading this country. He and his men would always have to hunt them down and eliminate them if they ever dared to set foot on this land.

The men took another two days to make it back to the valley. Hammer paused on the ridgetop. The scar from the Ashtaws' stampede still darkened the fields, but the Ashtaws didn't notice.

Anyone who came to look would only assume that the Ashtaws had stampeded. Anything could have caused that. A Boultar attack could have caused it.

Scarecrow slammed his hand on Hammer's shoulder and forced him to turn away. "No more delays. It's time for you to become a man at last."

Hammer turned bright red and laughed. "I already am one the last time I checked."

His men kept teasing him as they marched him all the way down the canyon to the camp. His heart stopped when he spotted Vina talking to Enzi and a few other new people. She burst into a smile at something they said—and then she saw Hammer.

Their eyes met across the camp—and they both knew. She was of age now. Nothing stood between them. Nothing would stand between them ever again.

His people crowded around talking and celebrating the Godless' victory. This was their land now. No one could or would ever take it away from them.

The others cooked their food, shared it around, and the men recounted their tales of the stampede and their incursion deeper into the jungle to hunt down the last Renegade stragglers.

Hammer eased over to Vina's side and put his arm around her from behind. He didn't have to do anything with her right now. He didn't have to do anything with her at all. She was his wife. They had the rest of their lives to do whatever they wanted.

He kissed her hair and that was all. No one said a word about it. It was already done.

Hammer and Vina sat with their friends and laughed at everyone's jokes. The boys had the most to say about the stampede. They and Seron had actually seen it from the ridgetop. The stampede didn't look like much from the top an Ashtaw's neck.

Enzi, the new people, and the children exclaimed over the men's exploits. Some of the little boys asked questions about how the men had tamed the Ashtaws and how they used them to fight.

"You mean you can't use your weapons at all?" Loza's little son Gio asked.

"How could we use our weapons when we're so high up in the air?" Eager asked. "We couldn't reach the enemy even with an extra long spear."

Gio frowned. "I didn't think of that."

"We don't need weapons," Scarecrow added. "The Ashtaws' feet and legs are all the weapon we need."

"I'll take you up to the ridge tomorrow," Seron offered. "I'll show you the scar and point out where the Renegade village used to be. No one could survive."

"Is it safe for him to leave the camp?" Loza asked.

"It's as safe now as it ever will be," Hammer replied. "Our enemies will take time before they regroup enough to send anyone back into the valley looking for us or trying to retake this territory."

The conversation shifted after that. The men asked what had been going on in the camp while they were gone.

Enzi had become something like a custodian who guided and managed everything in the camp while the men went out on scouting and hunting parties.

The women treated him as a father figure. The little children treated him like a grandfather. Both roles suited him. He even held some of the littlest children on his lap to give their mothers a break.

Hammer glanced around. He didn't need to be here for this and it was starting to get late. All the couples sat close around the fire. Ant and Eleph. Cross and Sema. Lucky and Masha. Scarecrow and Daora.

Pitch, Omen, and Seron all sat next to women, too. Hammer froze with his gaze riveted on Rosta and Acrobat sitting next to each other. She sat with her arm around his shoulders from behind and her head resting on the shoulder nearest her.

Neither of them saw Hammer watching them. Both Rosta and Acrobat were too busy listening to the others talk.

That moment sealed the deal. Hammer got to his feet, took Vina's hand, and led her back to their own shelter. It was their shelter now. It was his as much as hers—but everyone already knew that.

No one broke off their conversation when Hammer and Vina left together. There was nothing to comment on.

They went inside exactly the same way they would every night from now on for the rest of their married life together. Hammer shut the door and pulled Vina down on the bed next to him.

He put his arms around her, shut his eyes, and she hugged him back just as tightly. They could both finally rest. The wait was over.

Chapter 35

Hammer strode down the valley and had to stop when one of the young Ashtaws scampered around him. It bumped into him and almost made him fall over.

He faced the creature and petted it. "Go play with someone else, little brother. I'll play with you another day."

"Why don't you put a harness on him and let him start getting used to it?" Cross asked from Hammer's other side. "You need a new mount."

"He's too small to be a mount for me. I need an adult." Hammer pushed the little Ashtaw away, but the creature only followed him when Hammer walked away.

Cross laughed. "He likes you."

"He ought to. I've known him since the day he was born."

The men kept going. Hammer knew almost every Ashtaw in the herd by now. The Godless had been living here for two years and tamed dozens of Ashtaws.

"Which Ashtaws do you want to train for combat next?" Cross asked.

"We'll stick with the young males," Hammer replied. "We'll keep taming the females so they let us handle their young, but we'll only take the males into combat. The females are too valuable."

Cross nodded just as a shout got their attention from up on the ridge. One of the men waved down at them from the northeast.

Cross shielded his eyes. "It's Lucky."

Hammer already recognized Lucky. Hammer waved back and he and Cross left the herd to climb the hill. The rest of their party skimmed down the ridgeline to meet up with them on the way. The band was bigger now.

The boys who had left Shadow's band had initiated and so had Seron. Seron had taken the name Restless. Lonion had become Flex. Ziti had become Lizard and Thuron had become Silent.

He really had become silent. He had suffered an injury to his throat during his initiation battle against the Cursed Sand. Ziti had fought a Stalkion. That left the Cursed Sand for Silent to fight.

He went down into the creature's hole, so none of the men had seen how the injury happened. He had suffered some kind of crushing blow to his neck.

He could still talk, but talking hurt him. He had stopped talking unless he absolutely had to.

None of that mattered because he had grown up to be one of the most ferocious warriors in the band. He had developed into a younger copy of his brother Scarecrow. The two men were cut from the same cloth.

They loved each other like no other and always fought together. Scarecrow couldn't have been prouder of his brother and vice versa. They had every right to be proud of each other.

Vuco hadn't survived his initiation. No one talked about him anymore.

The remaining three younger men had learned to ride and handle the Ashtaws alongside Hammer's original core group.

A whole new generation of uninitiated boys had also joined their band. The young sons of women rescued from the Bounty Hunters became just as enthusiastic about joining the Godless as Hammer and his men had been.

The boys came out on maneuvers with the men and learned how to ride Ashtaws in combat, too. No one had to stay behind anymore.

Even the women and girls came up to the valley to help handle the Ashtaws. The Godless started handling the youngest newborns almost as soon as they hit the grass—like this little male pestering Hammer right now.

The men continued down the ridge until they found Lucky standing his post. The Godless posted watches on the ridge all the time now.

The Godless had to repel the odd incursion, but they didn't happen often enough to cause any serious problems.

The Godless always handled incursions the same way. They lured their enemies into open places where the Ashtaws could trample the unsuspecting bastards into the ground.

Hammer looked around. "What's wrong?" he asked Lucky. "The country is clear."

"Not quite. Look." Lucky pointed across the countryside to the northeast.

The party looked down the hillside and across the jungle. A wide flowing river cut across the countryside over there. The river glistened and shimmered in the sun.

Banks, grassy knolls, and scattered clearings dotted the river along its length before the river vanished into the jungle.

Hammer and his men watched another group back down the river from the northwest bend to the southeast where the river disappeared. Twenty strangers fought tooth and nail against three Krakelows whipping, cracking, and hissing through the air.

The Krakelows divided, wrapped themselves around the combatants' limbs, and pulled some of them to the ground.

Hammer recognized the combatants' long black hair braided into ropes. Two-thirds of the combatants were men wearing loincloths stitched out of hides.

A quarter of the combatants were women wearing similar loincloths and tops sewn together at the sides and shoulders.

The remaining members of the party were children. The combatants pushed the children behind them to protect them from the Krakelows, but the adults couldn't even protect themselves.

"They're Godless," Lucky murmured.

"They won't make it," Scarecrow added. "Look. Their strongest men are already getting pulled down."

It was true. The Krakelows wrapped up three of the party's biggest men. The men couldn't move their legs and eventually fell over. They had to use their free arms to keep themselves alive.

None of the others could help these fallen men. Even the women had to fight with everything they had to stop the Krakelows from taking down anyone else or getting to the children next.

"Stay on watch, Lucky," Hammer ordered. "The rest of you—let's go."

He plunged down the other side of the ridge, picked up speed, and drew his blade running through the jungle on his way to the river.

He veered right and then cut back to the left to come up on the Krakelows from behind. They were all too busy fighting the other Godless band.

Hammer and his men burst out of the trees and attacked without warning. He charged deep into the group and hacked the three fallen men free first thing.

He had to turn in all directions to deflect Krakelow segments flying at him from all sides. He swiped his blade to cut them into smaller pieces. They fell to the ground and lay there squirming. They couldn't launch themselves anywhere once they got small enough.

The rest of his men flooded the area and chopped the Krakelows into even smaller pieces. Then the men had to go around and scrape all the segments off of everyone to whom they had attached.

Almost everyone in this other band had a piece of a Krakelow wrapped around some part of his or her body. Even the children had a few. Hammer pried a segment off one little girl's leg. She screamed when she saw the blood.

Her mother picked her up and kissed her. Hammer pulled his bowl of leaf paste out of his bag and held it out to the girl. "Do you want to do it or should I?"

She turned her head away, buried her face in her mother's shoulder, and sobbed while he spread the paste on her leg. "It will start feeling better, but you should drink some Gooji juice. All of you should."

"Thank you so much," the mother exclaimed. "We would all have gone down if not for you."

Hammer opened his mouth to answer, but one of the men interrupted him. The guy shook hands with Scarecrow. "Thank you so much for bringing your band to our aid. My name is Lifeless. I'm the Kral of this band. It's a pleasure to make your acquaintance."

"You're welcome. My name is Scarecrow and I am not the Kral of this band." Scarecrow pointed at Hammer. "He is."

Lifeless turned around. His eyes fell out of their sockets when he saw Hammer. "You?! You're the Kral off this band?!"

Hammer held out his hand. "My name is Hammer. Where do you come from?"

"We came from the north—beyond the mountains."

Hammer pricked up his ears. "Really? Do you know any other Godless bands up there? I know a few other people who came from there."

"We haven't gone back in years. We were just traveling through this area on our way south."

Hammer made another survey of Lifeless's party. He didn't have anyone with him who might be anywhere near the age of gathering. Lifeless couldn't be taking his people there.

Hammer had been keeping a close eye on Lizard, Flex, and Silent. They would all be coming up to the age of gathering in less than two years.

Hammer counted down the days before he would meet the other Clans at the gathering. Would he meet Shadow's band there, too? That would be interesting.

The women that Hammer's band rescued from the Bounty Hunters didn't bring any teenage girls with them—no one close to old enough for these three young men. Teenage girls didn't last long with the Bounty Hunters.

Hammer wanted to bring in new women for his men to marry. He wanted to hurry up and build his band into a bigger force that could handle more of the dangers they faced.

Lifeless held out his hand again. "We're grateful for your help. We'll be on our way. I wish you all the best."

He shook hands with Hammer again. Then Lifeless and his men rounded up their women and children and set off down the river heading southeast.

Hammer watched them out of sight. What was this gnawing feeling in his gut? He shouldn't feel this way about another group of Godless who happened to pass through his territory.

He and his people had enough to worry about from the enemies they already had. He didn't need to go looking for more of them right inside his own Clan.

These Godless didn't pose any risk to him or his band. Lifeless's people left Hammer's territory on their way south. Hammer had done did them a good turn. Now he would never see any of those people again.

"What do you think?" Scarecrow growled in Hammer's ear.

Hammer glanced over at his friend. Hammer knew Scarecrow too well not to recognize that glare, the hard set of Scarecrow's jaw, and the flash of dark fire in his eyes. Scarecrow felt it, too.

Hammer turned around to face the rest of his party. "I think, if we ever see any of those people again, we shouldn't tell them about the Ashtaws. We'll keep it to ourselves unless it becomes strategically necessary to tell them the truth."

Half of his men nodded. Even the boys nodded. They all must have felt this cloud of foreboding hanging over the encounter. Hammer didn't like this at all.

His band had pledged to drive all invaders out of their territory and keep this land for themselves and the next generation. Hammer never imagined the day would come when he would include another band of Godless in that pledge.

He didn't have to think of them as part of that pledge because they were gone. He set off back toward the valley, but he and his men walked this time. He needed time to think.

Chapter 36

Hammer heard childish laughter ringing through the jungle long before he got near the camp in the box canyon. He got within half a mile of the camp before a little toddler boy burst out of the bushes and collided with Hammer's legs.

"What are you doing out this far, Zino?" Hammer picked up the child, rested the boy on his elbow, and kissed him under the ear. "You better not have run away again. Mother will punish you."

"If you don't beat her to it, right?" Cross asked.

Hammer didn't get a chance to answer before Vina burst out of the bushes right behind Zino. She gasped in exasperation when she saw Hammer holding the boy. "How many times do I have to tell you not to run off!"

"What did I tell you?" Hammer asked the boy. "You have some explaining to do."

The other men laughed at him. Vina kissed Hammer and joined their party on the way back to the camp.

She carried their infant daughter, Milara, in a wrap tied around her upper body. A round head with a tuft of black hair stuck out of the wrap. Hammer couldn't see any other part of the baby.

The men scattered when they entered the camp. All the married men returned to their own shelters, kissed their wives, and settled down to play with their children.

Some of the men who had married freed captive women had adopted their children. Flawless had married a woman with three children all under the age of ten. All the other children had been born into the band in the last two years.

Hammer and Vina returned to their own place. Vina went about her work using one hand to support Milara and the other to do whatever task Vina had to do.

Hammer sat down and sat Zino on his lap. "Now listen to me, my son," Hammer began. Zino twisted his head around to peer up at him. "How many times have I told you not to go out into the jungle without a weapon?" Hammer asked.

Zino furrowed his brow. "Mother never said I had to take a weapon."

"That's when you were with Mother. You didn't need a weapon when you were with her. She would have defended you—but what about when you go out into the jungle by yourself? How would you defend yourself against Gorlocks and Crushers and Krakelows and Boultars then? Hmm? Answer me that."

Vina snorted at him from a few feet away. She made a face when Hammer glanced at her.

"I could have fought a Gorlock," Zino insisted.

"What would you fight him with—your bare hands? You go take a look at Cross's face. He fought a Gorlock in his initiation. He got those scars even with his weapons in his hands. A Gorlock would snap up an unarmed boy like you in seconds. Then what would Mother say when I came home and asked where you were?"

Vina laughed in the background, but she didn't interject.

"You should give me a weapon," the boy announced.

Hammer's eyes shot up. "Should I? Do you think you could carry my blade?"

"No! It's too big!" the boy countered.

"What weapon would I give you that you could use to defeat a Gorlock? Are you saying I should give you Scarecrow's axes?"

Zino glanced across the camp toward Scarecrow's house. He sat there playing with the son he'd fathered from Daora.

All the color drained from Zino's face when he saw Scarecrow's big axes lying on the ground. They weren't as big as Viking's, but Scarecrow's axes were plenty enough.

Then Zino's eyes darted to Eager's house. He had married a women freed from the Bounty Hunters.

Rosta tottered around her house trying to work around her enormous belly. She still went everywhere and did everything to serve Acrobat, feed him, and do whatever he needed no matter how difficult she found the work.

Eager fought with two giant kukris almost as big as Alien's. Zino immediately looked away when he saw Eager sharpening his weapons on his lap outside his house.

"I'll make you a bargain, my son," Hammer went on. "I'll give you my hunting knife—here." He pulled it out of its sheath. "The day you can defeat me with this is the day you can go out into the jungle alone without Mother. Do we have an agreement? Until you can beat me, I can't believe you could beat a Gorlock or even a large Gurlg chick."

Zino took the knife and studied it in his lap for a minute. He sat in silence for a minute before he struggled to stand up.

He turned around, flexed his knees, and held up the knife. "Defend yourself, Father!"

Hammer reacted too fast to realize what he was doing. He shot out his hand and plucked the knife straight out of the startled boy's hand. "Try again another day, my son. Do some growing up. Then we'll fight again."

Zino looked around in confusion when he suddenly realized he no longer held the knife in his hand.

Hammer put the weapon back in its sheath behind his back. His two-year-old son wasn't old enough to carry a weapon anyway—but Hammer already knew that. He just wanted to make a point.

Vina came over and put a bowl of freshly roasted meat in his hands. Hammer tipped up the bowl, dumped a piece into his mouth, and leaned back on his arm while he chewed.

Zino lost interest in Hammer as soon as their first altercation ended. The boy toddled off somewhere else to play with the twigs sticking out of the shelter wall.

Hammer surveyed the camp while he decided what to do next. He had been planning to train some of the younger male Ashtaws for combat tomorrow.

The vague feeling of unease about his meeting with Lifeless lingered in Hammer's gut even now. He didn't want to train the Ashtaws as long as Lifeless's band kept hanging around.

Hammer didn't even want to go near the Ashtaws until he satisfied himself that Lifeless really had taken his band out of the area.

Hammer couldn't explain his misgivings because Lifeless wasn't around. He was on his way out of Hammer's territory at this very moment. Hammer would never see any of those people again—unless Lifeless established territory for himself.

He wouldn't be able to do that because other Clans already laid claim to all the land in the south. Some of them might have been harmless Clans. The Followers lived in the south.

They still claimed the area as their territory. Other Clans left the Followers there to live in their own way.

Some Clans considered the Followers good for nothing other than bringing young women to the gatherings. Some Clans left the Followers in peace for that reason alone.

Then there were the Clans that didn't leave the Followers in peace. Some Clans attacked the Followers, stole their women and girls, killed the boys and men, marauded their territories for anything of value, and then moved into those territories to claim the land for themselves.

Godless didn't do that and Lifeless was Godless. He wouldn't molest the Followers to take their land.....unless Lifeless wasn't Godless after all.

Why on earth would Hammer think that about another Godless Kral? Lifeless gave Hammer absolutely no reason to suspect him of anything. Lifeless passed through the area and left it as quickly as he came. He didn't stay. He didn't intrude. He didn't molest.

He seemed to understand at his core that he couldn't stay in another band's territory—not even the territory of another Godless band. Lifeless would either have to subordinate himself to Hammer as Kral or challenge him to take over the band and the territory.

That word sent a thread of fire through Hammer's guts. *Challenge.* Hammer knew that word better than most other Krals did. Some Krals ruled for their entire lives without ever facing a challenge.

Hammer had faced his first challenge in his very first month as Kral. He had never faced another one, but he knew how to handle it if he did.

He tried to shake off the memory of his battle against Mammoth. Lifeless didn't challenge Hammer. Lifeless got the message loud and clear, moved on, and vacated the area. What could be more straightforward than that?

Cross came over and sat down next to Hammer just then. Cross held his one-year-old daughter in his arms.

She curled up against his chest and peered out at the world from inside the safe, protective cage of his arms.

Hammer pushed the matter out of his mind. "So?" Cross asked. "I suppose we'll be back to running skirmishes with the Ashtaws tomorrow."

"I suppose we will," Hammer murmured.

"I've been thinking we should start rotating which Ashtaws we use when we go against any intruders," Cross suggested. "We should give each of them a chance to face the enemy instead of using the same creatures every time."

Hammer shrugged. "That sounds like a good idea."

"We have enough of them now," Cross went on. "They'll get out of practice if we leave the new ones behind each time."

Hammer nodded. "Right."

Cross studied him. Hammer looked away.

Cross had become the person Earthquake had pretended to be when the band first left Shadow's territory. Cross had become Hammer's righthand man and closest confident apart from Vina.

Hammer needed someone like that. He had known it when he first left Shadow's band. Maybe that was one of the reasons why he had tried to trust Earthquake so much. Hammer needed someone to talk to and confide in about everything on his mind.

Cross really was that person. Hammer really did trust Cross—in everything.

Cross didn't have to pretend or put himself in that position. He just naturally assumed it because he was the person Hammer trusted the most. He trusted all his men to the ends of the Earth, but Cross would always hold a special place in Hammer's life.

They talked of other things for a few hours. They talked about everything other than Lifeless and his band's incursion into Hammer's territory.

He shouldn't even think of it as an incursion because he could hardly call it that.

Hammer had killed Renegades for even passing through the jungle adjacent to his territory. He hunted them down and slaughtered them without mercy just for the crime of traveling somewhat near his territory.

He had let Lifeless go because he and his people were Godless. Did Hammer make a mistake about that?

He didn't ask Cross and Cross didn't bring it up. That on its own told Hammer a lot. Cross didn't protest when Hammer ordered the men to keep quiet about the Ashtaws. None of the men protested.

What more confirmation did Hammer need that they all felt the same thing and came to the same conclusion?

Chapter 37

H ammer bent over the spit and cut a hunk of meat off the haunch hanging from the crossbar. Someone had forgotten to take the meat off the spit before everyone went to sleep last night.

The meat had gone cold overnight, but it still tasted fine. Hammer was just licking the juice off his fingers. The rest of his men woke up, came out of their houses, and started to eat breakfast with their families.

Hammer stiffened when he heard footsteps running through the jungle outside the box canyon. Flawless raced into camp and almost collapsed panting and sweating in front of Hammer. "Come up to the ridge!" Flawless husked. "Come now!"

Hammer didn't hesitate an instant. He cast a hard look around the camp and made eye contact with half a dozen of his staunchest men. They all watched and listened to Flawless.

Hammer didn't take the time to check that everyone followed. They all dropped what they were doing, grabbed their weapons, and took off running up to the ridge.

Flawless led them back to the Broken Tooth. He really did collapse against a rock and almost rolled off it. He shut his eyes and pointed eastward. "There!" he croaked. "Over there."

Hammer's eyes riveted on a coil of smoke rising between the distant trees. It was the unmistakable sign of a campfire.

"Who is it?" Restless asked.

"Who do you think it is?!" Scarecrow fired back. "There is only one group around here that would camp within spitting distance of our territory. Use your brain!"

"Take it easy, brother," Hammer told him. "Stay calm. Is it them, Flawless?"

Flawless didn't raise his head off the rock. He kept his eyes shut, gulped, and nodded. He didn't speak above a whisper. "I went to check before I came to get you."

That explained why Flawless was so exhausted. He must have left his post, run down the ridge into the jungle, scouted the campfire to see who it was, run all the way down to the box canyon to raise the alarm, and then run all the way back up here to lead Hammer to the Broken Tooth where he and the men would see the sign for themselves.

"The bastards didn't even try to leave the area," Scarecrow snarled. "They're messing with us on purpose to challenge us."

"You stay here and catch your breath, Flawless," Hammer ordered. "The rest of you—come with me—all except for you, Lizard. You take Flex and Silent and skirt their camp from the north. Don't show yourselves no matter what you do. Stay hidden, and if anything goes wrong, come back up here, get Flawless, and go back down to the box canyon to defend the camp. Understand?"

The three young men nodded.

"The rest of you remember what I said," Hammer went on. "Don't say a word about the Ashtaws no matter what. If Lifeless or any of his people ask how we won this territory, just say we did it by fighting—which is the truth. Now come on. We need to deal with this."

The three young men took off running northward along the ridge. They wouldn't drop down into the flat ground or enter the jungle until they got far enough away to avoid detection.

Hammer set off straight downhill from the Broken Tooth. Flawless stayed behind alone. Everyone else went with Hammer to back him up.

He deliberately slowed his pace when he entered the trees. He actually stopped a hundred yards from the campfire so he would be able to calm himself down—and to give his men a chance to calm down.

He shook the tension out of his shoulders before he trusted himself enough to continue. He made plenty of noise so Lifeless and his men would hear Hammer's party approaching. Lifeless and his men all grabbed for their weapons.

Lifeless sagged in relief when he saw who it was. "Oh, it's only you. You had us worried there for a minute." He waved at his camp. "Come on in. Take a seat."

Hammer didn't move. "Is something wrong? You said you planned to leave the area and continue south. Did something happen? Is one of your people hurt?"

"We will continue south. We just stopped here for the night. Come share a meal with us. We still want to thank you for your help yesterday."

"You shouldn't stay here," Hammer insisted. "This country is crawling with Renegades and Bounty Hunters—and you're encroaching on the territories of two other Godless bands. You can't stay. You should leave immediately before someone gets the wrong idea."

Lifeless completely ignored Hammer's subtext. "We will leave. We're in no rush. Come sit down. I insist—or I might get the wrong idea."

Hammer hesitated. He couldn't offend another Kral by outright refusing his offer of hospitality.

Lifeless's attitude set all of Hammer's alarm bells ringing. Hammer had basically just told Lifeless point blank that he was intruding on Hammer's territory.

Lifeless knew Hammer was Kral of his band—which meant Hammer must have territory. He wouldn't be here if one of the territories Lifeless was intruding on wasn't Hammer's territory.

Lifeless cast the most passing glance at the men standing behind Hammer. "You have a good group here. You should bring your wives and children up here. We would like to extend them hospitality, too—in gratitude for your help yesterday."

Hammer made a split-second decision, said, "Would you please excuse me for a minute?" and turned around. He grabbed Restless by the elbow, steered him out of the group, and pulled him to a safe distance out of earshot from Lifeless and the others.

"Head back to the ridge, circle north, and take the three younger men back to the box canyon," Hammer whispered. "Warn Enzi and the women to arm up and be ready to defend the camp if anything goes wrong."

Restless nodded and walked away westward at a slow saunter. He kept walking slowly and casually until he passed out of sight.

Hammer returned to Lifeless's group. "I just sent one of my men to our camp to tell our wives and children about your invitation. They should be here soon."

Lifeless waved again. "Sit down, sit down! What's the matter? There's no danger here. These are my sons—Golden, Jump, and Winter."

Hammer approached the fire and sat down. His men surrounded him. Half of them sat down. The other half remained standing, but that appeared normal considering that there wasn't enough space for all of them to sit down.

Lifeless's men eyed Hammer's party across the fire. The women kept fussing with their children the whole time.

Lifeless sat down on a stump near Hammer and handed him a bowl full of roasted meat. Where did Lifeless get this meat? Did he hunt—right here in another band's territory? He had some nerve doing that without asking permission.

"I'm surprised a man as young as you became Kral of such a band," Lifeless remarked. "But then again, all your men are young, aren't they? Did you break away from another Kral?"

Hammer did his best to keep his tone neutral. "No, we didn't break away."

"How did you find wives for yourselves? Did you steal them from someone else?"

Hammer didn't answer at all. Was this man trying to insult Hammer to his face?

Lifeless pretended not to notice Hammer's silence. "This is a good territory you have. We could share it together."

"Two bands can't share territory," Hammer murmured under his breath. He didn't even try to keep the iron out of his tone. "One would have to become subordinate to the other."

"You've done well, but you're young," Lifeless went on. "You would need the help of older, more experienced men to help you cope with all the dangers out there. The Renegades or the Bounty Hunters could wipe you out if they attacked you here."

Hammer didn't answer that, either. Now he knew for certain that Lifeless was trying to insult him. Lifeless blatantly questioned Hammer's authority and competence as Kral of his band.

The same word crept back into Hammer's mind. *Challenge.* That's what this was. Hammer should have listened to his instincts instead of trying to brush them away.

Lifeless wanted to challenge Hammer. Lifeless wanted to take this territory for himself—which meant incorporating the current band into his own. Lifeless would become Kral of one combined band.

Lifeless would have to kill Hammer to do that. Lifeless would probably have to kill all of Hammer's men, too—either that or drive them all out of the area.

Then Lifeless and his men could take all the women from Hammer's band and make them a part of Lifeless's band. Hammer couldn't possibly come to any other conclusion from Lifeless's words.

He didn't come right out and challenge Hammer. That would lead to a one-on-one fight between the two men. Lifeless obviously didn't want that.

Hammer kept eating the food in front of him, but he took that time to measure Lifeless's men. They all looked strong, capable, and just as fierce and determined as Hammer's men.

Hammer's band had one thing going for them. They had already fought the Renegades and the Bounty Hunters more than once.

Lifeless obviously underestimated Hammer's experience—and all his men's experience. Even the three younger men and uninitiated boys had more experience than most Godless their age.

All these assaults and attacks had made Hammer's band hard, resilient, resourceful, and ferociously protective of the territory they had worked so hard to claim. No one would ever take that away from them.

"Just think it over," Lifeless went on. "We could be stronger together."

"I will think it over. It's an interesting suggestion. I'll discuss it with my people." Hammer stood up and handed back the half-eaten bowl of food. "Thank you for your hospitality, but you really should think about moving on. The bands in this area don't take kindly to intruders. They probably already think you've overstayed your welcome. Staying longer would be considered an act of war. I hope you have a safe journey south. I advise you to leave today—this morning. Your people are all healthy. You have no more reason to stay. I wish you well."

Hammer didn't give Lifeless a chance to answer before Hammer turned on his heel and walked off without looking back. Lifeless would be certain to understand Hammer's hidden meaning that time.

Lifeless would have to be too stupid even to lead his band if he didn't understand it. Lifeless must realize that Hammer was talking about his own band that would consider it an act of war if Lifeless stayed here.

Hammer already considered it an act of war. Lifeless had already crossed that line. He couldn't take that back—and he wouldn't take it back. He had come here for one reason only. He wouldn't leave until he accomplished it or died trying.

Chapter 38

"Can you believe the balls on that son of a bitch?!" Scarecrow snarled on the way back up the ridge. "I don't believe my ears!"

"He sure does like his chances," Cross remarked. "He doesn't realize we would have already had to fight Renegades and Bounty Hunters just to survive in this territory. I'm surprised he doesn't see that."

"Maybe he thinks we just got here," Lucky pointed out. "Maybe he doesn't think we've been in the area long enough to fight anyone."

"He's blinded by our age," Hammer replied over his shoulder. "He sees a bunch of young men. He thinks we just ran away from our Kral and set up here by ourselves."

"He actually had the nerve to say we stole our wives!" Scarecrow snapped. "I swear I'll break the bastard in half for that."

"You won't get anywhere close to them, brother," Hammer replied. "You'll be on top of your Ashtaw when it happens. Your Ashtaw will step on him and it will all be over."

"So have you definitely made up your mind to attack them?" Cross asked. "They haven't done anything yet."

"They haven't yet, but they will," Hammer replied. "I'm certain of it. Then we'll have all the justification we need to attack them and drive them out or kill them."

"Are you set on using the Ashtaws for that?" Eager asked. "Lifeless doesn't have that many people. It will be a lot harder to isolate them all in one area."

"We'll see how it goes. We'll definitely keep training our Ashtaws. We need them to be ready to fight. If worse comes to the worse, we'll lay another ambush by inviting Lifeless to dinner. Some of us will stick around and entertain his band around the fire with our wives and children. Then, at a given signal, the Ashtaws will come over the ridge, our people will bail out, and the Ashtaws can finish off Lifeless's band that way."

"I would rather kill him myself," Scarecrow snarled. "I wish I could see his face when I sink my ax into his rotten skull."

Hammer let that go. "How many extra weapons do we have?" he asked. "I want everyone to start carrying extra—including the women. We'll start leaving a few of our men behind at the camp to guard the place each time we go out. We need to start taking better precautions. We'll increase our patrols on the eastern side of the valley in case Lifeless launches an incursion from there."

The men entered the camp and found the women in a state of uproar over Restless and the three young men coming down there with the warning to arm up.

All the women were carrying weapons, so at least they took his warning seriously. It took a long time to explain everything to the women in a way they could understand the danger.

No one would stop talking about it for hours. Hammer and his men stayed up late into the night talking everything over and planning how to deal with it when it did actually happen.

Hammer didn't hear a single one of his men doubt him or suggest that he give Lifeless another chance to prove he didn't mean any harm. Every man here had smelled trouble the minute they laid eyes on Lifeless's band.

Hammer finally went to bed. Vina and the two children were already in there sound asleep.

Hammer slept apart from them. He didn't put his arms around them the way he normally would. He had to get up early in the morning. He didn't want to wake them up when he left.

He came out of his house to find all the men already out there waiting for him. They talked in low murmurs, checked their weapons, added things to their shoulder bags, and took their harnesses with them when they all trooped back out to the valley.

Hammer climbed up, paused on the southern ridgeline, and surveyed the Ashtaws below him. Cross's suggestion about taking different mounts came back to Hammer in that moment.

It was a good suggestion. The band needed as many mounts as possible that could actually perform in combat. The band had almost twenty that the men knew they could count on.

Hammer started to pick out which mounts to take instead of them. Rustling in the nearby jungle to the east distracted him.

He glanced down there and saw three Godless men moving through the canopy. They were Lifeless's three sons—Golden, Jump, and Winter.

An enormous male Ridgebeak with a wide, white frill of sharp feathers around his head flapped above the foliage. The Ridgebeak kept diving and trying to grab the men in its talons.

Winter threw a lasso at the Ridgebeak's feet and missed. The Ridgebeak must have faced that before. It dodged. The rope landed across the creature's toe knuckle and slid off the Ridgebeak's scaly skin.

"Will you look at this?!" Scarecrow breathed. "The sons of bitches are hunting right here in our territory! Oh, hell no!"

"Let's go!" Hammer called to his men, dropped his harnesses there on top of the ridge, and raced off down the hill.

His men sprinted right on his tail. The Ridgebeak kept diving for the men. Winter gathered his noose, tried again to cinch it around the Ridgebeak's talons, and landed it this time.

This was by far the stupidest way to hunt a Ridgebeak. For a start, the Ridgebeak could easily lift a man at the end of a rope if the noose did tighten around any part of the Ridgebeak's foot.

For another thing, the Ridgebeak could lift the man out of the branches to someplace he would be totally exposed to the Ridgebeak's attack. The branches protected the three men now. Winter would lose that protection if the Ridgebeak pulled him into the open.

Winter obviously didn't know this. He found this out the hard way once he actually succeeded in roping the Ridgebeak's foot. The Ridgebeak let out a spine-chilling shriek and ripped away from the sensation of getting caught.

He would have pulled Winter out of the branches. Winter realized the danger in a rare moment of common sense. He let go of the rope—which meant he and his brothers now had absolutely no way to capture the Ridgebeak.

The Ridgebeak still had its talons. It had the most perfect, deadly way to catch the men. The bird plunged again and again and crashed through the canopy trying to grab them.

Hammer and his comrades dove into the trees, swung up into the branches, and raced through the jungle trying to catch up with the three men before they decided to retreat.

The three men must have been trying to decide how to go about capturing and killing the Ridgebeak now without using a rope. The three men stuck around just long enough for Hammer and his men to show up.

Hammer let go of the branch he was holding and let his weight drop out of the canopy. He raised his blade, collided with Jump, and both men hurtled to the ground far below.

Hammer's maneuver took Jump by surprise. He twisted around trying to see who or what attacked him. He didn't figure it out in time.

Hammer raised his blade in one hand and the two men smashed into the ground full force. Hammer made sure to land on top of Jump so the other man's body cushioned Hammer's fall.

Hammer's weight hurt Jump even more. Then Hammer drove his blade into the corner of Jump's shoulder.

Jump groaned out loud when the blade impaled all the way through him and jabbed into the dirt underneath him. Jump grimaced in pain, but Hammer wasn't playing games this time.

He launched to his feet and Hammer kicked Jump in the head with all his might. Jump's head snapped sideways. Hammer kicked him again and then a few more times in the body. He left Jump lying there moaning in semi-conscious pain.

Hammer left the blade stuck into Jump's shoulder. The sounds of yells, struggles, and even screams echoed through the canopy overhead.

Hammer looked up just in time for Winter to come plummeting out of the canopy. He crashed down next to his brother. Winter landed hard on his side and curled into a ball groaning in agony, too. He didn't try to get up.

Hammer's men hauled Golden down by his hair. Golden had the misfortune to get caught by Scarecrow, but for some reason, Scarecrow didn't injure the guy.

Scarecrow yanked Golden to the ground and threw him down extra hard next to his brothers. "Get your piece of shit brothers out of here!" Scarecrow barked. "Take your rotten band and get the hell of our land! Tell your father we were merciful enough to leave you three pieces of trash alive, but we won't be so generous next time! Do you think you can summon the brainpower to remember all of that?"

Golden staggered to his feet and grabbed Winter. Winter was apparently not so badly injured that he couldn't stand up.

He stumbled a lot, but he managed to blunder over to Jump. Hammer took his sweet time pulling his blade out of Jump's shoulder. Hammer might have "accidentally" twisted the blade when he pulled it out.

Jump roared out in agony. Hammer backed up a few steps to let Winter and Golden pull Jump to his feet.

"You won't get away with this," Golden slurred. "You're children...you can't hold this territory from us. Everything you have will be ours....."

Hammer dove for him and slashed his blade across Golden's cheek. He jerked away yelling in fury, but he couldn't retaliate. Hammer's men had disarmed both Golden and Winter in the canopy.

The three brothers wove and staggered from side to side on their way deeper into the jungle. "You're still in our territory!" Hammer called after them. "Don't let us see you in it again or it will mean war! Tell your father I said so!"

None of the three men responded or even turned around. They blundered into the jungle and disappeared.

"We ought to lead the ants to their camp," Scarecrow muttered. "That would teach the little shits. Then their piece of filth father really would be lifeless. The name would actually fit." He laughed at his own joke.

Hammer patted him on the shoulder. "We'll have our chance. They can't possibly mistake this for anything other than an act of war. Now let's go get ready. We can expect them to escalate next time."

Chapter 39

Hammer lay flat on his stomach on top of the ridge, but he didn't face the Ashtaws' valley. The Ashtaws were the least of his worries right now.

His men stretched out on either side of him with the uninitiated boys on the far end. Flex, Lizard, and Silent weren't here.

Hammer had never met anyone better at scouting and surveillance than those three. They worked seamlessly, noiselessly, and could pass undetected in almost any situation.

"How long do you think it will take for them to come back?" Acrobat asked.

"It will take as long as it takes," Scarecrow replied. "You can't expect them to rush things. They might make a mistake and get caught. Then we would be in an even more critical position of having to rescue them *and* drive out the enemy."

"I don't care when they come back as long as they come back and tell us what we want to know." Hammer's head jerked aside. "There they are. They're coming now."

Everyone turned their heads and looked far to the north. The three younger men advanced out of the jungle miles away from where they left.

Hammer and his party pulled back from the edge of the ridge and retreated down the line of hills to rendezvous with Flex, Lizard, and Silent.

"So what did you see?" Hammer asked.

"They're arming just like you said," Lizard replied. "They're carrying a lot more weapons than we realized. They have whole bundles of weapons."

"We never saw that when we saved them from the Krakelows," Ant pointed out. "I didn't see that Lifeless's people were carrying any kind of baggage at all. They only had what they could carry."

"I thought the same thing," Lizard replies. "We didn't see anything then, but we did see it now. Lifeless and his people have a big stash of weapons over in their camp. They keep it hidden in the undergrowth. That's why we didn't see it when you went out to meet them. Silent thinks Lifeless staged that whole incident with the Krakelows to get us to come in and save them. He wanted to check how capable we were and how well we could fight. They hid the weapons somewhere in the trees so we only saw what was right in front of us."

Hammer turned to Silent. "Really? That is incredible."

Silent dipped his chin once in a brief nod. He didn't reply other than that.

"Did you hear them talking about when they plan to attack?" Hammer asked.

"Tonight at sundown," Lizard replied. "We still can't be sure they even know where our camp is, but that's when they plan to launch their attack. We did hear them talking about coming west—so we figure they've been following us each time we leave. We came back to the valley each time we parted from them. They probably think our camp is over here. At least...I hope that's what they think."

Hammer clapped him on the shoulder and then did the same thing to Flex and Silent. "You all did really well. I'm proud of you. This information is going to win it for us. You three are priceless."

"Thank you," Lizard husked. "It was the least we could do."

"Let's go down to the camp, get our harnesses, and tell everyone what we're doing. Then we can get back up here and mount up in time to intercept the bastards before sundown. I'm going to leave you three, Restless, and the boys down in the camp just in case we're wrong about the bastards coming west. I don't do this to punish you. I'm doing it because I trust all of you to protect our wives and children in case something goes wrong."

"Of course," Lizard replied. "We understand perfectly. You can count on us."

"Lifeless's band is small enough. We won't need so many Ashtaws just to make our point. If I'm right, they'll run for it and leave the area. If we squash a few, we'll call it a bonus."

Lizard gave the men the rest of the report on the way down the canyons. He described what a sorry condition Jump was in, but he was still walking around and preparing himself to come out and fight tonight regardless.

"What a moron Lifeless is," Cross remarked. "He just doesn't take the hint, does he?"

"He sounded like he was out for revenge," Flex added. "He really sounded like he agreed with Golden. Lifeless thinks we're children and we need him to step in and be a father to us by teaching us a lesson."

"Wow!" Eager exclaimed. "He really is a moron."

"He doesn't post a watch, either," Lizard added. "He and his men stood around talking right there by the campfire. Lifeless didn't set any of his men to cover the area or see if anyone was approaching close enough to listen."

The men only stayed in camp for a few minutes—just long enough for Hammer to explain the situation to Enzi and the women.

Hammer went through the camp, made sure all the women had enough weapons, and repeated that he wanted all of them to stay alert and ready to defend themselves until the men returned. They all agreed. Even Rosta agreed even though she could barely move.

Hammer and his men returned to the ridge just as the sun started to sink toward the western horizon. It was time.

The men headed down into the valley. Hammer still found himself looking around for his first mount. He had really come to love her, but she had died giving birth the previous year.

Her loss still stung. He didn't want another mount even though he'd spent the last year using other mounts. Coming to the valley always made him miss her. Now he had to take another mount just when he needed a mount could really trust.

He trusted plenty of them. He had ridden five different Ashtaws between then and now. They all behaved perfectly and obeyed his every command, but they weren't her.

He had developed a special relationship with her. He didn't see how he could ever have that with another Ashtaw, but anything was possible.

He stopped where he was when three different Ashtaws came toward him. Two were young males. The third was a female.

He felt instantly drawn to her even though he and his men had agreed to use males instead. Maybe that was the secret. Maybe he had a soft spot for the females because his first mount had been female.

His men all had their favorites, too. Getting everyone to change their mounts each time would be a battle to say the least.

All three Ashtaws lowered their heads to nuzzle him. He threw caution to the wind and slipped his harness around the young female's head.

He realized while he tied it on that he might be setting himself up for a lot more heartache. Getting attached to another female could lead him to the same problem if she died giving birth, too.

Getting attached to any Ashtaw would cause the same problem. One of them could die from anything. The Ashtaws' sheer size seemed to cause them health problems. Some Ashtaw or another regularly turned up dead on the grassy valley floor.

Okay, that might be an exaggeration. They didn't *regularly* turn up dead on the grassy valley floor. It had happened maybe three times in the last year—which was still a lot considering that the creatures died of some natural cause.

They didn't get attacked by Boultars or any other dangerous creature. They just dropped dead for no apparent reason.

The young female stood quietly while he tied on his seat harness, mounted up, and she raised her head. He steered her toward the eastern ridge.

The men had grown accustomed to using the Broken Tooth as their staging area whenever they wanted to take their Ashtaws on maneuvers outside the valley—especially maneuvers to the east.

The flat spot just there offered a perfect vantage point for the men to look down on the countryside east of the valley. They could see miles of territory between the ridge and the edge of the jungle.

The men could even see over the top of the jungle to territory beyond the carpet of trees. The men just couldn't see anything going on inside the jungle.

Scarecrow squinted at the sky. "The sun is going down. They should be showing themselves any......"

He broke off when the men spotted movement in the trees. It started as a subtle wave of hidden shadow building to something darker.

Lifeless and his men surged out of the undergrowth in a sudden burst of energy. His three sons accompanied the rest of the men of Lifeless's band.

Jump still staggered a lot. He could barely stay on his feet. Hammer actually felt sorry for the guy. Hammer would never have made a man go out to battle if he was that injured. He really needed to stay home in bed, but Lifeless apparently didn't think of that.

The other men ran well and they all came armed. They came armed with the typical array of Godless weapons—axes, kukris, and a few regular blades.

None of the Lifeless's men carried metal Renegade blades like Hammer did. He was one of the very few of his band who still used them.

It didn't matter what kind of weapon any of them used. Lifeless and his men charged to the center of the flat ground out there. They kept pushing forward heading for the valley. They must have really thought Hammer's band camped here.

Hammer kicked his mount. "Go! Go!" he yelled.

All the Ashtaws surged forward, broke into a run, and thundered down the hill at top speed.

The Ashtaws had a long, smooth, loping gait that kept their heads suspended high above the ground. The Ashtaws hardly moved their heads at all when they ran. It made for a very smooth, almost floating ride through space.

Hammer's mount picked up speed. So did Lifeless's band. He and his men didn't register at first that they were running straight into the path of a dozen full-sized Ashtaws coming at them full speed.

Lifeless and his men checked themselves and then scrambled to retreat fast enough. They didn't get there in time. Jump staggered and went down under Eager's mount. Half of Lifeless's men stumbled away and scattered into the jungle.

Lifeless, his remaining sons, and a few others tried only once to stand their ground. That instant of delay sealed their doom. The Ashtaws barreled over the top of them and crashed into the jungle.

Hammer caught a few fleeting glimpses of the fugitives scurrying around on the jungle floor trying to stay one step ahead of the Ashtaws. The trees slowed the creatures down and saved these people's lives.

Hammer didn't slow his mount down. She plunged into the jungle and kept going. The resistance of so many breaking trees infuriated her. She seemed to take personal offense that anything would dare to slow her down.

She shoved harder to get through that resistance. She didn't see the people running in front of her. Hammer kept spotting them here and there.

He didn't try to steer his mount to trample them. He didn't have to. She kept swerving from one direction to another. She trampled two more people that he definitely saw. He didn't see the others.

He drove them all the way to Shadow's territory and reined his mount at the boundary. He actually didn't know where the boundary was or if there even was a boundary between his and Shadow's territory.

Hammer decided not to take his Ashtaws into Shadow's territory. That really would have been pushing it too far.

Hammer reined his mount backward and turned westward for home. His men kept turning their mounts this way and that trying to flatten each and every member of Lifeless's band.

Hammer's men couldn't have succeeded. The jungle was already getting too dark for the men to see their enemies fleeing into the shadows. He rounded them up and gave the order to fall back. They had accomplished their mission.

Hammer and his men released their mounts back into the valley and then spent four hours searching the jungle for any trace of Lifeless's men—or their women.

Hammer didn't know where Lifeless had stashed his women before the battle. They might still be inside Hammer's territory. Should he be worried about that?

He and his men didn't find anything. They had no choice but to give up the search and go home.

Chapter 40

H ammer climbed up to the ridgetop the next morning and stopped at his usual spot. His men came with him, and this time, they didn't need any of their scouts or watchmen to alert them that someone was coming.

"Now what?" Ant muttered. "Can't we just get one day out of the year to live in peace? I swear these people come from all over the country to take a shot at us."

"They're women," Cross pointed out. "They're Godless women. They look like Lifeless's women."

They did look like Lifeless's women. They looked more and more like Lifeless's women the closer the men got to them.

Hammer and his comrades circled the valley, dropped down to the flats leading to the jungle, and followed the tree line north to meet up with the approaching women. All five women came. Three carried children. That was all the women and children in Lifeless's band.

Hammer stopped at a distance from them and measured the women while he waited for them to catch up to him. None of them had come armed—not even with a simple hunting knife.

That on its own told him something was seriously wrong. What Godless Kral in his right mind would send his women out into the jungle unarmed?

The women had all been armed when they fought the Krakelows. The women had *not* been armed in Lifeless's camp. Hammer hadn't noticed that before. He should have realized then that something was off.

"You have to help us!" one of the women blurted out as soon as she got close enough. "Please! You have to help us!"

"Why do you need help?" Scarecrow asked. "You have your own band. Go with your men. Ask them for help."

"They aren't our men!" The woman's voice spiked to a shriek. She crushed the little boy in her arms in a death grip while her features quivered and spasmed all over the place. "They captured us! You're real Godless! You have to help us! They captured us from our own Clans! None of us are Godless! Please! You can't send us back! They beat and abuse us all the time!" She lost the fight to control herself and broke down sobbing. "Please help us! You're our last hope! We can't live like this anymore!"

"They....they captured you?!" Hammer rasped. "They're Godless! Godless don't take captives."

"I know!" she bawled. "You're real Godless! Please help us! They're marauders! I don't even know if they are Godless or just posing as Godless to make everyone think they're okay! They go around the country attacking other Godless! Please....please help us!"

"We should have known," Scarecrow snarled.

Hammer stepped forward and held out his arm. "Come on. Come with us. Let's go. We'll take you somewhere safe."

The woman in front of him staggered once when she tried to take a step. She really started crying when she heard what he said. "Thank you!" she choked. "Oh, thank you!"

"Stop," he murmured. "You're safe now."

He guided the woman forward. All the others followed. Most blinked back tears of terror and desperation.

He got them all moving toward the south. "Ant, take Flawless, Pitch, Lucky, and Eager. Go back up the ridge and keep a sharp lookout for any of the Lifeless's people coming back. If this doesn't trigger them to attack, nothing will."

The party split up. Hammer and his men drew their weapons and guarded the women all the way down the canyon.

Hammer delivered the women to Vina, Loza, Eleph, and the others. Hammer didn't stick around long enough to make sure these women found places to stay tonight. No one knew better than the Godless women how to take care of these former captives.

He paused at the head of the box canyon and watched the Godless women lead the newcomers inside. The newcomers completely broke down emotionally when the Godless women treated them kindly.

The crying mothers set off the children. Hammer turned away and led his men all the way back up to the ridge. "Any second now....." Ant remarked once they all resembled.

"Did you see anything?" Hammer asked. "Anything at all?'

"Nothing," Ant replied. "They're lying low wherever they are."

"Of course they're lying low," Eager interjected. "How many men do you think they really have left? They can't have more than ten. I would say they probably have less than five. That's what I saw. They would have to be irretrievably stupid to come after the women with so few."

"Let's remember who we're dealing with," Flawless added. "I can't even remember how many irretrievably stupid things these people have done."

"Starting with impersonating Godless," Hammer added. "How stupid do you have to be to pretend to be Godless and then go around attacking other Godless?"

"It makes you wonder how they've gotten away with it for so long," Omen remarked.

"We don't know they've gotten away with it," Cross pointed out. "Lifeless might have started out with a lot more people—like a lot more. He could have been losing people left and right all the way here. What used to be a large, strong band might have dwindled to this and now they're on their last legs."

"Lifeless isn't even alive anymore and they lost all their women," Scarecrow added. "So technically they aren't even a band anymore. They're just a bunch of guys with very little common sense. I don't know about you, but if I had that few men, I would run in the other direction."

Hammer had to laugh. The men kept shooting rude remarks back and forth at their enemies' expense. Things really didn't seem to be going well for whoever was left of Lifeless's people.

One of his no-good sons might be taking over as Kral. Whoever it was might get the idea to come for revenge no matter how many men he had.

"We should go out there looking for them," Restless suggested. "We shouldn't let them prowl around on our land to organize and do whatever they want."

"We would have to split up to do that," Hammer decided. "Our numbers are our advantage and they still don't know where our camp is. If they come, they'll come here. We'll stay here, keep an eye on things, and stick together until they show themselves. One of them might have a brainwave and decide to leave the area after all. If they don't do anything, we won't do anything. We won't have to."

The men stayed on watch for the rest of the day. Hammer kept all but two of his men on the eastern side of the valley.

He sent pairs to circle the rest of the valley just in case. He didn't want to take any chances that any enemy might be approaching from any side of his territory.

They didn't. Everything stayed perfectly quiet, but he didn't feel right about leaving the valley unattended even to go to sleep.

He sent word down the canyon that he and the men had to stay on watch tonight. He organized his men in shifts so they could take turns sleeping. Everyone else stayed awake and watchful until morning.

Chapter 41

Hammer woke up at the first light of dawn. He hadn't slept on the ground in a long time. It brought back memories of the journey that Hangman's band had made from Renegade territory to the northern mountains and back south to Shadow's band.

Living here lulled him into a state of relaxed comfort. He and his comrades had faced a lot more danger back then.

The sensation of sleeping on the bare ground heightened his senses and kept him extra alert. Maybe he should start having his men sleep on the ground more often to keep them watchful and their senses sharp.

He climbed up the rocks and ate some of the food out of his bag while he waited for the others to wake up. Two-thirds of his men were still on watch from last night.

They kept a close eye on the country to the east, but he saw from their relaxed posture that Lifeless's men hadn't shown themselves all night.

Ant climbed up the rock and sat down next to Hammer. "How long do you want to watch?"

"We'll watch for the rest of today. If they don't show themselves, we'll leave it alone and assume they left the area unless they specifically make some move against us."

The others milled around, ate, drank from their water gourds, and talked some. No one acted stiff or annoyed that they had to spend the night on the ground.

No one acted tense or on edge. None of the men expected anything to happen even as they all kept watch in case it did.

The sun migrated higher. Questions crept into Hammer's mind. Maybe he didn't need to take these precautions after all. Lifeless's remaining men might have already left the area. Then all this standing around and waiting would be a giant waste of time.

He glanced over his shoulder toward the Asthaws. They were much more important than anything Lifeless's band did.

That moment when he turned his head brought his line of sight around to the north. He wouldn't have seen his enemies approaching if he hadn't turned his head right then—or he wouldn't have seen them.

"There they are," he growled. "They're coming."

His words sent a shockwave through his men. They all snapped alert in seconds. Most drew their weapons and swiveled north to meet the enemy.

"I guess they weren't heading south after all," Lucky remarked. "They're coming from too far north. They must have retreated there."

No one else said a word as ten men advanced down the tree line. The invaders stayed out in the open between the ridge and the jungle—right where Hammer and his men couldn't fail to see their enemies coming.

Hammer waved his men forward. They filed down the slopes and positioned themselves where the intruders would be able to intercept Hammer's band. Golden led the party. Hammer didn't see Winter in the group.

Hammer did see a bunch of strangers who hadn't been with Lifeless's party during the Krakelow attack. These strangers hadn't been in Lifeless's camp when Hammer and Lifeless had shared such a pleasant conversation.

These strangers also hadn't been with Lifeless when he tried to attack the valley. How many more men did Golden have hidden out of sight?

Cross might be right about Lifeless being Kral of a much larger band. He could have been traveling with a good-sized fighting force. He kept them in reserve until he needed them.

"Your father is dead," Hammer began. "Haven't you learned by now that we aren't children for you to trifle with? Do you fancy another battle against our Ashtaws?"

Golden closed up his face in a scowl. "I don't know how you did it with those Ashtaws and I don't care about that. You're holding our women. You stole them from us...."

"We don't need your women, punk!" Scarecrow fired back. "We have our own. You keep yours to yourself."

"Your women came over to us willingly," Hammer interrupted. "They came of their own free will and begged us to take them. They said you stole them from other Clans, that you kept them as captives, and that you beat and abused them—which means you, your father, and all your stinking lackeys here aren't really Godless at all. I don't know what you are, but we are Godless. We're real Godless—which is exactly why your women came to us to get away from you. There never was a woman or a child born who called on me and mine for help who didn't get it. We'll defend them against you and stop you from taking them back. You should know better than to play games with us. I don't know how many men you have hiding out there in the jungle, but you have a very simple choice to make. Move on and leave my territory or you'll all die here. Let that be your last warning."

"I don't believe you!" Golden snapped. "I don't believe you didn't steal them."

"That was you, asshole," Restless cut in. "You stole them."

"Prove it," Golden countered. "Prove they crossed over to you willingly."

Hammer checked himself before he answered. "If I do that, you'll turn around and walk away. These women are free to come and go as they please. They can decide which band they choose to belong to. I'll bring them here and they'll decide. Once they do, you'll leave my territory with or without them. Their decision will be final. Is that clear?"

Golden nodded once. "Of course."

Hammer turned to Lucky. "Bring the women up here. Don't bring the children."

Lucky took off running for the southern canyons. Hammer and his men stood and waited in open confrontation against Golden and his men.

The wait gave Hammer all the time he needed to evaluate the people in front of him. These men were as big, as strong, and as fierce as any Godless warriors he'd ever seen.

Some were as big as Viking, though none of them was as big as Alien. Lifeless must have kept his strongest men in reserve.

Silent must have been right about Lifeless staging that Krakelow attack. A real Kral would have brought out his best and strongest warriors to protect the women and children.

Hammer thanked his lucky stars that Lifeless was already dead. Hammer would have had to track the guy down and kill him a second time for that.

He had actually put his women and children in danger to lure Hammer's band into a trap. Lifeless had actually let the Krakelows attach some of their segments to children just to make the ploy convincing enough.

He had armed his women to fight Krakelows—on purpose. What kind of fiend would do something like that?

Lifeless—Golden—they had left these women unattended and unguarded in the jungle. Lifeless had hidden the women and children somewhere while he launched the assault against the valley.

The women and children had never been in danger from the Ashtaws. The women and children had never been anywhere near the Ashtaws or the assault.

Golden had also left the women and children unattended and unguarded. He must have. The women and children wouldn't have been able to escape and come over to Hammer's men if the women had been guarded.

Of course Lifeless and Golden had left the women unguarded. The men didn't care about protecting their women. The men thought they could just steal new women from somewhere else if anything happened to these women.

Putting those pieces together told Hammer all he needed to know about the people in front of him. Golden would follow in his father's footsteps. All of them would. That was exactly the reason they were here right now.

If they succeeded here, they would keep doing exactly the same thing somewhere else. They would finish with Hammer's band and move on to the next Godless band.

Who would be next—Shadow's band? Hangman and Mora were over there. Viking and Nagana were over there.

All of Hammer's men's families were over there—all their mothers and younger siblings and Red's men who had been taking care of and raising Hammer's men since the beginning.

That was the moment when Hammer made up his mind to kill every single last one of these marauders. He didn't know if they were real Godless—whatever the hell that meant. He really didn't care which Clan they belonged to or if they belonged to a Clan at all.

He wouldn't let a single one of them leave his territory. He had made a commitment in his mind to turn this territory into a black hole.

His enemies fell into the black hole. They never came out. They never survived to leave his territory or to tell anyone what happened to them. They just vanished off the face of the earth.

The same thing would happen to Lifeless's band—Golden's band—whoever's band this was. None of them would walk away. They had their chance.

The outcome of this meeting with the women meant nothing. Hammer would wipe these marauders out one way or the other. He would hunt them down one at a time if he had to.

They would show themselves when they attacked him. Golden knew better than to hold anything back this time. He would bring his entire force against Hammer.

Golden knew about the Ashtaws. Hammer didn't see how Golden would be able to counter the Ashtaws—and in that moment, Hammer made the decision not to use the Ashtaws against these people.

The Ashtaws gave Hammer a massive advantage against his enemies, but the Ashtaws did have one distinct disadvantage. They were too big. They couldn't pinpoint a single individual—not unless that individual stood in one place.

Even then, the Ashtaws didn't even understand who to kill or even that they were supposed to kill anyone. They just walked around where Hammer and his men directed them.

Golden knew Hammer could use the Ashtaws against the marauders. Golden would expect that. He would expect Hammer to leverage the Ashtaws' size and strength.

Golden would never expect Hammer to attack on foot and hand-to-hand like regular Godless. That on its own would tip the balance in Hammer's favor.

Lucky came back with the five women and none of the children. The women trembled, but they climbed out of the canyons and strode up the countryside more determinedly than Hammer expected. Lucky must have told the women what was going on.

The women lined up across from Golden's band, but the women stayed close to Hammer's men. The women didn't let themselves get too close to Golden and his thugs.

"You had no right to run away!" Golden snapped. "You belong to us!"

"Get out of here!" that one woman shrieked. She did all the talking on behalf of the women. Hammer didn't even know their names yet. "We never belonged to you! You're thieves and murderers! You're plunderers! You were never Godless! Don't come near us or our children again! How dare you suggest that these men took us from you?! We've been trying to escape for years! We aren't your prisoners anymore!" She spun around and accosted Lucky who still stood next to her. "Give me a weapon!"

She lunged for him and snatched the kukri from his side before he had a chance to stop her. She charged out of position and raised the kukri to strike at Golden's men.

Flawless and Eager grabbed her and wrestled her back into Hammer's group. She kept yelling in broken sobs while she struggled to attack her enemies.

"There you go," Hammer interjected. "You have your answer. Now it's up to you."

"You won't get away with this," Golden snarled.

"You said that last time and we did get away with it," Hammer replied. "It was only a matter of time before you tangled with a band more powerful than you. What did you think was going to happen—that we would lie down and let you kill us all and steal our women? Get off my land. Don't let me see your face again unless you're ready to defend yourself."

Golden bared his teeth a few more times before he and his men retreated. They backed away a dozen yards and then turned and hiked all the way back north in the direction from which they came.

The woman's sobs broke the uncomfortable silence. "Take the women back down the canyon, Lucky, and then come straight back here."

"Don't you want to post a guard around the camp?" Lucky asked. "What if these idiots make a play for the canyons?"

"That won't happen because we're going to go after them first. Come back here as quick as you can. We'll wait for you."

Chapter 42

Hammer and his men climbed a long way down the canyons and into the dense jungle, but the men didn't return to their camp in the box canyon.

The men wouldn't return to their wives and children until the men eliminated all of Golden's remaining people. Hammer didn't know how many people Golden still had. That didn't matter.

The Godless men vaulted into the branches and took off at high speed back up to the jungle east of the Ashtaws' valley. This was Hammer's territory. No invader could set foot here without losing his life.

The men spread out the farther north they traveled. Hammer didn't want to leave even one corner of his land unsearched.

Of course Golden didn't take his people south. They occupied a ravine surrounding a small streambed far to the north—much farther north than the place they had staged that Krakelow fight.

Golden and his men might even have withdrawn to some other band's territory. Hammer honestly didn't care about invading another band's territory—not when it came to erasing these monsters from existence.

Hammer and his men dropped out of the branches in a silent whirlwind of death and destruction. They attacked Golden's band unawares while the invaders were still standing around checking and assembling their weapons to make an assault on Hammer.

Did these men plan to attack the box canyon? Was that their plan all along—to hit Hammer where he was most vulnerable?

Golden's men recovered more quickly than Hammer anticipated. The enemy fought back and pressed Hammer's band out of the ravine.

Four of Golden's men came after Hammer. Golden must have told his people to eliminate Hammer first. They cornered him against a dense thicket of trees. He couldn't retreat any further, so he launched into the branches.

His enemies followed. They could climb as well as any real Godless, so maybe they just turned rotten somewhere along the line.

They hounded him all the way to the top of the canopy. He tried a dozen times to get into a position where he could counter their moves, but their numbers made it impossible.

He was just considering doing something drastic when a Ridgebeak plummeted out of the sky, smashed through the canopy near him, and came perilously close to grabbing him in its talons.

The bird missed and lifted itself back into the air, but it didn't leave. It hovered there and made a second dive. Hammer had to avoid both the Ridgebeak and his enemies.

The enemy Godless took advantage of the moment, circled beneath Hammer, and tried to drive him upward into the Ridgebeak's grasp.

He made a split-second decision, jumped off his branch, and let gravity take over. He might be one man against four, but he knew this territory better than Golden's men did.

He took off at high speed racing through the jungle, but he chose his route with care. He stuck to the open places where the Ridgebeak would be able to see him and follow him.

He burst out onto the riverbank where he and his men had first rescued Lifeless's band from the Krakelows. Hammer sprinted onto one of the grassy knolls and spun around to face his enemies.

They closed in on him from all four sides and surrounded him in weapons. He wouldn't be able to get away from them.

He raised his blade to defend himself. Two of Golden's men rushed him from either side. He couldn't protect himself from both of them.

He ducked both assaults, stabbed one of Golden's men under the arm, and would have rolled out of the way to get clear of the other three.

He never got a chance to. The Ridgebeak dove out of the sky and slammed into Hammer's two adversaries hard enough to buckle them right on top of him.

The Ridgebeak smashed all three men down on the ground and tightened its claws around them to pick them up.

Hammer's maneuver trapped him underneath the other two. That one moment gave him time to slither out from under their bodies and escape before the Ridgebeak closed its talons all the way.

It crushed the two men in a bone-breaking grip, flapped its wings, and launched holding onto both of them. They screamed, dropped their weapons, and twisted over in the bird's clutches to try to struggle out of its talons.

The other two invaders rushed forward to help their friends, but the Ridgebeak was already rising too high. Hammer spun backward and hacked his blade across one of his enemies' necks. That left one.

The last free man grabbed his friends and pulled. His actions annoyed the Ridgebeak. It flexed its powerful wings to hold it aloft and, in one swift lunge of pure murderous power, it snapped its beak at the last man standing.

The beak crushed his skull and the sharp points at the tip of the beak impaled the guy through the chest.

His body folded onto the grass and the Ridgebeak launched into the air still carrying those two men. The Ridgebeak swooped away toward the jungle. It would carry the men back to its nest to feed to its chicks. Hammer wouldn't see those invaders again.

He grabbed their fallen weapons and sprinted back into the jungle. He only had to follow the sounds of conflict to find his men locked in battle against the enemy.

Hammer pivoted from one enemy combatant to the next and freed his men to go after the others. The enemy band saw the battle turning in Hammer's favor. A few of Lifeless's men broke away and ran for it while their comrades stayed behind and fought to the last.

Hammer teamed up with Pitch and Lucky, freed Omen, and the four of them went after three other enemy combatants who had cornered Ant and Flawless a dozen yards away in the undergrowth.

The Godless men worked to systematically eliminate everyone in view. That left the cowards fleeing from justice.

Hammer launched into the tree branches to run them down, but the enemy combatants scattered in multiple directions. Hammer and his men separated. He, Cross, Eager, and Scarecrow went after five men all fleeing north.

Hammer spotted Golden in the group and went after him in particular. Golden and his comrades didn't think to climb into the branches.

Hammer overtook them, dropped to the ground to block their way, and came face to face with Golden for the third time.

"Are you going somewhere?" Hammer demanded. "You said you wanted to share my territory. You wouldn't want to offend me by turning down my hospitality, would you?"

Golden's eyes widened. Then he remembered to harden his features. He raised his axe and braced himself for the fight.

Hammer's men moved in on Golden's comrades five against five. Hammer blocked out everything else except Golden.

Golden charged. He used the same strategy that Mammoth had used in his challenge. Golden bet everything on his own strength and the size of his weapon.

Hammer reared out of range and the axe zinged past his face. He didn't even have to move to thrust out his blade and pierce Golden through the chest. He winced, but he didn't fall. He took a step closer.

Hammer pulled his blade out immediately after striking and took a step back to stay out of Golden's range. "What's the matter?" Hammer asked. "Did that hurt? Did you think I was just going to stand in one place and let you hit me?"

"Just finish him off, brother," Scarecrow muttered from the side. "Don't toy with him."

Hammer realized in that moment that Scarecrow, Cross, and Eager weren't fighting their adversaries anymore. The rest of Golden's men lay dead on the ground. He was the last one left.

He took advantage of Hammer's distraction and swung again. Hammer snapped awake, avoided the stroke, and stabbed. He didn't have time to aim at anything.

Golden came too hard and too fast. Hammer's blade plunged deeper into Golden's chest than Hammer intended. He really did plan to toy with Golden a little longer, but it didn't work out that way.

Golden collapsed on his knees and his axe fell out of his hands. He grimaced in agony and toppled onto his back. Hammer looked down his nose and the man writhing in front of him. Hammer's blade had stuck Golden six inches deep in the upper ribs on his left side.

His movements became more relaxed. He eventually wilted onto the ground. He still rolled his head back and forth and tried to look around, but he couldn't move apart from that.

Hammer glanced around and spotted a dead tree nearby. He grabbed Golden by the ankle and dragged him to the tree. Golden bellowed in pain, but he couldn't fight back.

Scarecrow, Cross, and Eager sprang into the branches and started climbing. Hammer circled the tree to its side and kicked the loose, rotten trunk over.

Abnormit larvae spilled out all over Golden. Hammer sprang away in time to avoid the flood. He launched into the branches and scaled up to sit next to his friends while they watched their enemy meet his well-deserved fate.

"Are you happy now?" Scarecrow asked.

"Yes," Hammer replied. "We can go home now—as long as the other men have finished off the rest of Lifeless's party."

Hammer backtracked. It didn't take long for him and his friends to locate all the rest of their men in the jungle. They spread out and followed every single fleeing fugitive who tried to run away.

The men worked together to wipe them all out. None remained.

The men didn't make it back to the box canyon until long after dark. They found Enzi and the women sitting up waiting.

Hammer expected more of a celebration to break out, but everyone kept it calm and serene.

Vina, Sema, Daora, Masha, and Eleph had spent the day building shelters for the five new women from Lifeless's band. Then the women had their work cut out for them feeding everyone.

Hammer and the others settled down with their wives. The children were already falling apart from fatigue, so the mothers wound up leaving early.

Hammer sat up around the fire with his friends and companions. They talked about their victories and all their plans for the future.

Hammer experienced again the deep certainty that all his visions for this band would come true. They were already materializing right in front of his eyes.

He and his people would build a legacy on this territory—a legacy that would last the generations just like all the great leaders and visionaries before them.

He didn't have to dream about it anymore because he was already in it. It was happening. He would put his stamp on history.

Future generations might not even remember his name, but they would live his legacy and build on it to make it even greater. It all started right here, right now, with these people around him right now.

The present belonged to them and so did the future. This world was theirs to rule, theirs to protect, and theirs to build with nothing to stand in their way.

End of Book 4.

Keep Reading

R ise of the Giants Series: Book 5: Hidden Kingdom

The brave warriors of Hammer's band of Godless Clan must forge their own path after separating from their families and the only life they've ever known. The world of dangers doesn't forgive the slightest error and Hammer must overcome countless obstacles just to keep himself and his comrades alive.

Hammer and his people return to the valley and get the idea to domesticate the Ashtaws the way Mora suggested. The project could take years and might even cost the men their lives, but this could be the secret to finally defeating the deadly enemies circling and trying to destroy the band.

Hammer must learn on the fly how to be the leader his people need him to be. He'll face challenges from the dangerous world around him and from internal conflicts and betrayals within his own band. Everything depends on him—including whether he and his people live or die.

You can find it at your favorite book retailer.

Sign Up Once--Get all Theo Mann's free books including brand new releases

S ign Up Once--Get all Theo Mann's free books including brand new releases

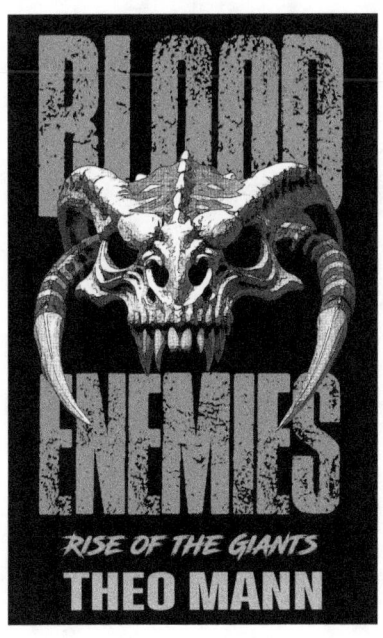

In a world where everything is out to kill you, humans must fight for survival every day against huge dangerous creatures and enemy Clans. The Godless Clan has enough to worry about already. They don't need to fight their own.

Sixteen-year-old Shadow knows exactly what to do when he discovers a girl from an enemy band hiding in the jungle. He takes her captive as a prisoner of war, but the Godless have a strict code of honor when dealing with women—even enemy women.

He and Katha will have to fight for their very survival and overcome generations of mistrust before they make it back to their people—who just might be the most dangerous enemies either of them has ever faced.

Sign up at www.theomann.com to read it for free

About Theo Mann

I write 70 books per year—and yes, before you ask, all these books are my original creative work. Nothing written under my name is AI-generated or ghostwritten because I write better than AI and any ghostwriter out there.

People don't read fiction for entertainment or to escape from reality. People read fiction to see their humanity reflected in another person's character and story.

This is my promise to you. When you read my books, you'll see your own humanity reflected in the characters and stories. I take this commitment to my readers very seriously. My books are an intimate form of communication between us. I would never disrespect my readers by turning that over to a machine or another writer. This is my bond between me and you as my reader.

I write 20,000 words per day as my daily work output. If anyone with a public platform would like to challenge me to prove this in a controlled environment, feel free to contact me on this website's contact page.

I worked as a professional ghostwriter for fifteen years. Now I'm on a mission to set a Guinness World Record by writing 700 books over the next ten years and 1400 books over the next twenty years, all originally written by me. See my website for the full book list.

I'm also the author of *Proof for the Existence of God* and the *Crimes Against Fiction* blog. You can find all my nonfiction work at www.crimes-against-fiction.com.

If you have a story idea, or if you would like me to explore a series in more depth, or if you'd like me to explore a character by writing a spinoff series about that character or world, leave me a message on my website's contact page. I answer all reader emails, so ask me anything, tell me what you liked and didn't like, and let me know where you'd like your favorite series to go. I would love to hear your ideas and find out what you'd like to read next.

Find out more at www.theomann.com.

Also by Theo Mann (so far)

Standalone Novels

Kingdom of Heaven

The Verge

Series

Onyx Series (Books 1-6)

Prideland Series (Books 1-4)

Ultra Meridian Series (Books 1-7)

Hellhounds Series (Books 1-7)

Battlefleet Series (Books 1-4)

Highland Heroes Series (Books 1-6)

Battalion 1 Series (Books 1-5)

The Network Series (Books 1-6)

Corrupted Coil (Books 1-5)

Rise of the Giants Series (Books 1-10)

The Edge of Chaos Series (Books 1-5)

The White Series (Books 1-7)

www.ingramcontent.com/pod-product-compliance
Lightning Source LLC
Chambersburg PA
CBHW052025020726
47501CB00004B/1254